THE ~~~~~~ MAN

Gladys Maude Winifred Mitchell – or 'The Great Gladys' as Philip Larkin described her – was born in 1901, in Cowley in Oxfordshire. She graduated in history from University College London and in 1921 began her long career as a teacher. She studied the works of Sigmund Freud and attributed her interest in witchcraft to the influence of her friend, the detective novelist Helen Simpson.

Her first novel, *Speedy Death*, was published in 1929 and introduced readers to Beatrice Adela Lestrange Bradley, the heroine of a further sixty-six crime novels. She wrote at least one novel a year throughout her career and was an early member of the Detection Club along with G. K. Chesterton, Agatha Christie and Dorothy Sayers. In 1961 she retired from teaching and, from her home in Dorset, continued to write, receiving the Crime Writers' Association Silver Dagger Award in 1976. Gladys Mitchell died in 1983.

ALSO BY GLADYS MITCHELL

GLADYS MITCHELL

The
Twenty-Third
Man

VINTAGE BOOKS
London

Published by Vintage 2011

2 4 6 8 10 9 7 5 3 1

Copyright © the Executors of the Estate of Gladys Mitchell 1957

Gladys Mitchell has asserted her right under the Copyright, Designs
and Patents Act 1988 to be identified as the author of this work

First published in Great Britain in 1957 by
Michael Joseph

Vintage
Random House, 20 Vauxhall Bridge Road,
London SW1V 2SA

www.vintage-books.co.uk

Addresses for companies within The Random House Group Limited
can be found at: www.randomhouse.co.uk/offices.htm

The Random House Group Limited Reg. No. 954009

A CIP catalogue record for this book
is available from the British Library

ISBN 9780099563273

The Random House Group Limited supports The Forest Stewardship
Council (FSC®), the leading international forest certification organisation.
Our books carrying the FSC label are printed on FSC® certified paper. FSC is
the only forest certification scheme endorsed by the leading environmental
organisations, including Greenpeace. Our paper procurement policy can be
found at www.randomhouse.co.uk/environment

Printed and bound by
CPI Group (UK) Ltd, Croydon, CR0 4YY

CONTENTS

CHAPTER I

The Hotel Sombrero de Miguel Cervantes

THE island of Hombres Muertos was aptly named. They sat, these dead men, twenty-three of them, around a stone table in a cave on Monte Negro, the highest mountain on the island and so called because of the dark, sculptured waves of lava which had flowed from the crater and congealed above the cavern.

No one knew the names of the dead men or why their bodies had been placed where they were. There was a legend that they had been kings of the island before the Spaniards conquered and named it. The Jesuits followed the Conquistadores and built a college and a church in the village they named Reales. Reales grew into a city with a cathedral and a bishop. There were installed in the Cathedral a solid silver altar and silver lamps from Spanish America. Later came the harbour and a long, concrete Mole; later still, tourists and the sale of souvenirs.

The cave, with its grisly occupants, was one of the show-places of the island. It ranked with the three-thousand-year-old dragon tree, the banana plantation, the botanical gardens, and the cigar factory, and there were men in Reales who made a fair living by acting as guides to the cave, where sat the robed, masked, and mummified kings.

From the sea, the island had the appearance of a stark, serrated mountain range, black against the eye-dazzling blue of the sky, and that was almost as Caroline saw it from the deck of the liner *Alaric*, six days out from Liverpool and due to make Reales the first port of call. It was half past five in the morning, and she stood by the rail in her dressing-gown and looked towards Hombres Muertos. She could make out the Mole and a huddle of houses dominated by the Cathedral. Behind these houses were white-walled villas on the long, green slopes of a hill, and beyond these slopes rose the mountains, menacing, dark, and sharp against a green and primrose heaven.

There was no breeze, and the delicious, temperate air of the early morning gave no indication of the heat of the day to come. The sea was calm and very clear. It rushed in silent, translucent glass from the cut-water of the liner and flared out towards the ship's wake. It had a mesmeric, evocative effect on the watcher from the deck above. Caroline, her mind never far removed from the deed which had altered her life, found herself brooding again on the reasons for her own and her brother's escape from England to Hombres Muertos.

This black mood was dispelled almost at once by the discovery that she was not alone. At her elbow a beautiful, resonant voice was quoting from John Masefield.

'*In the harbour, in the island in the Spanish seas, are the tiny white houses and the orange trees, and, day-long, night-long, the cool and pleasant breeze of a steady tradewind blowing.* All seem to be ours except for the cool and pleasant breeze. Hot weather is promised for today.'

Caroline turned and smiled. She knew the voice although it was the first time that she herself had been directly addressed by the speaker.

'Good morning, Dame Beatrice,' she said. 'Are you thinking of going ashore?'

'Not only of going ashore, but of staying ashore,' the small, spare, black-haired Witch of Endor replied. 'I am taking a holiday, and Hombres Muertos appears to be the one place whither none of my acquaintances is bound.'

'We're staying ashore, too. My brother and I, you know. Telham had had a bad breakdown and we thought it might be a good place in which to recuperate.'

'Your brother?'

'Yes. We haven't the same surname. I'm married – that is, I'm a widow. My name is Lockerby. Where are you staying on the island?'

'At the Hotel Sombrero.'

'Oh, good! So are we. Oh, I forgot, though. You want to get away from people, don't you?'

'Only from old acquaintances. I am no misanthrope. It will be very pleasant to have someone to talk to at the hotel.'

She nodded and walked briskly away. Caroline picked up the towel which she had flung on to the rail, and sauntered off to the open-air swimming pool.

By the time that the passengers were beginning to go in to breakfast, the ship was fast to the Mole. On the quayside the local itinerants were setting up a Babel of salestalk. There were ferocious outbursts of argument and high-pitched, foreign laughter. They had brought their wares alongside before the ship had docked, and were offering embroidered shawls, pyjamas of generous cut and gaudy hue, basket-work, carvings, beads, and fruit, and were hoping to reap a harvest before the tourists had a chance to visit the shops in the town.

By half past nine those passengers who had decided to remain on board were nearly in deck-chairs with their feet up, and those others, the majority, who had heard the call of the island, were already stepping ashore.

Dame Beatrice Lestrange Bradley found herself following Caroline and her brother to a line of taxi-cabs beside which laden camels lurched, grunted, and spat, and panniered donkeys, stoically disregarding thumps and curses, were pulled, and sometimes thrust, towards the edge of the Mole, so that their burdens might be unloaded on to the small black steamers which were to take bananas, wine, and basket-work to Europe.

Behind Dame Beatrice walked a tall young man with a pale face, short, dark-brown hair, and an expression of reckless dissatisfaction. She had noticed him during the voyage and had put him down as an ex-convict. As psychiatric consultant to the Home Office, she knew a good deal about the reactions and bearing of released prisoners, and the young man, whose name on the passenger list was given as Clun, bore, she decided, the unmistakable signs.

She wondered whether he intended to stay on Hombres Muertos, or whether he had come ashore for the few hours that the ship would remain in port.

He caught her up just before they reached the taxi-rank.

'I trust you are bound for the Hotel Sombrero,' he said. His voice was pleasant. 'If so, I wish you would share my taxi.'

'Very kind of you,' said Dame Beatrice, 'but I am not going immediately to the hotel. I propose to do some shopping.'

'Ah,' said the young man, unabashed by this transparent excuse, 'then I think I'll catch up those two people in front.' Before he could overtake Caroline and her brother, however, they had given directions to the driver of the first taxi in the rank and were off. The young man took the next cab and Dame Beatrice took the third and drove to the shopping centre of Reales where she purchased some picture postcards and a small basket before going back to the waiting taxi.

The hotel porters had made themselves responsible for the collection and transportation of luggage, and she gave them mental praise when she discovered that her trunk and suitcases were already in her room. The Customs formalities had been of the briefest. Short-term visitors had been allowed to go ashore after signing, on board the *Alaric*, a declaration that they had nothing on which duty should be paid. From what she had observed, as she watched the luggage being taken ashore, of a perfunctory scrawling on a trunk here and on a suitcase there, the Customs officials found little reason to suspect that anything illicit was being smuggled ashore, and did not care much, anyway.

She unpacked and went down the wide, cool, stone staircase to lunch. At a table for four were Caroline Lockerby and her brother. The tall, pale young man who had invited Dame Beatrice to share his taxi was standing at the entrance to the shuttered dining-room and was scanning the tables. He saw Dame Beatrice at once.

'Why, look,' he said, 'those two people from the boat seem to have spare chairs. Who are they?'

'They are Mrs Lockerby and her brother,' Dame Beatrice replied.

'Do you think they'd like us to join them? Family party, wouldn't you say? I can't abide eating alone.' There was something peculiar in his tone. He walked towards the table at which Caroline and her brother were seated, and pulled out a chair for Dame Beatrice. Telham gave him an appraising glance, reminding Dame Beatrice of the attitude of an older brother towards a younger one, and nodded as the introductions were made.

The four made an ill-assorted quartet – Caroline in her late twenties, beautiful after the fashion of the pre-Raphaelite painters, but with eyes whose passion Burne-Jones never painted, the two young men, the one dark, pallid, and restless, the other fair-haired with strained, weak eyes and a mouth which mocked at himself, and, a truly incongruous figure, the spare and upright, black-haired, quick-eyed psychiatrist, humorous, shrewd, and mellowed. On her yellow, claw-like hands the precious stones with their witchcraft fire of rubies, opals, and emeralds, glowed in magnificent rings.

Young Clun put his fingers on her yellow wrist. Her hand was palm-downwards on the table.

'You seem to be worth robbing,' he said. Dame Beatrice looked down at his hand and he took it away. She flexed her fingers and grinned.

'Yes,' she said pleasantly, 'quite worth robbing – up to a point, dear child. Beyond that point, of course, not.' She glanced at his face. Clun shrugged, but his eyes fell away.

'As a matter of fact, it wasn't robbery,' he said. 'It was brought in as manslaughter. I hit a bloke a little bit too hard. Three years. Quite a packet for the all-too-human mistake of not realizing what the poor corpse would look like, you know.'

There was a crash. Telham had leapt up and pushed his chair from the table with so much violence that it had

fallen over. His face was scarlet. He made Dame Beatrice
an awkward, stiff little bow.

'You won't expect me to sit down with a murderer,' he
said. His sister rose, but in a composed manner.

'Please forgive us,' she said. She put her hand on her
brother's arm, and the pair walked over to an empty table
in a different part of the room. It was another table for
four, and the brother and sister seated themselves with
their backs to the places they had left.

'Well, I'm damned,' said Clun mildly. 'What bug, do
you suppose, has bitten *them*?'

'Manslaughter,' replied Dame Beatrice. 'And Mrs Lockerby, I gather, recently lost her husband.'

'Well, hang it, how the hell was *I* to know?'

'You couldn't know – unless, of course, you knew.
Would you care to order for both of us? I can eat anything except the island pork. Veal, I am glad to notice,
does not appear on the menu.'

'You know,' said Clun, when they were served, 'you're
the sort of person who gets told things. You seem what
they call a born confidante.'

'Naturally. It is my profession.'

'A barrister? Yes, you *could* be. Don't care much about
barristers. Mine failed to get me off, yet I should have
thought there were extenuating circumstances. Provocation, for instance. Doesn't provocation count for anything
in the eyes of the law?' A twisted smile came into play.
She wondered what the provocation had been, but he
wanted her to ask him and for this she was disinclined.

'I am not a barrister,' she said.

'A doctor, then? The medico let down the prisoner at
my trial. Would the blow have killed the man before he
fell down the stairs? Yes, it would. Perhaps it wouldn't.
Sit on the fence and don't commit yourself. It was really
pretty to hear him. Anyway, the ayes had it. You ever
been in prison?'

'I have not had that experience, but I *am* a doctor. I
am also a psychiatrist and a specialist in nervous diseases.'

'One of those "lie on the couch and spout any rot that comes into your head" merchants? Somehow, I shouldn't have thought it. You seem, if you don't mind my saying so, more like a rather cynical but sporting aunt. *Are* you an aunt, by any chance?'

'Certainly I am, and a great-aunt, too.'

'I knew it well, you'd better adopt me as an extra nephew. I have a feeling that we are going to get on rather well.'

'What, *precisely*, did you do to be sentenced?'

'I got tight and punched a chap and he tumbled downstairs.'

'Extenuating circumstances, I think you said.'

'None, great-aunt. He did not fall: he was definitely pushed.'

'I do not need another great-nephew.'

'Oh, well, there was no harm in trying. See you later, alligator.'

Dame Beatrice grinned, looking much like the creature in question. Clun smiled in response, made her a jerky, ironic bow, and, waving aside the waiter who was bringing ice cream and a profusion of the fruits of the island, sauntered out. Dame Beatrice finished her lunch and was about to get up from the table when the brother and sister came up to her.

'I say,' said Telham, the flush still visible on his cheekbones, 'I ought to apologize, but, well...' He glanced at his sister.

'No,' she said. 'Not now. One day I'll tell Dame Beatrice all about it. What are we going to do this afternoon?'

'I', said Dame Beatrice, 'am going to sit in the sun and watch lizards.'

'Lovely. Telham and I thought of going down to the beach. They say the bathing here is delightful, and this hotel has its own private path down the cliff – a wonderful zigzag affair with the most marvellous views from every angle.' But her panegyrics rang false, thought Dame Beatrice. She herself did not get into the sunshine as soon as she had hoped. She was taking coffee in the shaded lounge of the hotel when a small, spare woman who might once have been very good-looking, came up to her and demanded: 'Are you a bird-watcher?'

'I am interested in all wild life,' Dame Beatrice cautiously replied.

'Field-glasses?'

'I beg your pardon?'

'Do you possess field-glasses?'

'Certainly I do.'

'Oh, good. Then you won't need to borrow the club ones. I like to lend those to the natives. You would be surprised at the interest they take.'

'In watching birds?'

'What else?'

'David watched Bathsheba, you know.'

'Really!' said the fanatic. 'What an idea!' Dame Beatrice gazed at her retreating, upright, narrow back with an indulgent leer.

Just as she was finishing her coffee, a rotund man, with china-blue eyes and the complexion of mahogany furniture, put a tall glass and a bottle of tonic-water on her table and seated himself beside her.

'Introducing Daniel Nathaniel Snodgrass,' he said jovially. 'A poor pseudonym, madam, but mine own. Actually, my name is Peterhouse, and my motto is that we British should stick together.'

'Laudable, but unfortunately I am not British,' said Dame Beatrice, summing him up as mentally unsound.

'But – the hotel register?'

'Oh, that!' She dismissed it with a wave of her yellow claw. 'I mean, I am not British in the matter of sticking together. I am, to borrow a word, an isolationist.'

'Well, well,' said Mr Peterhouse, conceding the point almost contemptuously, 'so am I, in my own way, of course. That is to say, I am a botanist.'

'This island surely must give you scope.'

'Oh, it does! Orchids, for instance. I have sent to Kew

Gardens several specimens for which they themselves have had to find names.'

'That is indeed a wonderful achievement, but is not an exploration of the island fraught with danger to life and limb?'

'To both, I can assure you. Ravines, crevasses, caverns, mountain fastnesses – I have explored them all. The trouble, of course, is Tio Caballo.'

'A local landowner?' (Not that 'Uncle Horse' sounded a likely name for a feudal lord, she thought.)

'A local brigand, madam. Twice have I lighted upon his hide-outs. Once, when I was in pursuit of *Cavernus epiglottis,* whose antecedents are found only in New Mexico, as you probably know, I stumbled upon Caballo and his band and was held to ransom. The fact that I had no money but was carrying a case of rather strong cigars of local manufacture won me my freedom. I also had to promise to pray for Caballo's soul. He is a deeply religious man and risks getting into trouble by sneaking into the Cathedral to hear Mass. I was able to redeem my promise by proxy. A small donation secured the services of Brother Pedro-Maria, a fellow botanist, who lives in the monastery at Puerto Santo, a few miles up the coast, and he took care of the matter for me.'

Dame Beatrice nodded genially.

'And your second adventure?' she asked.

'Not quite so happy. Caballo and half the band – they number eight or nine men – were off on some, no doubt, illegal errand, and I rounded a bluff high up in the mountains to run into his lieutenant, José el Lupe. José, not a bad fellow in his way, had need of a disguise so that he could visit his girl friend here in Reales. When he is rich enough they will marry. He took my clothes and lent me some of his, not that we are anything of the same build, but I would not have offered any criticism of the arrangement except that his garments were verminous. I ventured to point this out. The Spanish for lice is *piojos.* José was most amused.'

'I begin to see what your motto involves. All Britons on this island should stick together. With a posse of clean-limbed Englishmen at your back you could penetrate the territory of Tio Caballo without fear of reprisals or the necessity for prayers. What about forming a club and lending the members field-glasses so that they could espy the bandits from afar?'

'That woman is mad,' said Mr Peterhouse solemnly. 'I hope she hasn't been pestering you? She always waylays people who are fresh to the hotel. She's a menace. Of course,' he added hurriedly, as he caught Dame Beatrice's eye, 'we do lead rather a dull life here, in a way, so far as the hotel is concerned. One does rather like to see new faces. Are you staying here long?'

'A month at least – until the next ship calls, you know. Longer than that if I like it.'

'Do you play bridge?'

'No.'

'Then I advise you to begin. There's nothing to do here in the evening except to play bridge.'

'Then I shall do nothing in the evenings.' She nodded, put down her cup and strolled out. '*Cavernus epiglottis?*' she thought. 'How ridiculous!'

By three o'clock in the afternoon she was sitting in brilliant sunshine watching the lizards. The heat was intense, but, like the lizards themselves, Dame Beatrice appeared to thrive on it. She saw several saurians, some of European-Mediterranean, some of North African type, and there was one fine creature, twenty inches long, who lay sunning himself for half an hour or more, his throat pulsating and his reptilian eyes fixed (she felt certain) on her own.

'*Locerta simonyi*,' said Dame Beatrice, addressing him affectionately, 'I wonder what brought you to the Island of Dead Men? You are not indigenous here.'

'Not what. Who,' stated a voice behind her; and a very handsome man, wearing the kind of linen shirt, shapeless drawers and thin, worn blanket which the island peasants affected, seated himself beside her. 'It was I, Karl Emden, who introduced *Locerta simonyi* to this island. He, like Beelzebub, is the Lord of Flies. You are staying with us at the *Sombrero*, I believe?'

'Yes, I am spending a holiday here.'

'I have lived here for two months. Delightful place! I saw you sitting in the lounge drinking coffee. I wouldn't encourage Mrs Bluetit Angel, if I were you. She's mad. Did she talk about birds? It's her only subject, so she's certain to have got on it. Charlie Peterhouse, too, the silly old pest. *He* collects plants. Did he try to get you to play bridge? He's the biggest cheat on the island. You don't want to get into any set where *he* manipulates the cards. Have you met Ruiz yet? If not, you will. He's a bit of a bore, actually. Got a son doing well in South America. Ruiz is all right, I suppose, but to listen to him you'd think he was lord of this island. Oh, you'll find them all out in time. Luisa, now, his daughter. She acts as book-keeper, so watch your bill when you get it. Are many people staying off for a holiday? I wasn't in to lunch. Amaryllis – the current issue, don't you know – kept me busy, so we had a snack and a drink at Puerto del Sol, down the coast. Pretty little place. You ought to go and see it while you're here.'

'I expect I shall, if it is worth a visit. I am here for a rest as much as anything.'

He surveyed her spare, upright figure quizzically.

'You don't look like one who has much use for rest,' he said. 'You look very much on the alert. I suppose you've been a professional woman of some sort?'

'I still am, I hope. I am a psychiatrist.'

'Good Lord! Just the woman! I could do with a checkup. Do you care to have a patient? I don't think I'm bats, or have suicidal tendencies, or a split personality, but I'm exercised in my mind and I'd like to confide in the right sort of person. The right sort of person would seem to be an elderly lady – men don't like me, for some reason. Don Juan is seldom popular with his own sex. Jealousy, I suppose.'

'I must interrupt you,' said Dame Beatrice. 'I am here on holiday. Your complexes and difficulties must be taken elsewhere.'

'Yes, but you don't know what my difficulties are. I've only one, actually. It's concerned with murder.'

'Have you committed murder?'

'No, of course not. Never mind. Tell me about the other people who are stopping off. I'm told that we generally get half a dozen or more at this time of year.'

'I know only of three, apart from myself.'

'Are they all three together?' His voice was strangely eager.

'I hardly think so. There is a young man named Clun who seems to have been released from prison very recently.'

'Prison? What had he done?'

'He had slaughtered a man.'

'Murdered him? My God!'

'No. He "hit him a bit too hard", to employ his own euphemism. Then there are a brother and sister. *He* is in a highly nervous state, it seems, and *she* is recently widowed. A very beautiful young woman, passionate, if I judge aright, but apparently self-controlled. It is a self-control which could easily snap, I feel. Her name is Lockerby.'

'And nobody else stopped off?'

'I think there is nobody else.'

'My God!' said the young man again. 'What a collection! And you're all staying at least a month, until the next ship calls, of course?'

'There is an airfield, is there not, on the island?'

'Yes, a tiny one. There's not much flat land here, as you can imagine. So you think you might fly home, do you? And what about the other three, I wonder?'

'I have no idea. My plan was to stay a month at least. I do not much care for flying. I greatly prefer the sea.'

'I've no money. That's my trouble,' said the young man. 'If I had, I'd leave here tomorrow. You're not thinking of coming back to the hotel yet, I suppose?'

'I am thinking of logger-headed turtles, skinks, geckos, and eels,' responded Dame Beatrice, transferring her attention to an attractive, bright-green lizard some seven inches long which was flicking its tongue in and out and appeared to be smiling. 'I think I'll go down to the beach.'

The path was a broad walk broken every twenty yards or so by flights of steps. After the tropical luxuriance of the hotel gardens, where grew date palms and oranges, flowering shrubs, and ferns as tall as trees, the path, which was bordered by castor-oil plants, aloes, and the prickly pear, was arid and very dusty. At one of the hairpin bends a primitive sort of man came into view. He was watering the path from a goatskin, but when she reached the beach she might have been on the Riviera. She found a chair which was not shaded by a striped umbrella, and sat in the sun for an hour watching the bathers and the sun-bathers, until Caroline Lockerby, in a short, elegant wrap of orange and white towelling, open down the front to show the briefest of bathing costumes, came and sat on the sand beside her.

'I can't get Telham to come out of the water,' she said, 'and I'm dying for a cup of tea. Do come back to the hotel and let's have it on the terrace: I'm sorry about lunch,' she went on, as they climbed towards the shady gardens, 'but, if I tell you the circumstances, you'll probably understand. What have you been doing with yourself?'

'I met one of the hotel inhabitants who appears to have gone native,' said Dame Beatrice. 'He was asking all about the new arrivals at the hotel. I don't think he found my descriptions interesting.'

They climbed to the terrace and sat down. Below them the mountainous coast, bent like a friendly arm around the bay, stretched to the shadowy distance. To the right the Mole, the shape of a dog's hind leg, separated Puerto de Reales from the tree-lined Avenida Maritima, a newly constructed road which had become a favourite promenade for the townspeople when the heat of the day was over. Far away, but easily distinguishable because of its height

and the everlasting snow on its mountain summit, towered Santa Maria de Nieves. It had always been regarded
as sacred by the natives of Hombres Muertos and had
been dedicated by the Spaniards to Our Lady of Snows.
From where they sat, Monte Negro, with its cave of dead
men, was not visible.

'It is a beautiful place,' said Dame Beatrice. 'I'm very
sorry Laura couldn't come.'

'Laura? Your daughter?'

'My secretary. I am the personification of Macbeth's
wish for Lady Macbeth – I bring forth men children only.
Laura is no luckier. She has just had a boy. I remained in
England long enough to stand godmother and then I
came here to muse upon the mutability of secretaries and
the tendency of young women to substitute husband and
baby for the services of morbid psychology.'

'Morbid psychology?' Caroline suddenly stiffened.
'Could you cure Telham?' she asked.

'Cure him?'

'Take him out of himself. You saw what he was like at
lunch. He was there when Ian was killed. He doesn't get
over it. That's why I want to talk to you. What happened
was fairly beastly. Ian was my husband. Well, they were
out together one night, coming home from a rather vulgar
pub-crawl. They got mixed up with some louts in a street
fight. I don't know how it began. Telham ran away, but
Ian, who was always hot-tempered, stood his ground. Telham felt ashamed after a bit, and went back. Ian was
dead. Somebody had – what they call "attended to" him.
I wasn't allowed to see the body. His father identified him
at the inquest. The police couldn't find any evidence. There
were no witnesses – at least, no one came forward, and
Telham wasn't able to describe any of the youths well
enough to be much help. I ought to tell you that I was
almost through with Ian, but, all the same, it was a rotten
way for him to finish up. Telham can't forgive himself.
That's why he reacted as he did when that awful young
man talked about hitting too hard and not knowing his

own strength. Telham's quite raw inside. It's driving him
mad to think he ran away and left Ian to face it all.'

'Remorse acts like that,' said Dame Beatrice. There was
a pause. 'I couldn't treat him without his consent and
cooperation, you know,' she added in a tone of finality.

'It's not as though he could have *done* anything if he *had*
stuck by Ian,' said Caroline angrily. 'He'd have been
killed, too – or maimed for life – and where's the sense in
that?'

There was another short pause. Caroline looked defiant,
as though she sensed disapproval in the air. But Dame
Beatrice expressed nothing of that kind. She said:

'But isn't he maimed for life now? I don't think any
treatment could restore his peace of mind. A woman may
be able to forgive herself for cowardice, but I do not believe it of a man.'

'But think of all the people who have shown fear, and
then gone back and won the V.C. and things like that!'

Dame Beatrice looked at her with sharp interest.

'Um – yes,' she said, very doubtfully.

'But Telham went back!' said Caroline wildly. 'I tell
you he *did* go back to help Ian!'

'I can do nothing to help *him*.'

'But why not?'

'I should find out all the wrong things.'

'I don't know what you mean!'

'Neither do I, my dear. You are very fond of your
brother, are you not?'

'We're very fond of one another. I almost brought him
up, although there are only four years between us. I was
fourteen when my mother died. Telham was too young to
lose his mother at ten years old.'

'I agree. I also see a waiter who is coming to provide us
with tea.'

The waiter, a thin young man with melancholy eyes,
came up and solicited their order.

'China tea. Nothing more,' said Dame Beatrice. Caroline involved herself in a lengthy speech in Castilian

Spanish. The waiter looked perplexed and returned with the usual set tea.

'I don't want it,' said Caroline, when the waiter had left them. 'Oh, dear! What on earth am I going to do?'

'Don't eat it,' said Dame Beatrice; she spoke lightly, knowing perfectly well that Caroline was not referring to the over-sweet cakes and poisonous-looking sandwiches, but to the morbid preoccupations of Telham. 'Please believe me', she went on in a different tone, 'when I insist that there is nothing I can do for your brother.'

'You mean his case is hopeless?' Caroline poured out tea for them both and avoided Dame Beatrice's eye.

'I do not regard him as a case, otherwise I would do as you wish.'

'He's in hell,' said Caroline, 'and you refuse to do anything to help him!'

'It does not seem to me a task for laymen. Tell him to go to a priest.'

'We have no religion, I'm thankful to say!'

With this, Caroline got up abruptly and went into the hotel. Dame Beatrice poured herself out a second cup of tea, and added a thin slice of lemon. She had just taken a refreshing sip – it was very good tea, for Ruiz understood his English guests – when she was joined by a young American girl who was visiting the island with her father.

'I have never', said the new arrival, 'gotten around to the English theory that tea is a social vehicle. No, *sir*. I guess the Boston Tea Party settled for me in this respect.'

'Speak English, sit down, and help me dispose of these revolting sandwiches,' said Dame Beatrice.

'Sure. I guess you are *the* Dame Beatrice Bradley. I've read your books. I'm just mad about psychiatry. Could I trouble you to sign my book? I'd appreciate it very much if you would.'

'With pleasure. Tell me, what do you make of a man staying in the hotel who wears peasant costume and is extremely handsome?'

'He's a wolf.'

'By that I am to understand –?'

'Nobody's safe when that guy Karl Emden is around. He's as fresh as they come. Ask me; ask Luisa Ruiz; ask Pilar, the room-maid. One thing: he's quitting the hotel pretty soon, or so I hear.'

'Quitting the hotel?'

'Going to get him an apartment in a cave. There's a big troglodyte community in the foothills of Santa Maria de Nieves. He's going there to get local colour, and I sure hope it's a black eye.'

'Dear me! You sound very vindictive!'

'Sure am. Not that I can't take care of myself, but it does make me real sore when these heels take it for granted every girl they meet is going to fall for them. As I say, he's even dunked a doughnut with Luisa Ruiz, and she's no film star. I guess old Papa Ruiz has chucked him out of the hotel, and that's why he says he's leaving.'

'I doubt whether that is the reason,' said Dame Beatrice. She spoke absently. She was thinking of the reaction of the handsome young man with the German name when she had described to him the newest guests at the hotel, 'I think someone has turned up whom he doesn't want to meet.'

'Then I guess it's that Mrs Lockerby,' said the girl. 'If he's played Don Juan with her, he'll need to watch his step, and, when I say that, I'm not kidding. I'd just hate to meet *her* down a dark alley on a dirty night if I were a guy who'd stood her up.'

'I don't know why your dear papa paid to send you to an expensive school,' said Dame Beatrice. 'And don't you come from Boston?'

The unabashed American laughed.

'Sure, but I aim to be democratic,' she said. 'Pop likes me to talk good, like I was English or something, so I only get to practise my native wood-notes on strangers.'

'Then the sooner I cease to be a stranger the better,' said Dame Beatrice.

CHAPTER 2

The Dead Troglodytes

'I AM organizing', said the ubiquitous Mr Peterhouse, looming over the small table at which Dame Beatrice was at breakfast some mornings later, 'an excursion into the mountains. I wonder whether you would care to join my party? We shall go by mule, donkey, or litter; the last to be borne by lousy but sure-footed porters. We propose to visit the cave of Los Hombres Muertos. It is an outing which no one should miss. The cost I can let you know later.'

'So there really *are* dead men on the island,' said Dame Beatrice. 'I thought there must be. And they inhabit a cave, do they? Yes, I should like to join your party. You speak with muted enthusiasm of the litter, I notice. Do I understand that you yourself at some time have patronized its porters?'

'It would scarcely be a possible means of progress for one of the tougher sex, dear lady.'

'No, you are right. I shall not patronize it. But for you it would be a different matter. You have before you the historic example of King Edward, Hammer of the Scots. Was he not borne northwards in a litter? As for me, I shall compound for a donkey. I have never owned one, but they have a reputation for sure-footedness, and, although undoubtedly obstinate, they are said to be faithful. Then, too, they appear, with credit to themselves, in literature. One thinks of the noble ass of Lucius Apuleius; of Stevenson's little Modestine; one remembers that the immortal Sancho Panza rode upon an ass, not to speak of the prophet Baalam.'

'We start at eight tomorrow morning,' said Mr Peterhouse, ignoring with dignity these irrelevancies. 'It is not a long journey, but it needs to be taken slowly, for the track is rough and steep. Then, too, one does not willingly travel during the hottest part of the day, and one does wish to leave time for a thorough exploration of the cave. Besides, we *must* get back in time for dinner.'

'Yes, I do see that *that* is essential! Very well, then, I look forward to eight o'clock tomorrow morning.'

As Dame Beatrice was about to leave the dining-room, Caroline Lockerby came across to her from a table in an alcove. 'Have you finished breakfast? If so, come and sit in the garden,' she said.

'On the terrace, then.'

Caroline waited until her elderly companion had settled herself against the wicker back of her armchair and then she said: 'This expedition. What's it all about?'

'A pleasure trip, I gather.'

'To visit a cave full of dead bodies? I don't want to go, and I know Telham doesn't, but it's not very easy to refuse. Mr Peterhouse is a harmless old thing, and when we tried to stall he looked so upset that I gave in at once. The trouble is that that awful man Clun is going as well, and – well, mountain heights affect Telham and, really, I don't want another row.'

'Possibly we need not travel in very close propinquity. Could not your brother ride in the rear of the party?'

'Yes, if he can be persuaded to, but I'm afraid he's a bit of a thruster. We ride on mules, I understand?'

'I have compounded for the harmless, necessary ass. I might possibly get Mr Clun to ride beside me to be my prop and stay upon the journey. Is he chivalrous towards the aged and infirm, do you suppose?'

'I should very much doubt it. Do you think he's staying here long?'

'I really have no idea. A homeward-bound ship calls every month, of course.'

'If he's only here for a month I shall persuade Telham to put up with him, but if he's here longer than that, I really think we must move to another hotel. My brother is in no state to have a murderer around.'

'A harsh description, surely? There may have been extenuating circumstances. In fact, Mr Clun himself implied that this was so, although he denied it later.'

'Oh, Lord!' exclaimed Caroline suddenly. 'Here come those frightful people from Santa Catalina Island! They all speak dreadful Spanish!'

Dame Beatrice followed her gaze. Into sight at the top of the steps which led to the beach had come a man, a woman, and a boy of about eleven. Each parent held a hand of the boy, who was protesting vigorously.

'Poor child!' said Dame Beatrice, in a dispassionate tone which hardly conveyed sympathy.

'The idiots!' said Caroline violently. 'People ask for what they get! They've brought up that brat so badly that now they've got a white elephant instead of a son!'

'They seem elderly to be the parents of that child.'

'Oh, he's adopted. Their name's Drashleigh. He isn't their own. At least, so I was told. He's an experiment. They want to bring him up without any inhibitions, the beastly brat. He almost drowned me, yesterday evening, in that horrible pool by the rock-gardens.'

'He seems sufficiently frustrated at the moment.' Dame Beatrice eyed with detached and critical interest the attempts of the boy to free himself. His voice came shrilly across the peaceful garden.

'It's not fair! You're all against me! Let go! I want to walk by myself. I'm not an idiot!'

'If we do let go, you must promise not to go back to the beach,' said his father.

'Promise, now, Clement,' said his mother.

'All right, all right, all right!' shouted the child. The parents exchanged glances across the top of his head, then the father nodded and they released their grip on his wrists. Like a deer, the boy leapt away and tore to the top of the steps up which he had been dragged. The father patted the mother on the arm. She sank on to a garden seat. The father plunged after the boy.

'Be careful! Be careful!' called the woman. Then she

got up and walked towards the terrace. 'Oh, dear! How hot it is!' she said. 'Is this anyone's chair?'

As the woman seated herself, Caroline got up.

'I promised to play rummy,' she said, and sauntered indoors. As a gesture, it could hardly have been more pointed. The newcomer turned her head and gazed for a moment at the swing doors through which Caroline had disappeared.

'And all because Clement pushed her into the ornamental lake yesterday,' she observed in a bitter tone. 'I offered to pay for her frock. I could hardly do more. It was just his boyish sense of fun.'

'Ah, yes,' said Dame Beatrice. 'It is fun for your husband, too, to run after him in all this heat. It does seem kind of so young a boy to keep his elders amused.'

Mrs Drashleigh gave her a very sharp glance, but Dame Beatrice's yellow countenance was non-committally bland.

'Of course, Clement is not like other children,' said his foster-mother. 'We believe in absolute freedom. Any psychiatrist will tell you...'

'Pardon me, but there is at least one who will not.'

'I meant to say –'

'You see, I am a psychiatrist myself.'

'Oh? *Oh!* Then you'll be just the person!'

'I am afraid I must contradict you.'

'But Clement –'

'I am here on holiday, and, in any case, my methods would prove too drastic for Clement, I fear.'

'Oh, I don't mean shock treatment or anything of *that* kind! I thought an analysis under light hypnosis would be best.'

Dame Beatrice cackled. 'Hypnosis would certainly be necessary,' she agreed. She got up. 'I am glad your son did not push *me* into the ornamental pond,' she added.

'Well, for *your* sake...' Mrs Drashleigh began.

'For his,' said Dame Beatrice. She smiled kindly and strolled towards the steps down which father and son had disappeared. It would be interesting to see the end of the chase, she thought.

Half-way down she met Mr Drashleigh toiling terrace-wards. He was alone. He mopped his brow and seemed relieved to have an excuse to pause for breath.

'The hotel should install a lift, I think,' he said. 'You will find it a long pull up if you are thinking of descending to the beach.'

'Yes, I think I will turn back with you,' said Dame Beatrice. 'Are you and your wife proposing to join the party tomorrow?'

'What party?'

'The party which is to visit the cave of dead men.'

'Oh, *that* party! I could wish it elsewhere! That is why Clement is being so tiresome today.'

'Indeed?'

'Yes, I'm afraid so. Mr Peterhouse invited my wife and me to go, and was thoughtless enough to do so in front of the boy. Well, of course, we could not take a child of his age to see anything unpleasant like that. It might colour his whole outlook for years to come. I could not think of exposing him to such horrors!'

'No doubt you are quite right. I remember, however, that my own son, at about the same age, insisted upon visiting a kind of grotto in the south of France where were exhibited the embalmed remains of the abbots of the local monastery.'

'*Insisted?* You did not allow him to go!'

'Indeed I did. I thought it the lesser of two evils.'

'In what way?'

'It satisfied his curiosity, which might otherwise have turned morbid, and it convinced him that, as a chamber of horrors, the spectacle had been overrated.'

'That is one way of looking at it, of course.'

It was clear to Dame Beatrice that he did not think so, and she changed the subject by asking him what he thought of the hotel. He was still telling her when they reached the terrace.

'But where is Clement?' asked his wife.

'Sitting on the moored raft out in the bay, dear. I could see him before I got right down to the beach, so it was obviously useless to go further.'

'Oh, dear! He *is* being difficult, and all because we refused to take him to that disgusting cave! Well, I suppose we must just sit here until he chooses to come back.'

'No, dear. He must be taught a little lesson. Let *him* come and find *us*. Come along to the suite.'

Caroline rejoined Dame Beatrice as soon as the fatuous couple had gone.

'Well?' she said, seating herself in the chair which Mrs Drashleigh had vacated. 'Did you enjoy a cosy chat?'

'Yes. Mrs Drashleigh has asked for my professional services for Clement.'

'The only professional services that would do any good to that frightful little monster would be those of an undertaker, I should think.'

'Come, come! Live and let live, you know.'

'That little fiend has the same mentality, exactly, as those brutes who killed my husband! I can't *stand* him! And I think his stupid parents ought to be hanged!'

She burst into tears and rushed into the hotel. Dame Beatrice remained where she was. She was not easily shocked, but there was something infinitely shocking about the hatred which Caroline felt for the boy. As she was thinking thus, he appeared at the top of the steps. He was a sturdy, freckled child with almost white hair, a very white skin except where the sun had scorched it, and a sullen droop to his mouth. He was wearing bathing trunks and rope-soled shoes and carried a brightly-striped towel. He was not at all an unattractive figure. He climbed to the terrace, flung the towel on the ground, and seated himself upon it. 'Hullo,' he said.

'Good day, Clement,' Dame Beatrice responded. 'Where did you get the towel?'

'Why do you want to know?' The question was not insolently put. He really meant what he said.

'You did not have it when you broke your promise and skipped for the beach.'

'Oh, it belongs to somebody, I suppose. I needed one, so I took it.'

'I sincerely hope that you will not contract any of the more scabrous forms of dermatitis, then.'

'What's that?' A fleeting look of alarm changed his normal expression of boredom to one of interest.

'There are several rather loathsome forms of skin disease which can be caught from using somebody else's towel. Didn't you know?'

'Oh, slosh! I don't believe that sort of rot! Who told you?' But his voice was more high-pitched than usual.

'I am a doctor. It is my business to warn people about such things. Of course, if they choose not to listen, there is nothing more I can do.'

'Oh, slosh!' said Clement uneasily. He got up, kicked at the towel, and then asked, 'If you're a doctor, can't you disinfect me? I used the beastly thing coming up. If it belongs to one of the islanders I might get leprosy!'

'Pick up the towel with this, then, and put it back where it came from' – Dame Beatrice produced a piece of paper – 'and hurry up. Time is of the essence in these skin diseases. The open pores, you know.'

He came back later to discover that she had a small bottle in her hand.

'This should obviate any possible ill-effects,' she said cheerfully. 'It smells good, too. Tip it into the bath when you have about six inches of water, preferably tepid. Use no soap. Conclude the ablutions with a cold shower.'

Ten minutes later Mrs Drashleigh appeared.

'I can't understand it.' she said. '*Did* you tell Clement to have a bath?'

'Yes.'

'Well, he's having one! Without any fuss! I can't understand it! He's never obeyed anyone before.'

'He thought it a case of necessity,' said Dame Beatrice. 'Obedience should depend upon that, don't you think?'

The party which set out next morning consisted only of Peterhouse, Dame Beatrice, Caroline, Telham, a local guide, and Mrs Drashleigh. They went in two cars to the hill village from which the mules were to be hired. A donkey for Dame Beatrice was not available, the reason, she suspected, being that for donkeys it was customary to charge a lower hiring-fee than for their unfertile offspring.

The village was dirty and charming. The wooden houses, stinking and insanitary, had balconies, courtyards, and galleries. The hillside beyond the village was terraced for crops. The cavalcade passed by the flank of a vineyard so widespread that the owners, as the guide, a short, swart, cut-throat man, explained, were obliged to move house frequently in order to keep it under complete cultivation.

The road the company were following degenerated into a narrow, precipitous path which zigzagged, black and dangerous, up the mountain-side until, at a thousand feet, it entered some beautiful woods of chestnut and laurel. In the clearings there was heather and where the belt of trees ended there was no other form of vegetation until the pine-woods began. At just on two thousand feet the party reached their goal and could see, beyond the cave, the dark-grey lava streams, immobile now, which had flowed in the sixteenth century from the huge volcanic crater up above.

The cave itself was rather disappointing. It was big enough – there was no doubt about that – but it penetrated only a comparatively short distance into the mountain-side. There was a sudden relief from the brilliance of the sun, an interlude of slightly alarming gloom, and then, as the eyes became accustomed to this, there were the embalmed dead men, all twenty-three of them, seated around their stone table in a dignified silence which seemed to rebuke the onlooker. Each was wearing a mask and his robes of state.

'There!' said Mr Peterhouse. 'Twenty-three dead men, and all of them kings! A sight worth seeing, I trust? Of course, all the bodies are mummified. They would not look so perfect otherwise. And what do you think of their robes and death-masks? Slightly Aztec in feeling, would you say?'

All that Dame Beatrice noted was that one of the dead kings was taller than the others, but she made no comment upon this.

'I would have thought African,' said Mrs Drashleigh. 'Zanzibar, you know.'

Nobody else contributed an opinion, and Caroline created an unpleasant diversion by clutching Peterhouse and suddenly screaming:

'He moved! The twenty-third one! I saw him move! Take me out! Take me out of here!'

Her brother swore nervously and gave her a slight shake. Mrs Drashleigh laughed, a sound rather like the neighing of a horse. Peterhouse clicked his tongue. The guide went up to the twenty-third robed skeleton and stared into its mask, then he spat for luck and announced abruptly that all would leave the cave.

A picnic meal had been provided by, and brought from, the hotel. As, by this time, it was past midday and the majority of the company were hungry, the food was hailed with considerable enthusiasm, especially as the preparation of the picnic dissipated the atmosphere induced by Caroline's inexplicable outburst. Mrs Drashleigh insisted upon presiding, in a somewhat officious manner, over the arrangements, but, freed from the onus of managing, or attempting to manage, Clement, she proved efficient enough, and, as she did mos tof the running about, nobody offered any objection to her as self-appointed organizer.

When the food had been disposed of and the last bottle of beer had been given to the guide, some of the party suggested that a further ascent of the mountain would be enjoyable. The opinion of Dame Beatrice, the oldest of the company, was solicited by Peterhouse. She replied:

'I should like to climb far enough to see El Pino de la Virgen, which, I understand, is at two thousand five hundred feet.'

The guide was pleased with this suggestion and fell in

with it volubly, explaining that the Pine of the Virgin was the biggest tree in the world, yes, and in the Garden of Eden also. Impressed, albeit not convinced, by these assertions, the party mounted their mules and resumed their mountain pilgrimage. The path was steeper than before, and appeared, to one, at least, of the company, very dangerous.

'I'm not going any further!' cried Caroline, suddenly. 'Look at where the rocks have fallen! We shall all be killed!'

Her brother, who was riding immediately behind her, begged her to stop being ridiculous.

'If it weren't safe, the guide wouldn't bring us. These fellows always think of their own skins!' he said. As though the island resented this aspersion on the guide, there was a rumbling sound and a large chunk of rock detached itself from the cliff-face and bounded, in a cloud of dust, down the mountain-side.

'You see!' Caroline almost screamed. 'I told you so!'

The guide, who was bringing up the rear, shouted a guttural command to the mules. These came to a halt, twitching their ears.

'It will be', said the guide calmly, 'of no danger to go on. Here always there falls a rock. One expects it. Never has the path to the Virgin seen an accident. It would be bad luck if no rock fell. The mountain signals to the Pine that there will be money to put in the box. Only those without piety will wish to turn back now.'

He received support from Peterhouse.

'Quite right, you know,' he said earnestly. 'Something in these old superstitions. Knew a couple once. Turned back at about this point on the route. Mules ran away with them and galloped them over the edge. Took days to locate the bodies. Smashed to bits. Not one whole bone in either of 'em. Terrible thing. So come along, Mrs Lockerby. Up with the bonnets of Bonnie Dundee.'

'I shall go back to the cave and wait where we picnicked,' said Caroline. 'I don't need anybody with me.'

'I'll certainly go with you,' said Mrs Drashleigh. 'I've seen so many of these Catholic shrines. They're much the same everywhere. We can't lose the way, guide, can we? It seemed to me there was only one path.'

'No, *I'll* go with her,' said Telham.

'You won't. You know you want to go on. I shall be quite all right by myself,' said his sister, in a peevish tone which indicated that she was feeling embarrassed by her own nervous outbursts.

Mrs Drashleigh, however, insisted that she herself would far rather return to the cave and rest where the party had picnicked than continue the climb, so the two women turned about, with some assistance from the guide in manoeuvring their mules, and the rest went on to the shrine.

The track soon widened and appeared to be in quadruplicate owing to the flow of the lava streams. Around them were pines and *codeso*, and, on the left, appeared a small vineyard. Some stumps of trees could be seen, and the guide, with generous gestures, explained that the severed trunks could, from that point, be toppled down the mountain-side into the sea, where they were lumberjacked into rafts for export to the treeless island of Santa Catalina nearby, whence had come the two Drashleighs and Clement.

El Pino de la Virgen, with its shrine, stood in a clearing. The guide paid veneration and the visitors contributed money. Above the shrine was the crater, symmetrical, Satanic, and cindery. Dame Beatrice alone, on foot, climbed up to it and gazed down into its depths. She estimated that it was about two hundred feet deep and it was evidently quite extinct. The view, when she turned her back on the lava-streaked hole, was extensive if not exciting. She could see a path, almost wide enough to be called a road, and learned from the guide, when she rejoined the others, that as they had elected to see the shrine, this road would prove the easiest way back to his village where the mules had been hired.

'The mules like it better that way,' he concluded, in sombre tones.

'We must certainly return for my sister,' said Telham, shortly, scowling at the fair, broad road. 'She and Mrs Drashleigh will be expecting us.'

'Look here,' said Peterhouse, 'I know that road from here down to Ychos perfectly well. It's safe enough, too. You go back with Pedro to the cave, young fellow, and I'll take Dame Beatrice down from here.'

The guide, having arranged a meeting-place (ostensibly so that he could collect all the mules, but actually to make certain of his gratuity), agreed that the Señor Peterhouse was perfectly capable of taking Dame Beatrice by the safe and easy descent to Ychos, so the party separated, agreeing to meet again at the point from which they had set out.

Dame Beatrice and Peterhouse were able to ride side by side. The track was an old bridle-path and the mules could be left to look after themselves. The lava streams on either side of it appeared to have run at great and probably terrifying speed, but they were sometimes lost to view, for they had burst down the slopes of the mountain like cascades, whereas the bridle-path meandered in wide bends down the gentlest slopes it could find.

Soon the landscape became very beautiful. There were orchards and small farms, and a dazzling prospect of the sea. Shy, smiling people met the travellers and offered fruit for sale. Naked or semi-naked children, brown-skinned and timidly cheeky, begged for money or held out small bunches of flowers.

Lower still there were the villas of the wealthier islanders, with gardens and orange groves. The houses were covered with flowering creepers in startling contrast to the aloes and prickly pear which, here and there, bordered the road.

'What do you think', said Peterhouse, breaking a silence which Dame Beatrice thought strangely lengthy, 'is the matter with Mrs Lockerby? She doesn't strike me as an hysterical type. You're a psychiatrist, I understand. What, exactly, did you make of her this afternoon? Were her reactions normal? I nearly jumped out of my skin when she yelled out like that in the cave.'

'Did you? Of course, some people are affected very adversely by the sight of mummies, skeletons and, generally, the trappings of death. I was more impressed by her refusal to continue after the boulder had fallen. The odd thing is that she should have preferred to return to the cave, where she had had such a fright, rather than to go on. After all, the guide, who should know, had reassured us. Besides, although I am no geographer or geologist, it was clear to me that the boulders which fall, it seems, with some regularity, do not endanger the safety of people using the mountain road. They fall from the cliff on the right, which is below the level of the trackway. There were no boulders in the cliff-face on our left. If there had been, those *might* have fallen athwart the road.'

Peterhouse wagged his head in agreement.

'I understand the brother and sister don't care about that chap Clun,' he said, apparently under the impression that he was changing the subject of conversation. 'Reckless sort of fellow, I should think. Probably did well in the war and has been a fish out of water ever since. Of course, *De Bello Gallico* might help. One never knows. The Romans were the most extraordinary people the world has ever known. One can understand the Greeks, but the Romans, doing good by stealth and never even blushing to find it fame... Tell me what you think about the Romans.'

'Domineering, profiteering, and engineering.' He was certainly a little less than *compos mentis,* she thought.

From Ychos a double-purpose road, with a firm surface for cars flanked on either side by a kind of Rotten Row for camels, donkeys, and mules, took them back to the village from which they had begun their mountaineering. They waited for half an hour and then the rest of the party joined them. Caroline chattered (exhaustingly for her hearers) all the way back to Reales. Telham was silent, Peterhouse seemed tired.

CHAPTER 3

Twenty-four Men

SEÑOR RUIZ was a great believer in gala nights. A this hotel every fifth evening, Sundays included, was a gala night. An extra course was added to the dinner, streamers and balloons were provided, an orchestra, comprising two guitars, two tom-toms, three sets of castanets, a triangle, and a native instrument which consisted of a large jar with a bit of rubber fixed over the opening, was installed in the ante-room adjacent to the dining-room and the lounge, and a good time, it was to be hoped, was had by all.

The mountaineers returned to the hotel to discover that it was a gala night, and a glimpse of the decorations in the public rooms and the sound of the musicians tuning up in the ante-room persuaded Dame Beatrice that she had had a fatiguing day, and would dine in her own room. Staffing was no problem at the Hotel Sombrero. The receptionist, who chanced, on this particular evening, to be Luisa Ruiz, expressed concern, and assured Dame Beatrice that she would put Pilar, the youngest chambermaid, entirely at her service.

Pilar was pretty and was sixteen years old. In common with most of the girls on Hombres Muertos, she looked at least three years older than she was. She was anxious to attract attention and indicated this by much giggling, a factor which was apt to be embarrassing to the uninitiated. She was engaged to be married to a young man nicknamed Pepe Casita, so called because his mother lived in one of the smallest houses in the town. His real name was Gonzalo Guache, and he was strong and very jealous.

All this Dame Beatrice received from Pilar while her solitary dinner was being served. Pilar apparently considered it her duty to be in attendance during the whole of the meal, and broke off the conversation only to disappear with the remains of each course. Reappearing with the next dish, she resumed her artless narrative where she had left off. She spoke the bastard Andalusian of the island, but her hearer had little difficulty in following the general plot.

'And where', asked Pilar, at the end, watching Dame Beatrice peel fruit, 'did your honour go today? I guessed it was to the mountains, for you were with the Señor Peterhouse, and he goes always to the mountains, unless he sails dangerously to his island.'

'We went to the cave of the dead men, in the care of a guide.'

'Then you were safe from the bandits. They are brothers to the guides and do not molest an expedition.'

'The bandits?'

'*Sí. Tio Caballo y José el Lupe.*'

'Dear me! But we were safe from them, you say? What a very fortunate thing!'

'The cave of the dead men is a bad place. No one goes there except the guides and the visitors. The guides must make money and the visitors must make foolishness.'

'Foolishness?'

'*Sí, señora. La tontería.*'

'Have *you* ever been to the cave?'

'Mother of God, no!'

'Tell me more about Uncle Horse and José the Wolf. You say they are bandits. Do they kill?'

'No, no! That would not pay them so well. One can kill. One can then steal the money. But perhaps the money is not much. Better to take prisoners and ask a ransom.'

'I see. They are kidnappers.'

Pilar did not understand the word *secuestradores,* so Dame Beatrice tried her with an explanation which involved the word *niños.*

'Children!' exclaimed Pilar. 'There is one child here who should be taken by Uncle Horse, yes, and retained by him, I think, for the boy is a bandit already.' She described in detail some of the exploits of Master Clement Drashleigh and concluded, 'If his good parents did not love him they would be compelled to wish him dead. I think they wish him dead.'

Dame Beatrice had seen nothing of Clement or his father since her return from the excursion, but she could not help wondering what sort of day Mr Drashleigh had spent. It transpired, after breakfast next morning, when the Drashleighs joined her on the terrace, that Clement had been, for him, fearfully and wonderfully well-behaved.

'In fact,' said the fond and foolish father, 'I believe he has turned over a new leaf. I am so pleased with him that I have given him permission to bathe alone this morning.'

'Oh, dear!' exclaimed Mrs Drashleigh. 'You shouldn't have done that! You know how reckless he is!'

'He asked me to show that I trusted him, my dear. We had quite a heart-to-heart talk about things. I could not destroy his confidence.'

'Well, no, of course not. Oh, I dare say it will be all right. There are always plenty of people about down there. But I hope he isn't going into the water on top of that hearty breakfast.'

'No, no. I warned him of that, and he said that he had no intention of bursting! He is really extremely amusing when he likes.'

Time passed. Mrs Drashleigh embroidered, Mr Drashleigh read, Dame Beatrice did nothing at all with a great sense of pleasure in being completely idle, and at a quarter to twelve a waiter came out with the mid-morning glasses of sherry. Lunch was served at three. At just after two o'clock Caroline, (who seemed to have forgotten completely her hysteria of the previous day), Telham, and Mrs Angel came up together from the beach, sat on the terrace in bath-robes, and drank cocktails. At half past two they got up to go and get dressed. Mrs Drashleigh looked at her watch.

'You'll have to go down and get Clement,' she said to

her husband. 'He'll be late for lunch and he does so love
his food. I must just go up to our room and tidy myself.'

'Oh, dear, he'll come when he sees everybody leaving
the beach,' said Mr Drashleigh. But when another quarter of an hour had passed and many more guests had come
back for lunch, and there was still no sign of the boy, Mr
Drashleigh, still unwilling to make the descent and face
the long climb back to the hotel if this could be avoided,
went from group to group asking whether anybody had
seen his son on the beach. Obtaining no satisfaction, he
was compelled, even as the gong went for lunch, to go in
search of the missing child. Half an hour later he entered
the dining-room, red in the face, perspiring, fatigued, and
anxious.

'I can't find him *anywhere!*' he said. 'I suppose he'll
turn up when he's hungry, but I do wish I knew where
he is.'

He sat down at the table, but made a very poor meal.
There was no sign of Clement when lunch was over, and
his parents were, by this time, very considerably alarmed.
Dame Beatrice had her own ideas. She motored to Ychos,
prepared to maintain that the boy had gone to the cave of
dead men. She saw Clement, with one of the island guides,
descending the last turn of the winding road, just as she
got out of the car. 'I say,' he said, as soon as he came up to
her, 'there are *twenty-four* dead men in that cave.'

'Twenty-three. I counted them,' said Dame Beatrice.
'Pay the guide and get into the car. You must be hungry.'

'I am. I'm absolutely starving. I had no idea it would
take so long. I say, can you lend me any money?'

Dame Beatrice paid the grinning guide, and restored
the truant to his parents. The last sounds she heard, as
she went up to her room for a short siesta, were Clement's
clear, confident tones in argument with his father's bari-
tone utterance and his mother's thin, tired voice.

'But there *are* twenty-four! I counted them twice, I tell
you! I *could* tell you something else, something terribly
important, but, as you don't believe me, I shan't.'

'Curious,' she thought. She had considerable faith in
the assertions of children when the child could neither
gain nor lose by a plain statement of fact. 'There were
only twenty-three when *we* were there,' she said over her
shoulder as she left.

She lay in the darkened room and took a cat-nap, but
soon was wide awake again. The hotel was very quiet.
Everybody, she supposed, was either taking a siesta or was
on the beach. From force of habit she began to run a professional ruler over the various people she had met on
Hombres Muertos.

The most obviously interesting, from a psychiatrist's
point of view, were the brother and sister. Caroline's extraordinary outbursts at the cave were certainly sympto-
matic of emotional upheaval, and Telham's altered attitude, from near-hysteria to comparative calm, was, in its
way, not very much less startling. That there was a very
close tie between brother and sister was evident. What was
not evident was the reason for their apparent exchange of
parts.

Karl Emden had put in no further appearance at the
hotel. It looked as though the lively and informative
American girl had been right, and Dame Beatrice made a
mental resolve to visit the troglodyte community. It might
make an interesting study, she thought, in more ways than
one.

The ex-gaolbird Clun was another subject for speculation. She wondered why he had not joined the expedition
to the cave. It could have been that he thought it might be
better to avoid making one of a party which included Telham and his sister, yet he had not struck her as a young
man who would be deterred by any false delicacy from
doing anything he had a mind to do.

She thought of Tio Caballo and José el Lupe, and wondered how Clun would figure as one of the band. She
wondered whether to ask him why he had not gone to the
cave with the others, but she doubted whether he would
make a truthful reply.

The thought of the visit to the cave brought her to Peterhouse and Mrs Angel. About the former she no longer reserved judgement. He was abnormal and not altogether harmless. In the mind of the fantastic Mrs Angel, however, she thought that something solid, sensible, and even sinister might well have being. In other words, she thought that Peterhouse might be slightly mad, but that Mrs Angel, who seemed to have made herself into a caricariture, was, probably, beneath the façade she had chosen, completely, if unhappily, sane.

At six Dame Beatrice took a tepid bath and dressed in most leisurely fashion. In this she was assisted by Pilar, who, since dinner on the previous evening, had attached herself to the bedroom and its occupant.

'It is said', Pilar observed, as she fastened Dame Beatrice's dinner frock, 'that the Señora Angel has seen a vision.'

'Well, with a name like that, why not?' Dame Beatrice demanded. Pilar gave a shocked little giggle.

'The señora does not understand.'

'Don't I? Well, you had better explain.'

'The Señora Angel has seen the señorito carried away by devils.'

'Why not? It would be a likely fate.'

'The señorito spoke of twenty-four men.'

'And so?'

'There are but twenty-three in the cave.'

'Granted. What of it?'

Pillar giggled uncontrollably.

'But, see! If there are twenty-four, one is a *dead* man.'

'They are all dead men.'

'I mean recently dead,' said Pilar. 'Do you believe in dreams, Señora?'

'Only when I have considerable knowledge of the dreamer.'

'Would you believe that the señorito could be carried away by devils?'

'As I said before, judging from the little I know of him, I should think it not at all unlikely.'

'You jest, Señora. Yet he did go to the cave, and he did say he saw twenty-four dead men. One of them could be Señor Emden. If not, how can one account for the flight of the birds? Ah, I knew it had significance! I knew it!'

'The flight of the birds?'

'Twenty-five quails, Señora. I see now what was meant. I can count, can I not? It is the adding together that matters.'

'I believe so, in spite of Mr Chesterton. He maintained if I understand his writings, that two and two do not necessarily make four.'

'But God has made it so! Listen: twenty-three kings, and one man murdered, and one who has killed him. Twenty-five. No?'

'What makes you think it is Mr Emden who makes the twenty-fourth man in the cave? And why should anyone wish to murder him?'

'That has arranged itself, if you knew all, Señora.'

'Is there any reason why I should not know all?'

'Knowledge is worth a little money, Señora.'

'I am obliged and grateful for the information.'

Pilar looked at her distrustfully.

'You do not pay?' she asked. Dame Beatrice shook her head.

'Not for gossip which can be picked up on the Mole, in the *plaza*, in the restaurants, in the lounges of this hotel, no.'

'Then I shall tell you for nothing. I trust in your generosity. I am your *camarera*, am I not?'

'Not only my chambermaid but the inspiration of Pepe Casita, I believe.'

Pilar giggled.

'You have the understanding heart, although you are old,' she said.

'*Because* I am old,' said Dame Beatrice. 'Now cease to talk nonsense about money you will not be given, and unburden yourself.'

Pilar seated herself on the edge of a hard chair, held her-

self as erect as a nun, folded her hands in the lap of her
short black skirt, and addressed herself to the task in hand
by enquiring:

'Do you know that Señor Peterhouse owns an island?'

'It would not surprise me if he did.'

'He has taken my Pepe there. It is not more than a
rock. They have climbed. *Madre de Dios,* how they have
climbed!'

'For what purpose?'

'What purpose ever have men?'

'The riddle of the Sphinx.'

'I do not understand you.'

'What else should I know, that I know not yet?'

'Ah, that! What expedition makes your honour tomorrow?'

'I go to the island of Zlotes.'

'Who is to say whether you go there or not? You know,
Señora, it is a puzzle where goes anyone from this hotel.
The beach, the garden, the excursion into the mountains,
the steamer to Zlotes, the little boat from which men may
fish off Puerto del Sol – who shall bear witness? Often I
say to myself – yes, I, Pilar, who should be thinking about
my marriage or my next confession or a new dress – I say,
instead, that I do not know what one or another does
when he has had breakfast or lunch at the hotel and then
makes an expedition. What, I ask myself, of the Señora
Angel? What of the Señor Peterhouse? What, even, of the
couple who have yoked themselves with the wild boy who
came to them, an orphan, in their old age?'

'You give me food for reflection. Accept this poor token
of my gratitude.'

'A thousand thanks, Señora. You understand that I
must take a marriage portion to Pepe when I marry him?
But why did you refuse it before?'

'I have my own ways of doing things. Will Pepe make a
good husband?'

'He will, at any rate, make a husband. One cannot ask
more.'

Dame Beatrice went by steamer to Zlotes on the following morning, and it needed only an hour until dinner when she returned to the hotel. Her trip had been interesting and informative and she was tired enough to find pleasure in the thought of relaxing on the terrace for twenty minutes before she needed to go up to dress.

Of relaxation that evening, however, there was to be none at all. The whole hotel was humming with excitement. Clement Drashleigh had not been seen since breakfast. Search parties had been out; he had been traced as far as the Mole, but there he had disappeared and further search had been unavailing.

Mr Drashleigh had upset the whole economy of the hotel by offering so large a reward for news which would lead to the recovery of his son that every servant who could manage to sneak away had deserted his task and was organizing his own search-party from among his relatives and friends.

Dame Beatrice, confronted by the news as soon as she set foot on the terrace, went to her room and rang the bell. Pilar appeared and was catechized.

'Tell me more about Mrs Angel and her vision.'

'But there is no more to tell. You see, it was true. She dreams. The *niñito* goes. All are in search. What do you think? What will be, will be. No?'

'I suppose the police have been told?'

'Of what avail? All the hotel is searching. The police could do no more.'

'All the hotel?'

'Of a truth. I am the only person to wait at the tables except for Mercedes, from the kitchen, and she is *loco*. All the waiters are gone, all the cooks. There is Berto, the head waiter, and myself, also Mercedes. No others.'

'Good gracious me! And here am I in a state of semi-starvation!'

'When night falls, they will return. I will bring you a fish and some bread, here, in this room. Also wine. You shall not die.'

She was as good as her word. Dame Beatrice ate as much of a three-pound bass as she could, drank half a bottle of a local wine which tasted not unlike Marsala, and felt equal to dealing with the problem of Clement's disappearance. She had her own solution, and lost no time in testing it. She rang again for Pilar.

'*Tio Caballo y José el Lupe,*' she said.

'Yes?' Pilar looked puzzled. Then her face lightened. 'Ah, those types! Yes, it is more than possible. If the little boy had gone again to visit the cave of dead men – if Uncle Horse knew he was going –'

'Had, perhaps, dared him to go there again?'

Pilar nodded, put her hands on her hips, and swayed excitedly.

'Yes, yes! It could be! I think it was like that. But what can we do? We cannot hunt brigands during the wilds of the night.'

Dame Beatrice agreed, displaying a gravity that befitted the situation.

'Will the bandits ill-treat the boy?' she asked. Pilar looked astounded.

'Ill-treat him? Would anyone on Hombres Muertos ill-treat a child? No, no! Have no fear for that. If the child is made to vomit, it will be with rich food; if to cry, it will be after much wine; if he should seem to moan, it will be the bagpipes they teach him to play; if to scream, it will be with the laughter they make up there.'

'In other words, he'll be safe enough tonight and we may as well leave it until the morning before we attempt to rescue him?'

'It will be easier to pay the money. It will cost less in the end,' said Pilar.

'That may be so, but nobody pays money if he can get what he wants for nothing. Tell me, Pilar, everything you can about Mrs Angel.'

'That one? But I am forbidden to discuss the guests with other guests.'

'Don't be stupid. You know perfectly well what I want

to know. If you do not, I will tell you in words that cannot
be misinterpreted.'

Pilar gave a wilder giggle than usual, glanced round the
room, drew nearer to the small, spare figure in the dragon-
strewn dressing-gown, and whispered:

'It's true. They sell their daughters to that wicked old
woman. Yes! Three or four years she lives here, and always the cave girls, they go.'

'The cave girls?'

'Sí, Señora. No one else will sell daughters. They are
needed for the cultivation – the bananas, the terraced
lands, the sugar-cane. But the cave people have no cultivation. They are the old people of the island. Not Spaniards, not anything now. There is nothing up there,
nothing. They go into the cigar factories and spend their
money on finery, so their fathers and brothers sell them to
Mrs Angel and she pays for them to go to South America,
and they are never heard of again. But it is lawful, so they
tell me, because the girls all say they want to go.'

'I see. That might explain the field-glasses, I suppose.
No wonder she was flustered when I mentioned David and
Bathsheba.'

'Please?'

'Not a story you would know, Pilar. Does Mrs Angel
really watch birds?'

'Oh, yes. It is true. The boatmen take her round the
coast to the wild places. They say she climbs cliffs. She is
bold and strong. Also they say that she can make bird-call,
and that eagles feed out of her hand.'

Dame Beatrice ruled out the eagles, but was inclined to
believe the rest of the report. Mrs Angel, it seemed, was a
woman of parts compounded of good and bad, like the
curate's egg.

'And Mr Peterhouse?' asked Dame Beatrice.

'He? He has great curiosity. He takes much interest in
everything, but for no information is there payment. Pepe
has complained much of that.'

'What information does he seek?'

'Of the fish, the birds, the soil, the rocks, the crops, the houses, the number of children, the age of marriage, the cave people, the bandits – everything.'

'Including, I suppose, the plants and flowers.'

'No, Señora. Never of the plants and flowers.'

'I thought he collected orchids.'

'It may be so; he does not speak of them to Pepe. However, he climbs much, and always alone. Sometimes he puts out to sea and climbs mountains in other islands.'

'Is that not dangerous?'

'It may be dangerous. I know nothing of that. He makes maps.'

'Maps?'

'Sí, Señora. When I have taken coffee to his room I have found him busy making maps.'

'How do you know they were maps?'

'He has said so,' replied Pilar, with dignity. 'What is more, they were very pretty, with colours of green and yellow and red.'

'Brown?'

'Not brown, but I think to remember purple.'

Dame Beatrice went to bed thoughtful. Early next morning she set out, with Pilar's Pepe Casita for guide and guarantee, to look for Clement Drashleigh.

CHAPTER 4

Uncle Horse and José the Wolf

'WHERE do we go, Señora?' asked Pepe Casita.

'To the cave of dead men. You may sit in front, beside the driver of the taxi-cab.'

'Very good. And then?'

'Then I shall wait upon inspiration and rely upon your acquaintance with the bandits.'

'But, Señora, I know nothing of the bandits except what I have heard.'

Dame Beatrice was not inclined to take notice of this disclaimer. The taxi took them to the village from which Peterhouse had hired the mules on Dame Beatrice's first visit to the cave. The negotiations were conducted by Pepe, who haggled for twenty minutes and then returned to announce that he had secured two reliable animals at a low fee. They mounted these and soon were being borne along the mountain path to the cave.

'Look after the mules. I am going inside to count the bodies,' said Dame Beatrice.

'Alone, Señora?'

'Certainly. Fear not for me. I have my little gun.'

'I fear dead men, not living ones, Señora.'

'To each his own fears and his own precautions. Does Uncle Horse suffer in health from living up here among the mountains?'

'It is said', replied Pepe, cautiously, 'that he suffers from a fall he had two months ago. He has a pain in his back – here.'

'Well, you had better get in touch with him whilst I am in the cave. Tell him I can put him to rights and that I will do so, provided that he hands over the señorito safe and sound, and at once.'

'I do not know the bandits,' reiterated Pepe, with a charming smile and a shrug of his thin shoulders.

'It will be worth your while to get to know them, then. Whistle them up. They can't be far away, if they continually lie in wait for those rash persons who choose to visit the caves without a guide.'

With these confident words she gave a slight nod and walked in at the mouth of the cave. She had brought the torch which she always kept on her bedside table in case the electric light in the hotel failed. She switched it on, and counted the seated bodies. There were twenty-three of them. She searched each corner of the cave, lighting up every cranny with the torch, but of Clement's twenty-fourth man there was no sign. She was about to make closer investigation of the twenty-three who were there, when she heard a shout from the mouth of the cave.

'*Señora, el señorito!*'

Dame Beatrice emerged into the sunlight. There stood Clement, hatless and grimy. He was leading a mule and wore a slightly defiant smile.

'No bandits?' enquired Dame Beatrice, removing her own chip straw hat and placing it on his head. 'I shall not suffer from the heat of the sun, but you may, dear child. Wear this, on pain of death, until we get to the village. I repeat: no bandits?'

'They wouldn't come. They're shy. They're awfully decent, though,' said Clement, banging the hat well down upon his head. 'Still, the food was pretty lousy, and there wasn't any ice-cream, and all we had to drink was goats' milk and the local wine – both completely foul.'

'What made you visit the cave again? – I suppose that is how you came to be captured?'

'Well, yes. I simply had to, you know. I expect you can guess why.'

'I imagine', said Dame Beatrice, patting her animal's neck, 'that you counted the bodies again and discovered that, after all, there were twenty-three and not twenty-four of them.'

'Well, at any rate, I had to give Chiquito the ten pesetas I'd betted him. I had just given them to him when we found ourselves surrounded. Ugly chaps, most of them were. They sent Chiquito home after he'd sworn by various saints and people that he wouldn't breathe a word about where I was, but they grabbed me and my mule, and took me to their den. How did you guess where I was? – or did Chiquito unfold a tale after all?'

'As far as I know, he kept his word to the bandits.'

'If he *had* told, I should have had my revenge on him. Revenge is sweet.'

'Revenge? An outmoded conception. Experience teaches that it really *is* nobler in the mind to suffer the slings and arrows of outrageous fortune.'

Clement, it was clear, was not prepared to endorse this view. They rode down the narrow and forbidding mountain track in silence until he said:

'The trouble with these islanders is that they're not nearly tough enough. I was amazed at my treatment, especially as I told old Caballo right at the beginning, when he grabbed me, that my parents, far from paying money to get me back, would thank him for hanging on to me. Luckily, I can speak a fair amount of island Spanish – I learnt it on our own island, you know – but old Tio Caballo doesn't know any English except O.K. Everything, according to him, was O.K. The only thing that wasn't O.K. was the food and drink – in my opinion, at any rate. I shan't be at all sorry to get back to the hotel and eat a decent meal.'

When they did reach the Hotel Sombrero, his parents attempted to carry out their plan of doing nothing to inhibit him, but for once it broke down. Mrs Drashleigh was obviously affected by the reunion, and proved this by an outburst of nagging. Mr Drashleigh said:

'Now see what you've done to your mother! It has been very inconsiderate of you, Clement. Fancy going again to that cave, foolish boy!'

Clement defended himself with a mixture of fact and fiction.

'Well, I had to take a dare, didn't I? You wouldn't

want me to look a fool in front of a *native* like Chiquito Daria! And how was I to know that the bandits were on the prowl? *I* didn't ask to be kidnapped, did I? And I've saved you an awful lot of money, let me tell you! How? Well, all night long I howled like a wolf. It always gets on *your* nerves when I do, so I thought maybe it would get on *theirs*, and it did. I thought they'd gag me, but they hate being unkind to children, so they put up with it as long as they could, and then bribed me to leave off. I did, because my throat was getting sore, but I made them promise to let me go. I made them take a Church oath. They're terribly religious, you know. But Pilar's Pepe came along before they actually freed me, and talked a lot of Spanish like an automatic weapon and they seemed only too glad to see the last of me. And you'd better give Pepe some money. I think he left them a lot of cigarettes. They were terribly pleased, because it's difficult for them to shop down here in the town. They get their food and wine from the villages, but they can't get smokes that way – not American ones, which is what they like. I shall probably go along and see them again, some time, and take them some more cigarettes, if you go on at me much longer. I've had a worrying time, let me tell you.'

'Well, now you had better get some sleep,' said Mr Drashleigh. 'And, another time, learn to curb your curiosity. It is morbid in so young a boy to want to see dead people.'

'You took me to the British Museum, when I was eight, to see the Egyptian mummies,' argued Clement. 'But that was educational, I suppose!'

'You are not be impudent,' said Mr Drashleigh.

'Well, if it wasn't educational, I don't see why you took me. Mother, when you went to the cave, did you actually *count* the bodies?'

'No, dear, but I thought they were very impressive.'

'Was one a lot taller than the rest?'

'Taller? It might have been. I couldn't be positively sure.'

'Ah, well, it's just as well I *did* go to the cave, then. The first time I went, there were definitely twenty-four bodies, as I told people when I got back, but now there are only twenty-three. I had plenty of time to count them and look round a bit before the bandits caught me. And, I tell you, one of the dead men was quite noticeably taller than the rest. He was there when there were twenty-four, and he was still there when there were twenty-three, yet you say you didn't notice him. You *must* have noticed him, Mother. I bet Dame Beatrice noticed him.'

'Yes, I did,' said Dame Beatrice.

'Not on your first visit, though? Not when you went with Mother and Mr Peterhouse? Are you *sure?*'

'Go to bed, Clement, and stop pestering people,' said Mr Drashleigh, with unwonted firmness.

'I want something to eat; something decent. The bandits' food was horrible!'

'Very well. Pilar shall bring you a menu as soon as you are in bed, and you can have your meal on a tray.'

'And I can really have what I like?'

'Well, not shell-fish, my boy.'

'Who wants shell-fish? I tell you I want something to *eat*!'

He was hustled away, intoning, with the relish of a *gourmand*, a recital of all the dishes he would choose if these should be on the menu. The gong was sounded for lunch – very late, as usual – and Dame Beatrice went to the table which she shared with Clun.

After coffee on the terrace, he left her, on the excuse that he was going fishing out in the bay. Dame Beatrice, relaxed and slightly somnolent after her morning's expedition, lay back in a comfortable chair and speculated idly upon Clement Drashleigh. She wished she knew some way of persuading his foolish foster-parents to send him to an English boarding-school. Her thoughts were interrupted by the appearance of Ruiz, who came up to her and said softly, but in a voice hoarse with fury:

'If he had not left my hotel, I would have kicked him

out. I would have strangled him. Even now, if ever I meet him, the villain, the cesspool, the pig, I will tear him in pieces! I will have him deported! I am Ruiz! He has dared to attempt to compromise my daughter, my Luisa! But that she carries always in her stocking a knife which she would not hesitate to use in defence of her modesty, he might even have contrived to take advantage of her. He is a beast, an ape, a baboon!'

'Dear me!' Dame Beatrice remarked. 'You, my good host, appear to have cause for complaint. How much of a German is Mr Emden, I wonder? One cannot go by physiognomy, of course, so it is of no avail to say that he has not the appearance of a true Nordic of unmixed blood. One can sometimes go a little by accent, but his, so far as I have been privileged to hear it, seems to be that of Walthamstow overlaid by the B.B.C. An original mixture, one would be inclined to think, to trip from the tongue of a Prussian. You *do* speak of Emden, I take it?'

'Speak of him? I spit upon his name!' declared Ruiz, in the same low, vindictive tone. 'And he shall go. I, Ruiz, have said it. He shall return to the slum that spawned him!'

'Was he, by any chance, talking of Emden?' asked Peterhouse, who had come up before Ruiz had finished speaking, and who now took the cushioned wicker chair next to that of Dame Beatrice.

'Undoubtedly,' she replied. 'It was odd that Emden should vanish before we had time and opportunity to make his acquaintance.'

'I didn't like him,' said Peterhouse, 'and I consider that his departure from the hotel was opportune. If he really *has* insulted Luisa Ruiz, he will do well to keep away. Spaniards are notably temperamental where their womenfolk are concerned, and, so far as I can discover, this island has no law against murder.'

'Really? How very interesting.'

'What, do you suppose, made that extraordinary child pay two visits to the cave of dead men? Anything more than sheer curiosity?'

'Curiosity would have much to do with it, no doubt. He's an intelligent little boy.'

'Too intelligent to tell as much as he knew, I expect.'

'Now, why should you suppose that?'

'I have no notion, dear lady. Just a passing thought.'

'I believe that thoughts should linger. I am inclined to distrust vapours and thin airs.'

'Yes, and there's such a thing as thin ice,' said Peterhouse, half to himself. Dame Beatrice gazed at him and raised her black eyebrows.

'Thin ice?' she inquired. 'You believe we are treading on thin ice?'

Peterhouse shook his head.

'I believe we have not heard the last of Emden,' he said. 'I wish I thought we had. He's been on the island two months – no longer – and has contrived to set everybody by the ears.'

'Two months? He came here –?'

'You can check from the visitors' book, but, to the best of my recollection, this would be his ninth or tenth week in Reales. Now tell me about the man Clun. Is he really a killer?'

'I would not put it like that.'

'But he did kill a man, and was put away for a stretch in prison, I believe?'

'He killed a man in a fight, I understand, and went to prison for manslaughter.'

'An uncomfortable fellow-traveller! I shall steer clear of him. Is it true that he and that young fellow Telham had a quarrel?'

'Mr Telham arrived here in a highly nervous state, but his sojourn on the island seems to have done him good.'

'It hasn't done his sister good. I'm told she had a fit of hysterics in the cave of dead kings.'

'You are *told?* But you were there!'

'I was there? ... Oh, *so* I was! How stupid of me.'

It was a curious lapse of memory, Dame Beatrice thought, and lapses of memory were psychologically interesting. To relieve him from embarrassment, she referred to her impending visit to the troglodytes, adding that she supposed such visits were quite common.

'Certainly. Visitors to the island often go to look at the cave-dwellers. There are just one or two things to remember,' said Peterhouse, seizing on the chance to impart information.

'The outer room is clean, neat, unoccupied, and for show,' said Dame Beatrice. 'The inner room, divided from the outer by a curtain or screen, is the family dwelling-place and has to be smelt to be believed.'

Mr Peterhouse looked disappointed.

'I thought it would be new to you,' he said. 'But there is another thing. The cave-dwellers are quite untutored and are as grasping as savages. They have neither manners nor morals.'

'Then it is unfair to compare them with savages, who, so far as my experience goes, obey a stricter code than our own. But you say that the cave-dwellers are grasping. What, precisely, do they grasp?'

'It is not possible to be precise. Their tastes are catholic. The young girls have a tremendous liking for ladies' fancy handkerchiefs, particularly if these be edged with lace. Brooches and bracelets, necklaces and wrist-watches they also find highly desirable, and from gentlemen they are apt to extract cigarette cases, lighters, and tie-pins. Nobody begs for any of these things but the young girls. The boys are too proud and the older people are too dignified to be mendicants. On the other hand, the old women always have goods for sale – mostly rubbish, of course.'

'How very interesting. I heard that the parents sell the young girls to South America. Is there any evidence of that?'

'I have no idea. I shouldn't think there's much in it. The girls are the only members of the family who earn any money. They work in the cigar factories and on the banana plantations, you know.'

'But a lump sum down, and no marriage dowry for the family to find –?'

'Well, maybe. But if you got the story from Pilar I shouldn't put too much faith in it. What she doesn't know she invents, and her imagination is a lively one.'

'How long has Mrs Angel lived on the island?'

'She came here when *I* came, and I've lived here for twenty years.'

'You remember her as a young woman, then?'

'As a good-looking one, too. Of course, she wasn't resident in the sense that she is now. She was always cutting her stick and going off to South America.'

'Really? Oh, yes, Pilar the Unreliable seemed to think that Mrs Angel had interests over there.'

'Not so unreliable, you think? I agree that her information is occasionally correct. It's the use she makes of it, and the interpretation she puts on it, that make her a person to beware of.'

'I will make a note of it. How long will it take me to reach the cave-dwellers?'

'It depends.'

'On the means of transport, I presume. How many cave-dwellers are there?'

'A couple of hundred: not more; possibly fewer. The caves are part of an ancient stronghold and form two or three galleries, as it were, in a hillside. They are very interesting. Of course, they're all liars and thieves up there. They are not Spaniards. They are probably the only true survivors of the original inhabitants of the island. Take a guide, or you may run into Tio Caballo and his band. Their haunts are all over these mountains.'

'Tio Caballo and José the Wolf are sensible creatures. They would know that the chances of anybody wishing to ransom *me* are small indeed, and smaller than that word. I think we may discount the theory that they will capture me if I go without a guide.'

'They might even murder you, dear lady. There is no adequate police force on the island to take action in such an eventuality. I feel it my duty to warn you of that, and to beg you to take Pilar's young man, or someone else who is known to the band.'

'Pepe Casita appears to be a person of parts.'

'He's an out-and-out young villain! They will make a pretty couple, he and Pilar, when they're married. Nobody's money and nobody's reputation will be safe.'

'Dear me! And both of them so young! And Pilar, apart from her tendency, as you say, to shatter reputations, such a good, kind girl!'

Peterhouse snorted.

'She's an impertinent little busybody!' he declared. 'I wouldn't trust her even as far as I could see her. Do you know what she told Ruiz about me? She told him I manufactured dope up in the mountains and sold it to the sailors when the liners put in here to disembark passengers.'

'Dear me! That was extremely indiscreet of her. What made her think of such a thing?'

'I could not say. She likes to make mischief. I wonder what she will find to say about you? Nobody is safe from her exaggerations.'

'It will be interesting to find out what she says about me, then. I do hope that, if rumours come to your ears, you will keep me posted.'

'Be assured that I will. Where is the young man Clun? I saw him go by with a fishing-rod. I wonder whether he will take long to recapture the art? He can hardly have practised it in prison! You would be well advised to have as little to do with him as possible.'

'Oh, I scarcely think he will prove dangerous.'

'You think he has had his lesson? I doubt it. Once a killer, always a killer, you know.'

'Such is not my experience. Besides, Mr Clun had no intention of killing, I am certain.'

'He looks a violent, uncontrolled person. Personally, I shall take great care never to be left alone with him. I was not sorry when he did not join the party which went to the cave. I wish you could have come, though.'

'I did come, if you remember.'

'Oh, did you?' He looked thoughtful, but Dame Beatrice knew that he was suffering from a state of mental fugue. She shook her head, but decided that, at the moment, it was no concern of hers. He came to with a start. 'What were we talking about?' he asked. 'I'm so sorry. I think the years of sunshine have addled my pate. Do forgive me! Are you an expert on forestry?'

'No, I fear not. I know the names of several trees, but there my knowledge ends.'

'A pity. I was going to ask you whether you thought the Turkey oak would flourish here. I must find out from Kew. Perhaps they would send me some acorns to plant.'

He walked briskly away. Dame Beatrice followed him with her eyes. As though he felt that she had called to him, he swung round and came striding back.

'I was going to ask you', she said, 'to tell me more about the bandits.'

'Ah,' said Peterhouse, 'I can tell you no more than I have told you already. As for that boy, I shouldn't believe a word he says, if I were you. He follows people about, you know, and spies on them. I believe he knows perfectly well where Emden has gone. You ask him, and see whether he does not.'

'Why not ask him yourself?'

'I don't care to be answered rudely.'

'I call that a very unchivalrous reason. If one of us is to suffer, does not convention demand that you, the male, assume the mantle of heroism?'

'You are jesting with me, dear lady.' He smiled with his lips, disclosing large, uneven, yellow teeth, but the smile did not extend to his eyes.

CHAPTER 5

The Living Troglodytes

THE hotel grape-vine, it appeared, had apprised most of the guests of Dame Beatrice's determination to visit the community of cave-dwellers.

'Nothing could be easier,' Mrs Angel assured her. 'And on no account take any notice of Mr Peterhouse. He specializes in jeremiads. He believes that the poor old cave-dwellers deal in witchcraft and less innocuous matters. He really *is* a silly old man.'

'*Less* innocuous matters?'

'Sodom and Gomorrah couldn't hold a candle to that man's mind, and, if they did, it would explode.'

'Really?'

'You sound incredulous. My Talkie has gone! It was that wretched Karl Emden.'

'It is in the hope of seeing him that I propose to visit the troglodytes.'

'Their caves are extremely insanitary. Have you brought a small-tooth comb? But, whether you have or whether you have not, remember to take no notice of anything Mr Peterhouse tells you. A most unreliable man, and hopelessly misinformed. You need to beware of him, you know. I do not believe he can distinguish between fat and fiction, and his memory is faulty, too. He would make a very bad witness in a court of law. And on no account allow him to accompany you. The cave-dwellers do not like him.'

Dame Beatrice certainly did not propose to seek his company on her visit to the troglodyte community, yet she agreed with him that it might be as well to take a guide. She spoke of this to Pilar.

'Your Pepe. Is he at liberty to escort me to the community of cave-dwellers?'

'For how much?' inquired Pilar, who believed in the direct approach.

'That is for him to say.'

'Then it will be too much. Offer fifty pesetas. It is plenty.'

'What about thirty?'

'That', said Pilar readily, 'would also be plenty. Give him twenty-five.'

'Very well, and here are ten pesetas for yourself. Please ask Pepe to undertake the hire of the mules.'

'No, no. You must not hire mules for that excursion. You go there in state, in a motor car.'

'Why?'

'The cave-dwellers have their pride. They are always visited by motor car. No one would think of anything else. There is quite a good road.'

So Dame Beatrice, accompanied by a newly shaven Pepe Casita, journeyed to the caves of Nuestra Doña de Mercedes in a hired limousine of 1935 vintage driven by a reckless islander named Ignacio Verde on Pilar's idea of a good road.

'We are here,' announced Ignacio, skidding to a halt on the edge of a thousand-foot drop. 'I wait two hours. Or more. Or less. As you wish. Your time is mine. Let us say two hours, shall we?'

They said two hours; then Pepe led the way to the caves. These as Peterhouse had stated, formed part of what had been a stronghold of the islanders before the time of the Spanish conquerors and it overlooked a deep river valley. The entrances were walled up except for the narrow doors. These were all closed and there was nobody to be seen.

'They heard the sound of the automobile,' said Pepe, a graceful, sad-eyed youth wearing a distressing pin-striped suit of navy-blue and a fancy hat like a fringed lamp-shade. 'They are within. I shall shout.'

This he did, and, without waiting for the result, retired to the car which had brought them. A boy's face appeared round the edge of a door and was immediately withdrawn. A moment later a lacquer-haired, full-faced woman of about twenty-five appeared in the doorway and beckoned to the visitor.

'We are here since twelve hundred years,' she announced, 'and we are the native peoples of the island. Before us we have photography showing my father's family, my mother's family, and an iron candlestick, property of Philip II, Spanish Armada, of Madrid, the Escorial. You are English lady, yes? Please to look around, and then I sell you the island pottery, not made on a wheel, secret of this place since ancient history times. I am educated in a convent. You may rely on me.'

Dame Beatrice bought the piece of pottery and asked how many members there were of the woman's family.

'We are eighteen,' was the reply. 'Six dead. So twelve.'

'And you all live behind that curtain?' asked Dame Beatrice, pointing to a horse-blanket which decorated the back of the cave.

'Certainly, but I cannot show you. We show only the *sala de recibo*.'

'And do you take lodgers?'

'With twelve living here? Good gracious me!'

In the next cave, the hostess was a black-eyed, tousle-haired girl of about sixteen who seized the lace-edged handkerchief Dame Beatrice held out and then, with a shrill cry, disappeared behind the curtain which, again, separated the whitewashed front of the cave from the malodorous living-quarters.

The apparently ubiquitous family photographs, an old-fashioned gramophone, and a basket chair of island manufacture formed the principal features of the parlour. Dame Beatrice scrutinized the photographs and wondered how best to introduce the reason for her visit. She was not left alone very long, for the girl reappeared, accompanied by a negroid crone of uncertain age who walked with the aid of a stick.

'I am blind,' announced the crone. 'I have lived in this cave since birth. I love the Americans, all of you. The

Americans are good people. They always give money. I do not object to payment in dollars. I shall sell you a piece of pottery. The like is not to be obtained by your friends. Unique. Indestructible. I do not love Communists. I love the American nation. Give me much money.'

To one so single-minded, Dame Beatrice thought it might be well to introduce the object of her visit as bluntly as possible.

'Where does the Señor Carlos Emden lodge?' she asked, pressing a ten-shilling note into an outstretched hand.

'You must take back your money. I do not know,' said the old woman. 'I have heard nothing of a gentleman so named.'

'No? That is a pity. But the money is for you, not for what you can tell me. Have you really not heard the name before? Karl Emden. He came to live in a cave. He left his hotel in Reales to become a cave-dweller like yourself. He is fascinated by the people of this island.'

'No. He has not come. I should have heard. I hear everything. When you are blind you hear everything and you feel the sunshine. Give me more money. It is your duty.'

'Tell me about Karl Emden.'

'I tell you that I do not know him. He is not here. He is not one of us. From Reales, you say? I have not been in Reales for twenty-five years. Have you looked at the photographs of my sons and daughters? And of my brothers and sisters? Do you wish to buy pottery? Would you like to buy a bottle of wine or a basket chair? I will make you a special price. You are old, like me. I can smell it.'

So it went on, until Dame Beatrice had visited six of the curious homesteads. No one would acknowledge any acquaintanceship with Emden and she was forced to the conclusion that, whatever his intentions might have been, he could not have come to the caves. If he had, the cave-dwellers were saying nothing about it. She was interested. She returned to the hired car while she considered the matter. It was easy to see cause and effect, especially when the evidence was circumstantial, as she very well knew, but, all the same, there was something disturbing in the fact that, the day after the *Alaric* had docked, the most individual and (if one admired the dress of the islanders) the most picturesque guest at the Hotel Sombrero had elected to forego the comfort and good food provided by Señor Ruiz and had announced his intention of joining the troglodytes.

Pepe Casita, with the sympathy of his kind, realized that she was troubled.

'You do not care for the caves?' he inquired. 'They are of the beasts, those people. Well I know it.'

'They are most interesting. Did you know that the Señor Emden, who was staying at the Hotel Sombrero, told us that he proposed to go and live there?'

'In the caves?'

'Yes, in the caves.'

'Impossible, Señora.'

'Why so?'

'It is unknown to dwell in the caves for anybody but *habitante de las cavernas*.'

'I don't see why.'

'*Los trogloditas*', said Pepe earnestly, 'are not of our world. They are *primitivos*. They do not conform. Only visitors and priests go to see them. They are *piojosos*, You understand?'

'Only too well. But perhaps Señor Emden is interested in anthropology – and in lice.'

'I believe, Señora, that Señor Emden is dead. He is in the cave of dead men. I have it from Tio Caballo. There is no doubt about the matter.'

'You think that the bandits have murdered him?'

'Oh, no! Oh, no! Tio Caballo is a good man. He murders nobody except his enemies. How could Señor Emden be his enemy? He has lived at the hotel only since two months. Besides, we do not make enemies of the tourists. It is not good business.'

'All the same, Señor Emden seems to have stirred up trouble.'

'Yes,' admitted Pepe, suddenly gritting his teeth. 'Pilar tells me so. But that I know her to be a virtuous girl, and not a *coqueta,* I would not marry her. But Tio Caballo had no quarrel with Señor Emden. How could he? He has no women in his life. One cannot consider his elderly mother.'

The driver of the hired car, who had joined them and was moodily kicking the front wall of an unoccupied cave, turned his head and said abruptly:

'The Señor Emden is a pig. He gives no gratuities.'

As this observation did not help in any way, Dame Beatrice ignored it, but Pepe said:

'You have reason, my friend. Those who give no gratuities are without a soul. They are of the nature of the beasts.'

'I am anxious to discover what has happened to this man without a soul,' said Dame Beatrice.

'Without doubt, he is in the cave of dead men,' declared Pepe. 'That is for certain. Tio Caballo has told me so, and he is an honourable man who would not deceive even his mother-in-law, if he had one.'

Dame Beatrice was convinced, by this time, that there was no news to be obtained from the troglodytes. She was about to get into the car when it was surrounded by a bevy of girls who had just climbed the hill. Laughing, and pushing one another, they crowded round her. One begged for a brooch she was wearing, another for her watch. Half a dozen voices demanded handkerchiefs. The voices were good-humoured and vociferous. The eyes were vulpine.

Dame Beatrice, like a conjurer, began producing handkerchiefs. They fluttered from the ends of her sleeves, from the pockets of her silk jacket, from her handbag, from the inside of her sunshade. A breeze on the hillside carried them, and the girls ran shrieking after them. Dame Beatrice, having dispersed the company, went to the door of the next cave. Another elderly woman stood here.

'You need make no more inquiries for the gentleman you seek. He is not here. Nobody new has come to the caves,' she said civilly, in quiet tones, and in Spanish flavoured only slightly by the island *patois*. 'There was a mad Englishman who came, like yourself, to make a visit here, and who offered me much money to hide him, but I like not to associate with those who hide from their enemies. If the enemies find out, they make trouble.'

'Can you describe him?'

'No. I did not take notice. He spoke Spanish from a little book, and, even so, very badly. I think he went from me to Aroja Pieta, and I think she promised to hide him until a ship called. But he has gone now. Are you his grandmother?'

'No, we are not related. We were fellow-guests at the hotel. I heard that he wished to live here, and I was interested to find out whether he liked the caves.'

'I cannot tell you. No, I cannot help you at all. Aroja Pieta lives in the fourth cave from this one. You could speak with her.'

Aroja Pieta turned out to be a middle-aged woman with much coarse black hair and an expression of surprise due to the fact that she had plucked her eyebrows. Her skirts were kilted to display a petticoat made from a blanket, and she flourished a brush which, at the moment when Dame Beatrice called, was dripping whitewash over the earthen floor of her cave.

'I shall sell you no pottery,' she announced. 'It is rubbish. I have here Roman lamps and coins. Antiques. Very good. Not like the pottery, which is rubbish. Also I have trinkets. I have ivory, jade, a silk shawl, a bell for your he-goat. What would you like?'

Dame Beatrice settled for a necklace of which none but the largest bead was of ivory, and then referred to the object of her visit.

'The señor from Reales? The Englishman? A strange person, for who would inhabit a cave when he could command the best house in Reales? Believe me, he is in trouble with his enemies. Myself, I care nothing for his past, no, not an unripe fig, so, when the Señor offers me money to be permitted to hide in my cave until a ship comes for him from England, I say to myself, "Why not?" Who sent him to me? That she-ass Serafina Todos. She thinks much of herself because she was born in La Linea. What a place! The streets stink. She would like to know all my business, that one!'

'And the Englishman?'

'Do I not tell you? I am whitening the walls against fleas, as he has requested me to do, but he does not come back any more. If he had fallen down the mountain, I should have heard. He has not, therefore, fallen down the mountain. Where, I ask myself, has he gone? You are sure he has left the hotel?'

'Yes, I am certain. That is, if we are speaking of the same man.'

'There could not be two. This man comes at the hour of siesta. He goes to Serafina Todos who is fool enough to be proud of herself. He comes to me from her and makes much talk of money if I will whitewash the walls against fleas. What are fleas? We call them little brothers. So I say to the Englishman that I whitewash the walls tomorrow. You see how I keep my word.'

She slopped whitewash about her in a freehanded, haphazard manner to prove her point. Dame Beatrice stepped out of range. She knew the Spanish, inconsequential, vague 'tomorrow'. She knew, too, that the islanders (and this, she felt certain, was also true of the troglodyte islanders) had no sense of time. The only day of the week they seemed able to name with any certainty was Sunday and the only dates they seemed able to remember were those of the *fiestas*. It would be useless, and also misleading, to attempt to find out from Doña Aroja on which day the Englishman had made his appearance.

'Did you never see him again after that first time?' she asked. Aroja Pieta paused in the whitewashing.

'Never again. He comes. He makes the arrangements –

honourably, as I think. He goes. He comes not yet. I still expect him. It is not with the English as with some others. If they make an arrangement it will be honoured. Unless he is dead, he will come. Now you will give me money, because you have taken my time, but, unless you are related to him, I do not understand why you seek him. You should not believe a young man's promises of marriage. Young men do not want to marry old women except for their money. Are you rich?'

'Not rich enough to tempt a young man into marriage. Your other supposition would appear to be more reasonable.'

'So. You are his grandmother.'

'I want to know whether we are speaking of the same young man. Describe him to me.'

'How can I?'

'Was he dark or fair?'

'He had a pale face, very handsome, very white. Eyes of a libertine.'

'His hair?'

'He was wearing a big hat like a peasant hat. He carried also a blanket, like the mountain shepherds, but it was clean. He was afraid. His eyes went this way, that way. He spoke out of a little book. It was difficult to understand him. Now tell me truthfully why you have come here today.'

'I wished to see why he should come to live in the caves.'

'Ah, that! You shall come tomorrow, and I may have news for you. Now you would like to give me a little more money, not for trade; for the love of God.'

'Next time.'

'A mañana!'

'A mañana!'

Dame Beatrice returned to the car and so to the Hotel Sombrero, driven at breakneck speed along Pilar's good road, Ignacio removing his hands from the wheel at one or two hairpin bends in order, by using graphic gestures, to feature various accidents he had witnessed on that very mountain-side. Dame Beatrice mused philosophically upon the Mohammedan theory of Kismet. It began to emerge as a reasonable doctrine and one extremely soothing to the nerves.

Mrs Angel met her on the terrace.

'Well?' she said. 'Did you find out about my Talkie?'

'You mentioned it before. Pray elucidate.'

'My bird.'

'Then nothing came out about it.'

'What did you think of the caves?'

'I did not find them worth a visit, but the cave-dwellers did find my visit worth while.'

'Rapacious creatures!'

'I take it that they are very poor, so I paid as graciously as I could.'

She went into the hotel and met Peterhouse at the foot of the wide stone stair. He wagged a playful finger.

'So you went to the caves! I wish now that I had gone with you. How did you get on?'

'I was mulcted of much cash.'

'Undoubtedly. That is why you would have been better off with an escort who knew the ropes. I do wish I had thought of it. What a pity you did not suggest it! However, I am to blame.'

'It is gallant of you not to reproach me. All the same, I found out what I went to find out.'

'The habits of a troglodyte people? But, from what you told me before you went, I gathered that you knew something of their way of life already.'

'I went to find out whether Mr Emden had gone there to live.'

'Emden? I have studied him closely since he came to stay at the hotel, and I would not be surprised at anything he did. The man is crazy. There you have it in a nutshell.'

'It seems as though the man has disappeared.'

'Disappeared? What gave you that idea, Dame Beatrice? Do you mean voluntarily or involuntarily?'

'More than one otherwise inexplicable circumstance gave me the idea. As for your second question...'

'Well, he was a beastly sort of fellow, I am sure. It may be a very good thing if he has gone.'

'That may well be so. Nevertheless, I feel sufficiently interested to have made up my mind to trace all his movements up to the time he was last seen, which, it turns out, may or may not have been at the caves.'

'How do you mean?'

'I mean that Mr Emden may have been seen there by his murderer, and that his murderer is unlikely to have been one of the troglodytes, Mr Peterhouse.'

CHAPTER 6

The Twenty-Fourth Man

IT was no easier than Dame Beatrice had imagined it would be to obtain information leading to an understanding of Emden's disappearance. Tentative and tactful soundings led nowhere, and it was not until the disappearance excited general comment that anything helpful was forthcoming.

The first news that others besides Dame Beatrice (and these for more personal reasons) were interested in Emden's fate came by way of Pepe Casita. He turned up at the hotel one morning in response to a message from Ruiz.

'You have a party to go to the cave of dead men? You wish to have a guide? But none of the guides will go,' said Pepe flatly.

From their seats in the lounge and on the veranda, the guests could hear the argument which ensued.

'Not to go? And why? Are they all millionaires that they are able to turn down a party of eleven of my guests, new by air yesterday, who wish to visit the cave? Am I to lose my little-enough share in the profits because of these lazy pigs? Go back at once and say that I want two guides, nine mules, and two small docile asses to be ready in one hour from now at Ychos. Do not reply, but go.'

'Understand me, Señor. When I say the guides will not go, I mean it. Nothing will move them. They say the cave is a bad place now. Even the bandits do not like it.'

'What is there for them to do today? I speak of the guides, not the bandits. Is it, I ask, a day of fiesta? Is it a day on which they mourn their grandmothers? Or is it that they are emigrating to the island of apes where live their kindred? Stop being a fool, or you will never work with me again.'

'I tell you, Señor Ruiz, I tell you, Don Jorge, that the cave is bewitched.'

'*Cincuenta diablos! Maldito amuleto de apóstata! Encantar la caverna de los hombres muertos – Santo Pedro! Una risotada inflada!*'

'Truly, it is nothing to laugh at, Señor. I, Pepe, assure you that the guides will not go. I myself am not superstitious, as you know. I am not an ignorant man. But even I do not care to go near the ghost of Señor Emden. It is a bad ghost, owing money to all the wine-shops in Reales, yes, and inheriting the curses of fathers, brothers, husbands, lovers. Oh, it is a bad place now, the cave of the dead men.'

'Señor Emden? He is dead? Then the *niño did* speak the truth when he said he saw twenty-four bodies! *Madre de Dios!* What misfortune will this bring upon me and my hotel?'

'Emden dead!' One hotel guest muttered it to another, and the word was passed round. Those who were feeling slightly bored by the lack of excitement they had experienced so far in the island capital, with its meagre and mediocre gaieties, hitched their chairs closer to catch the rest of the conversation, but apparently it was over, for Pepe's voice was heard no more, and Ruiz, followed by his daughter Luisa, came into the lounge, Luisa carrying a large black book, the hotel ledger.

The guests began to chatter.

'It can't be so very serious,' said Mrs Angel, betraying by this example of wishful thinking that she suspected the reverse to be the truth. 'I mean, people disappear for the strangest reasons.'

'He's probably gone over to one of the other islands,' said Peterhouse. 'I don't really think we need worry.'

'I shall worry if he doesn't pay his bill,' said Ruiz, to whom this remark had been addressed. 'How much does he owe, Luisa?'

'Four hundred and fifty pesetas, my father. He paid a little last Saturday.'

'That is something. He has run from my hotel for his life, I think.'

'He's one of the dead men on Monte Negro,' said Clement, who had only just come in, and who had not heard Pepe's remarks. 'That's where you ought to go and look, unless the bandits have cooked and eaten him. Somebody's slugged that slob.'

'Really, Clement!' protested Mrs Drashleigh. 'Where *can* you have picked up such expressions? You know, Dame Beatrice, *I* think it may be a case of loss of memory. It is such a common complaint nowadays. I put it down to the rush of modern life.'

'Life doesn't exactly rush here, though,' said Clement.

'Ah, but he came here in a very peculiar frame of mind,' said Mrs Angel. 'If you remember, he seemed quite distraught. Then he began this business of going native. I thought he overdid it when he went for a fortnight without shaving. "Really, Mr Emden," I remember saying to him, "anybody would suppose you had need of a disguise!" That cured him of *that*, I'm glad to say. There is no more repulsive sight than that of a man whose beard is beginning to sprout. If they *must* grow beards they should grow them at sea, where there are none but other hairy men to look at them!'

'A disguise?' said Mrs Drashleigh. 'Do you really think so? That would account for much. He has gone in fear of somebody.'

'And, judging by this disappearance trick, the somebody has caught up with him,' said Clun, who was lounging in an armchair and, until this moment, had betrayed no interest in the matter under discussion.

'It wouldn't be you, by any chance?' asked Telham, in a tone which was intended to be light, but which succeeded in sounding insulting. Clun looked at him and did not reply. Caroline said quickly:

'It's probably somebody he owes money to. I always thought he looked the borrowing type.'

'The welshing type, too, then,' said Clun, 'and, now that I have counted twenty and swallowed my nasty temper (which, no doubt, you will remember, Telham, got me into serious trouble once before), I will inform you categorically that I *was* not, *am* not, and *shall* not (so far as I know) ever be, prepared to kill that silly womanizer. What is more, if you suggest such a thing again, I shall take considerable pains to twist your head off. There seems to be no law here against manslaughter, and, even if there were, the police, to coin a phrase, are a *spent* Force. Do I make myself clear?'

Telham walked over to where the speaker was sprawled and stood glaring down on him. Clun took out a cigarette case, scanned the contents, shook his head at them, chose a cigarette, and studied it with his head on one side.

'Tcha!' said Telham, with explosive suddenness. He snatched the cigarette from Clun's fingers and flung it in his face. Clun got up, swinging himself to his feet like an athlete.

'*This* can't kill!' he said, and smacked his open hand across Telham's eyes and the bridge of his nose. The former watered; the latter dripped blood. 'And now stop being a blasted fool,' Clun added, reseating himself and selecting another cigarette from the case, which had fallen on to the carpet.

'Please, *please!*' said Ruiz urgently. 'Mr Telham, go and wash your face. You are making your white trousers very nasty. Mr Clun, either you apologize to these ladies, or I kick you out of my hotel.'

'You've *got* to kick him out,' said Caroline furiously, leading her brother away. 'Either he goes, or *we* do. I'm not standing for this kind of thing.'

'Nobody will be kicked out,' said Luisa Ruiz, who had been studying the hotel ledger but had witnessed the physical exchanges. 'The señores will fight a duel. That is the proper procedure when insults have been offered and reciprocated.'

'Swords or pistols, Telham?' said Clun, with outrageous cheerfulness. 'As for the ladies, I apologize wholeheartedly for not putting up a more entertaining and instructive show.' He got up, followed the brother and sister to the door, took Telham's free arm, and said sincerely, 'Sorry, old man. Beastly sorry. But you did begin it, you know.'

To the general surprise, Telham unhooked his arm from that of his sister, muttered something which nobody but she could catch, and went out arm-in-arm with Clun.

'Well!' said Mrs Angel. 'And what are we supposed to make of that?'

'The lion lying down with the lamb,' suggested Mrs Drashleigh, with a nervous titter.

'Or with a wolf in sheep's clothing,' said Dame Beatrice.

The next piece of information came from Tio Caballo. In the very early hours of the following morning he sneaked down from his mountain eyrie, took refuge in his mother's house in the slum quarter of Reales, and sent his sister to the hotel.

'My brother, Rodrigo Cunez, says you have promised to cure him. I must not give another name here. He said you would understand.'

Dame Beatrice went with her at once. The evil-smelling little house was one of a huddle of dwellings just behind the Cathedral. Dame Beatrice supposed that it formed a before-and-after-service refuge when Uncle Horse attended Mass.

The bandit was seated in the inner and more malodorous of the two rooms which composed the ground floor of his home, and rose politely when Dame Beatrice came in. His mother, whose wrinkles were caked with the dirt of several weeks, and who was completely toothless, came in with the visitor, escorting her as though the noisome den was a palace. Her hair was as black as Dame Beatrice's own, but, unlike Dame Beatrice's, was as coarse as a pony's mane and thick with rancid grease.

'This', said Señora Cunez, 'is my son. I am not proud of him. He cheats me, his mother, and expects me to protect him. He is an ape.'

'With a slight dislocation,' said Dame Beatrice in

English. 'He must take off his shirt,' she added in Spanish.

'You have great power,' said Señora Cunez. 'I will send in the priest. Not good is it for a man to take off his garments, even before an old woman, except there be a witness.'

The priest was run to earth by one of a swarm of half-naked children who thronged the open doorway. Dame Beatrice greeted him courteously. He scowled at her after the manner of the island village priests and muttered something under his breath.

'It is necessary', said she, 'that this poor man should receive remedial treatment. Advise him to take off his shirt.'

After an impassioned dialogue between the two men, off came Uncle Horse's shirt to disclose a remarkably clean body, albeit a somewhat hairy one.

'And now,' said Tio Caballo, when he had been allowed to resume his garments, 'I will do for you what you will, for, although you have given me so excruciating an agony, I am grateful to you.'

'You shall tell me the story of the twenty-fourth man,' said Dame Beatrice.

Uncle Horse broke into voluble speech. How did she know (he inquired) that there had been a twenty-fourth man? Of what type was he? Was it possible that the Seño-ra could not count? It did not seem likely... What was Uncle Horse to make of it? What was this twenty-fourth man? Surely, if there was such an individual, he was an impostor.

'You must show me', said Dame Beatrice, 'the redun-dant bones.'

'But whose bones? I know nothing of bones. The Se-ñora has misunderstood me. I have said nothing of bones.'

From these statements he declined to deviate. Dame Beatrice left the house with her firm conviction unaltered that the twenty-fourth man was Karl Emden.

Armed, thus, with faith rather than with sight, she be-gan her investigations. Having made contact, in two senses, (since she had manipulated his bones), with Tío Caballo, she felt that there was nothing to fear from the bandits. Her comings and goings on the mountains would be remarked, no doubt, but would provoke no other re-action.

Early on the following morning she hired a mule, de-clined the services of a guide, and set out alone for the cave on Monte Negro. The early morning air was fresh and clear, there was cloud on the summit of the mountain and she had an exhilarating feeling that she was pene-trating, in her dotage, Cloud-Cuckoo-Land.

Not far from the cave she met an uncouth man of (as nearly as she could judge) some forty years of age, who saluted her by stretching his arm across the path. Dame Beatrice halted.

'You have found them?' she asked. 'Señor Cunez has revealed to you their hiding-place?'

'We speak of bones,' said the stranger. 'Come with me.' He led her, jerking her mule by the bridle and exhorting it, in the island Spanish, to bestir itself, to a shelf of rock from which a precipice dropped three hundred feet to a dry river-bed. This, in the rainy season, was a torrent, boulder-strewn and with deep and dangerous holes, but in summer it looked like a particularly badly-surfaced track.

'Down there,' said Dame Beatrice's guide.

'Is there a way down?'

'Yes, but one needs courage.'

'I have a good head for heights. Lead on.'

After giving her thin and wiry body an appraising glance, he obeyed. Who, or what, had made the path they followed, Dame Beatrice did not know, and there seemed no point in asking for enlightenment. She found the going difficult but not dangerous. Hand-holds and foot-holds seemed man-made, for they were found at fairly regular intervals. In less time than she had been prepared for by her first sight of the gorge, she and her guide were at the bottom and he was picking his way across the potholes in the bed of the stream.

In the side of the gorge on the opposite side was a cave –
or, rather, a ramification of caves. From the pocket of his
disreputable trousers her guide produced a powerful
electric torch which he shone on the glistening walls, and
the oddly-assorted couple followed passage after passage
until even Dame Beatrice's bump of locality failed her and
she ceased to be able to memorize the turns and angles of
the way. She guessed, however, that she was penetrating
the principal stronghold of Tio Caballo and José the
Wolf.

It was the Wolf, in fact, who was there, at the end, to
greet her. The passage they were following ended in a
gigantic natural hall with a roof so high that the light of
the torch gave only an eerie impression of Cyclopean walls
which ended in velvet blackness. The Wolf was seated on
a heap of blankets in front of a wood fire. He was a tall
young man whose only claim to his nickname, so far as
Dame Beatrice then, and subsequently, could discover,
was the possession of a pair of extraordinarily long eye-
teeth which gave to his smile the effect of an animal snarl.

He introduced himself and continued:

'Good day, Doña Beatrice. I hope you have not incon-
venienced yourself to make this difficult journey. You are
interested, I believe, in the king who has been dethroned.
We rescued him from an ignominious situation, and have
arranged to return him to his own place, which now is
occupied by a usurper.'

'I am indeed interested in the kingly bones; even more
so in those of the usurper. It would please me very much if
I might be permitted to examine this dethroned monarch.'

'Willingly. Carlos, kindly trouble yourself to display the
twenty-third man to Doña Beatrice.'

Carlos, who had been seated in the shadow beyond the
range of the firelight, came forward. He bowed, disappeared, and returned with another of the band. They
vanished into the shadows and came back, after a short
time, carrying something which they dumped, with little
ceremony, in front of José el Lupe.

The object thus rudely presented was the mummified body of a man of slightly less than medium height (Dame Beatrice deduced) which had been reduced to shrivelled and monkey-like nonentity.

'This', she said, when she had made her examination, 'is not the body I seek. Conduct me to the cave of the dead men.'

There was some delay about this. Rapid conversations went on in the local *patois* and there seemed to be acrimonious argument. Dame Beatrice bided her time with the patience born of vast experience. In the end the group of gesticulating bandits came to her with their difficulties.

'We have nothing to do with this.'

'We are peaceable men. Our assassinations are our own business.'

'We know nothing of these island kings. They were not of our blood.'

'What have we to do with the English lord?'

Dame Beatrice took up the last speaker.

'The English lord? Name him.'

'Who is he but the señor who is lost?'

'Name him.'

'Do we not speak of the señor who lives like the islanders? He of the blanket? He who dresses like a shepherd?'

'You have not named him.'

Their armour of circumlocution was not proof against her persistence. They were, after all, very childlike.

'We speak of the Señor Carlos Emden,' said the bandit Carlos sullenly.

'Then let us go and see his dead body.'

This practical suggestion met with strong disapproval. Men advanced into the firelight from the depths of the cave, materializing – no longer disembodied voices – like a horde of grimacing ghouls. José the Wolf was equal to the situation.

'Are you men or lice? Are you cowards, afraid of the dead men's dinner-party? Carlos, the torch and a quick walk, if you please! It is insufferable discourtesy in you all to keep a lady waiting. Enrique, Gonzalo, Pablo, you will go with Carlos to escort Doña Beatrice to the cave. Take lanterns. It will be better to go by the river-bed, so that people who see you will not know the object of your search.'

Sullenly the escort fell in. Dame Beatrice was led through the labyrinthine cavern once more, and, sooner than she had anticipated, she and her bandits were picking their way among the pebbles and boulders of the dried-up watercourse. This wound round the foot of the mountain and they followed it for several miles. At last Carlos, who was in the lead, called a halt.

'We are now', said he, 'in line with the cave. It is where we found the twenty-third king. Here.' He pointed to the ground. 'We must clamber up this cliff. It is a steep climb, not dangerous. We will eat before we attempt it.'

He produced *gofio*, the unleavened bread of the island, cheese, and fruit, and the five of them perched themselves on boulders for a picnic. The bandits offered no conversation, but champed and swallowed, or spat out bits of fruit-skins and pips, in what Dame Beatrice recognized as a comradely and sociable manner. At the end of a quarter of an hour of stolid mastication, and a swig all round from a flask of raw, red wine, the escort rose as one man, and Carlos led the way to the bank and began to climb. The woods were thick here on the mountain-side, and formed an effective screen up to a thousand feet. After this there was nothing but heather until they had climbed to the next wooded slope. Above this was the cave, which they reached by a narrow gulley between two lava streams.

When the party were all assembled at the mouth of the cave, the bandits lit their lanterns, crossed themselves, and advanced towards the stone table around which the dead men were stiffly and majestically seated. Dame Beatrice made a rapid count, and then, accompanied by Carlos, who seemed not to relish the task, she inspected each cadaver closely.

'Here we are,' she said. 'Ask your comrades to gather

round. I must have witnesses.' She stripped the mask from the swathed head of the tallest dead man. The bandits, who had gathered round, recoiled and crossed themselves. 'Here, you see,' she said, 'is the face of Mr Emden. Help me to lay him flat and take off his robes.'

CHAPTER 7

Owls and Pussy-Cats

'STABBED in the back, and with an islander's knife? So we know where we are,' said Peterhouse, 'and that is something. Now the authorities will have to deal with it. Not that they're the slightest bit of good. They will probably think that the fact that a modern man has joined the kings in the cave will add to the attractions for tourists.'

Pentland Drashleigh took it upon himself to report to Ruiz, and to order him to call in the police. Ruiz became excited, and retorted that his hotel had always borne a good name.

'What are the police?' he demanded with impassioned rhetoric. 'Dogs, cowards, assassins, creeping cut-purses, usurers, spies! I tell you, you can trust them with nothing! This Emden was an Englishman. Why should my hotel be turned into a sty for these pigs of policemen? If an Englishman is killed on Hombres Muertos, is it my fault? Can I help it if other Englishmen wish to send him to hell? It is you others who must see to it. I will not countenance the police. They would eat my food, drink my wine, and ravish my daughter. No, I tell you! A thousand times, no! If the police come here, I tell them at once that the English do it. You!' He pointed dramatically at Mr Drashleigh. 'You, perhaps, are the man!'

'Very well,' said Dame Beatrice, coming to the rescue. 'There is much in what you say, Señor Ruiz. I have had experience of investigating the causes of unnatural death, and am prepared to undertake the duty of finding Mr Emden's murderer. I shall rely upon the willing cooperation of you all.'

'Clement,' said Mr Drashleigh, 'must be taken back to our home on Santa Catalina. He cannot be mixed up in this horrible business.'

'He has contrived to mix himself up in it,' Dame Beatrice pointed out, 'but I agree with you in principle. He cannot, however, be *taken*. He must be *sent*. As a public-spirited and enlightened man, you will appreciate that you and your wife must remain here, pending some result of our inquiries.'

'Yes, yes, of course. But the boy must go. For one thing, his life may not be safe. It seems to me that, but for his naughtiness in going to the cave in the first place, the subsequent substitution of Emden's body for that of one of the kings would never have been discovered.'

'The bandits know of the substitution, of course, because it was they who discovered the mummified body after it had been tumbled down the mountain-side. All the same, I think it very unlikely that they would have reported the matter, as Clement did. I understand your feelings perfectly well. By all means get the boy away from here, although, if he has told all he knows, I do not think he can be in any physical danger.'

'I am greatly concerned for his safety, none the less.'

Theodora Drashleigh did not share these fears. She even went so far as to reproach her husband for wishing to make Clement (as she expressed it) into a nincompoop.

'But, my dear,' said Mr Drashleigh, 'if the boy's life is in danger –'

'It can't be, Pentland! Clement is a high-spirited, naughty boy, but he knows no more than he has told us. I am sure of it. And he is not to be allowed to run away from danger, real or fancied. It would stunt his spiritual growth. You know our compact. You must abide by it. You promised.'

'Very well, Theodora. All I say is that you are taking an unwise risk and must accept the responsibility it entails.

He sought Dame Beatrice and begged her to add her arguments to his own. She set out his point of view clearly to Mrs Drashleigh, but Clement's foster-mother was not to be persuaded.

'Clement is in no danger. It's to be inferred that everything that he knows about this distressing business he has confided to us,' she insisted. 'Are you really thinking of interesting yourself more deeply in the affair? I refer to what you told Señor Ruiz.'

'More deeply?'

'Well,' put in Pentland Drashleigh apologetically, 'one cannot help but know of your *alter ego*, you know.'

'I have no *alter ego*. I am, first and last, a psychologist. I could even tell you why you wish to take Clement away from this island and why your wife wishes him to stay.'

'I have no concern but the boy's safety. My wife has no concern but the proper development of his character.'

'Pull devil, pull baker,' murmured Dame Beatrice in her beautiful voice. Drashleigh looked startled.

'I assure you we are wholly at one over Clement!' he said hotly. 'We see him steadily, we see him whole.'

'It is just as well to see him steadily. I will answer your question before we tread on dangerous ground. I meant what I said. I propose to solve the problem of Mr Emden's death.'

This (to begin with, at any rate) was, from her point of view, in the nature of an intellectual exercise, for she had no idea and did not, at that stage, intend to formulate one, of what she would do when she discovered the identity of the murderer. Information, mostly of a negative kind, was soon forthcoming, and did not, at first, seem helpful. The first conversation in which she joined was between Caroline and Mrs Angel.

'I *knew*,' said Caroline . 'That day we went to the cave, I *knew* something was wrong. Badly wrong. Terribly wrong. And it was soon proved.'

'Are you psychic, Mrs Lockerby?' Mrs Angel leaned forward with an avid and unpleasant expression upon her once-lovely countenance.

'Psychic? I've never thought so until now, but, really, it was the most extraordinary feeling, and it left me thoroughly unnerved. Dame Beatrice will bear me out.'

'Certainly. The fall of rock, no doubt, is the incident to which you refer,' said her leering sponsor.

'I could no more have gone any further along that road than I could have made myself walk into a furnace. I was completely terrified. I've never felt like it before, and I certainly don't want to have a repetition of it. It was bad enough to go back to the cave, but it was certainly preferable to taking that dreadful mountain road,' declared Caroline.

'But you didn't go into the cave, of course?' inquired Dame Beatrice. 'You rested where we had picknicked, I suppose.'

'As a matter of fact,' Caroline admitted, 'I did take a peep into the cave. I persuaded myself that it was idiotic to think that one of the kings had moved.'

'And was it?'

'Was it what?'

'Idiotic to think that one of the kings had moved.'

'I've no idea. What do you think?' It was a strangely defensive answer.

'I am like the youth in the poem. My thoughts are long, long thoughts. Also, in this case, my will is the wind's will.'

'I don't know what you mean.'

'That does not disconcert me.'

'Telham,' said Caroline quickly, 'thinks that the bandits murdered Mr Emden.'

'What have they gained, I wonder?'

'I suppose, if they did do it, they robbed the body.'

'We cannot tell. No inventory was taken, before the murder, of the contents of Emden's pockets. But, if he was murdered by bandits, the motive could only have been robbery, as you say. I thought, though, that the bandits preferred to hold their prisoners to ransom.'

'He'd lived here a long time, though, hadn't he? He may have made enemies.'

'Two months is not a long time.'

'He seemed like one of the islanders.'

'He was probably a romantic. I see him as a Steven-sonian figure. I think I will go and talk to Señor Ruiz.'

'Is it true that Emden tried to compromise Luisa Ruiz?'

'I heard something about it.'

'If he did, you surely need not look elsewhere for a motive; and Ruiz would have had knowledge of the cave of dead men.'

'So had we all.'

'We?'

'Emden was murdered after the *Alaric* docked, you know. Does that suggest nothing to you?'

'There is such a thing as coincidence.'

'You have taken the words out of my mouth. I must certainly speak to Señor Ruiz.'

The proprietor of the Sombrero was in his private sanctum. This was a room reminiscent of a monastic cell. It had a door into the lounge and another into a tiny, ground-floor bedroom. Dame Beatrice knocked at the door which led into the lounge. Ruiz opened it, and, not surprised, it seemed, by the visit, stood aside, bowed, and indicated that she was to enter. The room contained a large crucifix confronted by a prie-dieu. There were also an armchair, a small chair, a table, a telephone, and a bookcase which housed a complete set of the *Encyclopaedia Britannica*.

'You wish to complain about my hotel, Doña Beatrice?' asked the square-faced, dark-visaged proprietor of the Sombrero; but he smiled as he spoke, his previous passion forgotten.

'By no means. I find the arrangements excellent. It is upon another matter that I would like to speak to you.'

'About Señor Emden, no doubt. You will have realized that I had cause to dislike him. I know of your work. You will wish to know what I can tell you about his death. It is little. Did you determine the time when he died?'

'Yes, but approximately only. From what I saw in the cave, I should say that he had been dead for about four days.'

'In other words, he must have been killed the day after your ship docked and you came to my hotel?'

'Exactly. At what time of day I could not determine.'

'You will wish to know how I conducted my affairs on that day.'

'I wish to know whether Mr Emden's papers were in order.'

'We are not anxious here to make difficulties.'

'I see. Had he a passport?'

'That, yes.'

'Please conduct me to the room he occupied. I should like to see that passport.'

'You wish to ascertain from which country he came? I can tell you that. He carried an English passport. Still, you would prefer to see it for yourself. Come with me.'

The bedroom which had been allotted to Emden was locked. Ruiz opened it with a master-key. There was nothing to distinguish it from a dozen other bedrooms in the hotel. It was a double room containing two beds, one of which had not been made up. The dead man's luggage consisted of a small trunk and a couple of suit-cases. These were unlocked and an examination of their contents provided no clue to their owner's violent death. The odd thing was that he had not taken them with him when he left, if he had really intended to live with the troglodytes.

The passport was in the top right-hand drawer of a dressing-chest. It appeared to be in order and the photograph was recognizable.

'One would think he would have taken his passport with him, also his luggage. It has its interest, yes?' said Ruiz.

Dame Beatrice admitted that it had its interest.

'I would like', she said, 'to speak with Doña Luisa, your daughter.'

'You will ask her whether I had cause more than once to show anger against this Emden? You may ask her what you will. As for myself, if I could meet this slayer of Karl Emden, I would kiss his hand,' said Señor Ruiz, with feeling. 'I will bring Luisa from the kitchen. A good daughter, one would say. I beg you to question her. I assure you I have nothing to fear.'

He went out and returned in a moment with his daughter. Luisa Ruiz was short and plump, with a red mouth and a skin of the colour and something of the texture of magnolias. To Dame Beatrice she was not the epitome of beauty, but her body was seductive and her head had a haughty carriage which many might find attractive. She was courteous and cheerful.

'The Señor Emden? His behaviour was not that of a gentleman. One felt sorry for him, but I am not sorry to find him dead.'

Ruiz got up and went out. Luisa, at this, seated herself, put her neat feet together, and smoothed her plain black frock.

'When did Mr Emden begin making himself tiresome?' asked Dame Beatrice, encouraged by this conversational attitude.

'Oh, very soon. He was here since two months, and in a week he proposes to escort me to the bullfight, although he is aware that I have an understanding for four years with Miguel Plaza, who learns hotel management in Barcelona in order to return here and inherit his father's hotel in Puerto del Sol. I have explained that, in Miguel Plaza's absence, I go to the bullfight only with my relatives, but he was crude, that dromedary.'

'To put it bluntly, Señorita,' said Dame Beatrice, 'I am to understand that if your father, or any other relative of yours, had made up his mind to kill Mr Emden, he would not have waited two months to do it.'

'That is so. A Spaniard does not wait upon vengeance.'

'I am so certain of it that I shall not consider any of your relatives as possible murderers, Doña Luisa.'

'It would be foolish to do so, Doña Beatrice. May I return to my duties?'

'By all means, Señorita. I thank you for your cooperation. It is necessary, you will appreciate, for those of us who had no hand in Mr Emden's death to be cleared of suspicion.'

Luisa smiled, transfiguring her usually heavy face.

'In England killing is important. Here, on Hombres Muertos, too, we are civilized. But the authorities have many bodies; they fall down the mountain-side, they smash up automobiles, they are drowned in the sea. It becomes uninteresting, and Señor Emden was nothing to our people. I think he was here because he was in trouble.'

'In trouble?' This sounded promising. 'What makes you think so?'

'Since two months, no letters, no, not even a letter bringing money or bills. I say to myself that such a man, without friends or creditors, is running away from his home, and tells no one where he is gone. Then, to our maid Pilar, and even to me, Luisa Ruiz, he makes shameless proposals, so I think perhaps he has left a wife behind him so that he may not make honourable ones. That also looks like trouble. One would expect letters from a wife, no?'

'He might be divorced.'

'I had not thought of that. It is not in my religion.'

'What do you think about his body being found in the cave of the dead kings? Did that surprise you?'

Luisa shook her head, but not, it seemed, in answer to the last question.

'No islander would have put it there, Doña Beatrice. I can assure you of that,' she said. 'And certainly no islander would throw a dead king down the mountain for the bandits to find. None would do such a barbarous thing.'

The funeral of Karl Emden took place in the English church, which was tucked away in an obscure quarter of the town. Nobody knew which Christian denomination, if any, he had belonged to, so it was agreed, without much argument, that the English church was the obvious compromise. The body, bereft of the trappings of kingship, had been inspected in the cave by a resplendent officer of the island police. He had tugged the knife out of Emden's back, balanced it in his hand, made an ejaculation of contempt, and flung the weapon down the mountain-side.

'There is a less degree of putrefaction than would have been the case if he had lain in the sun,' he said. 'I will report to that effect. You must bury him at his own expense. The city cannot pay.'

'There's always something splendid and invigorating about funerals,' said Mrs Angel, when this one was over. 'Somehow they give one something.'

'What sort of something?' asked Clun. Mrs Angel gave a slight scream.

'Who is it who asks?' she demanded. Clun was silent. 'You who have killed,' yelled Mrs Angel, in an un-controlled and rather dreadful tone, 'can you do nothing but pose these stupid questions?'

'I beg your pardon,' said Clun, displaying no sign of repentance, 'but I do have a prejudice in favour of saying what I mean. It was wrong of me to expect that such a prejudice would extend itself to my friends.'

'Friends, indeed!' exclaimed Mrs Angel. 'As though anybody respectable would want to be thought the friend of a gaol-bird like you.'

'My dear – Mrs Angel,' said Ruiz, who had come into the lounge prepared with a civil expression of hope that the funeral had gone according to plan. The strange little pause did not pass unnoticed by Dame Beatrice, to whom it suggested a not improbable theory.

'Well,' snorted Mrs Angel, 'he has no more sympathy for that poor murdered man than for –'

'The bloke I served my time for. No, I haven't,' said Clun.

'You didn't even come to the funeral. You might have shown that much respect.'

'Why?'

'They say dead men's wounds always bleed if the murderer comes near,' said Clement. 'If you'd all been decent and let me come to the funeral, I would have kept my eyes open and told you whether the murderer was in the church or at the grave.'

'Nonsense,' said Mr Drashleigh. 'The body was enclosed in a coffin.'

'The blood would have seeped through the coffin.'

'Be quiet, Clement!' said Mrs Drashleigh. 'You are not to say such things.'

'Then I shall grow up inhibited, like you said I mustn't. Besides, I like to talk about blood and corpses and murders. I think they're interesting – much more interesting than flowers and music and poetry and all the things *you* think I ought to like.'

'Of course they are,' said Dame Beatrice, 'but most interesting of all is the Shakespearian admixture of all six. If you would care to go for a swim with Miranda here, she will acquaint you with some of the finer speeches in *Macbeth*.'

'I hardly think –' said Mrs Drashleigh.

'Then you shouldn't talk,' shouted Clement. 'And you needn't think that's rude, 'cos it's a *quotation*, see?'

'Feel?' said Clun, and clouted the seat of his shorts. Clement turned on him in a fury.

'I'll *knife* you for that!' he shrieked.

'Can't take it, huh?' said the American girl, at the psychological moment. Everybody looked pained except Dame Beatrice and Clun, who laughed. Clement made a face at them and grinned.

'Knife you?' repeated Peterhouse, half-aloud. Clun turned on him furiously.

'Oh, don't be a clot!' he said. 'The kid's all right. *He* isn't the one who did for Emden, but I've a pretty shrewd idea who is, and, in case present company is interested and, for once, possibly not excepted, I may add that I propose to do nothing whatever about it. I didn't like Emden –'

'You scarcely met him!' exclaimed Mrs Angel impulsively. Clun scowled at her so fiercely that she begged his pardon.

'I didn't like what I'd heard about Emden,' he said in amendment, 'and I have not the faintest objection to speaking ill of the dead.'

'Come, come,' said Mrs Drashleigh.

'I mean that. Emden was a mean, dirty skunk, and whoever did for him did a damned good deed. However, as I was about to say when I was interrupted –'

'I really *do* beg your pardon and I do *so* agree with what you say,' murmured Mrs Angel.

'– if anybody listening to me now thinks I might as well be silenced since I seem to know so much, I will add that the name of the person I suspect of killing Emden is in an envelope in the possession of Jose el Lupe, who will hand it over to Dame Beatrice Lestrange Bradley in the event of my sudden demise at the killer's hands.'

'Is this true?' demanded Peterhouse. Even Caroline and her brother, who had attended the funeral but had taken no part in the conversation which was going on, looked interested and slightly apprehensive. Clun laughed, and, as he strolled off, said, over his shoulder:

'No, but I like to worry some of the people some of the time. My prison life has made me sadistic.'

'Well, don't you dare work it off upon Clement!' said Mr Drashleigh, in a sudden shout.

'Really, Pentland,' remonstrated his wife, 'we cannot expect the world to use Clement as we would have him used. That is one reason why I am determined that he shall remain with us on Hombres Muertos instead of creeping safely away to Santa Catalina. And now, Dame Beatrice,' she added, 'I think I speak for us all in promising to do everything possible to aid you in your inquiries.'

She looked hopefully from one to another of the assembled guests, but nobody seemed anxious to support her. The nearest to any sign of agreement came from Telham, who said:

'Quite, quite, but I do think it's a job for the police.'

'I think it's a job for all of us,' said Mrs Angel. 'It's rather a disgraceful thing if an Englishman can be murdered on this little Spanish island and nobody do anything about it.'

'Let's check our alibis,' said Peterhouse. 'For my own part –'

'As we have no information as to the exact time of the stabbing, and as we have no scientific knowledge of the effect of the temperature of the cave upon the preservation of the remains,' said Dame Beatrice, 'I fail to see that alibis have any real significance.'

'That justifies itself,' said Ruiz.

'I could not agree more,' said Clun.

'Then it's just a question of information,' said the American girl. 'Too bad Pop and I are for the great open spaces pretty soon. I just do hope we're not under suspicion, Dame Beatrice?'

'No, no. There is no justification whatever for suspecting either of you.'

'How not?' inquired Ruiz. 'Do you know the name of the murderer?'

'I am not prepared to answer that question at present. Knowledge is not necessarily power. I want proof, and, so far, I have none that any court of law would accept.'

'That is a pity,' said Telham. 'This uncertainty is spoiling our holiday.'

'It is spoiling my brother's chance of recovery,' put in Caroline. 'We came here for peace and quiet. I wanted to forget about murders. I have suffered enough from sudden death. Why did this wretched Emden have to be murdered here? And what business is it of yours if he did?'

'It is a matter of professional curiosity,' Dame Beatrice replied. 'To a psychiatrist, murder is the most interesting study of all.'

Caroline snorted.

'I call it morbid and macabre', she said, 'to take interest in such awful wickedness.'

'Then the Bible is both morbid and macabre,' said Dame Beatrice, calmly.

CHAPTER 8

Mark Antony's Oration

'You need not think', said Clement, 'that my father had anything to do with it. I kicked Emden's shins as hard as I could, but I didn't breathe a word to a soul. I am *not* a cissy, no matter what Attwood may say.'

'Attwood?'

'A boy at home. Before we went to live on Santa Catalina, you know.'

'And Attwood thought you a coward?'

'Well, he didn't really, of course, but he was always trying to get under my skin. Just because he went to school and I didn't – not that I didn't want to, mind you! – he thought he could say what he liked. So when Emden caught up with me after I'd ducked him in the bay and gave me a hiding – he punches, you know – I mean, he did – I didn't let on. So my father didn't know. So he didn't kill Emden. So Q.E.D.'

'I see. And your mother?'

'My mother? Oh, no, really! You can't imagine *her* sneaking up behind a man and sticking a knife in his back, can you?'

'No, I cannot. Tell me, Clement – boys know this sort of thing – how easy is it to obtain possession of one of those knives the islanders use? Can one buy them?'

'I don't know. I haven't seen any for sale, but I'm mostly on the beach. I don't get pocket-money, you see, so there's nothing for me to buy. My parents get me most things I ask for, though. Anyway, I'll find out from my friends and let you know.'

'Why don't we give Clement pocket-money?' asked Theodora Drashleigh, surprised but not offended by the question. 'For two reasons. On Santa Catalina Island, which is our home, there is nothing to buy. Everything we need, except some of our food, is sent to us from London. Here, we do not wish to encourage Clement to go into the town. It is as simple as that.'

'Do you know that Emden struck Clement?'

'Struck him?'

'Punched him.'

'Good gracious, no!' There was a pause. 'What had Clement done?'

'Ducked him.'

'Clement is a very good swimmer.'

'People object to being ducked, even by very good swimmers.'

'Yes; Clement is high-spirited. Boys will be boys.'

'An euphemism, surely, for "boys will be pests". But that is of no importance at the moment. What kind of souvenirs can be purchased here?'

'Ah,' said Mrs Drashleigh, with unexpected shrewdness, 'don't tell me! I know what you're after! Native knives!'

'Exactly. Do you possess one?'

'No, but Pentland does.'

'Does?'

'Oh, yes, that's the point. You must not think me lacking in intelligence. He *still* does, so, you see, his was not the knife you found buried in Mr Emden's body. Oh, but he might have possessed two such knives, so my argument has no point. Have you spoken to Mrs Angel? If Emden struck Clement, which would be *our* motive for murder, hers would be that wretched bird.'

'Bird?' said Mrs Angel, in reply to Dame Beatrice. 'Oh, you mean Talkie. But I told you about that.'

'I did not realize that Talkie was a bird. Were you fond of it?'

'You must not imagine that *I* killed that dreadful man, Talkie or no Talkie,' said Mrs Angel earnestly. 'But, of course, I was fond of it! Talkie was a rare specimen, a black oyster-catcher. I spotted him on the beach at Puerto del Sol. We became great friends. He was a charming fellow, greedy, impudent, and cunning. Then that beast killed him. I was livid with rage. But I did not know it had happened at the time when it *did* happen, otherwise you could have condemned me at once. I would kill anyone who injured a bird. After all, we are descended from birds, are we not?'

'And from reptiles,' said Dame Beatrice, contriving to look like an alligator and at the same time contorting her mouth into a bird-like beak. 'Now, who else had a motive for compassing the death of the brute-apparent, I wonder?'

'That horrid child Drashleigh,' said Mrs Angel, investing the words with venom.

'Yes. I know he had had a misunderstanding with Mr Emden, and got the worst of an encounter with him.'

'Misunderstanding, indeed! He snooped on Emden, and Emden did not present a pretty picture! I believe the frightful boy blackmailed him!'

'I understood that Emden struck the boy for ducking him when they were swimming together in the bay.'

'I know nothing about that. It would have frightened Emden. He could not swim. The beach shelves steeply. In two strides one is in thirty feet of water.'

'Interesting,' said Dame Beatrice. She sought out Clement, and found him prodding the earth in the hotel garden. He did not look up, although he must have heard her footsteps on the path. She seated herself on a bench beneath a tree and eyed the back of his head. Clement soon gave way in the war of nerves.

'Oh, hallo,' he said. 'I say, it's hot. It's hotter here than on Santa Catalina Island. Can I fetch you an ice or a cushion or something?'

'No, thank you, Clement. You need not trouble to find out whether I can purchase an island knife, either. I have information that your father possesses one.'

'My father?' He swung round, still in a squatting position, and looked up at her. 'Does he? I didn't know that. Wonder whether he'd buy one for me?'

'I should think it extremely unlikely.'

'Well, there's one thing,' said Clement, defiantly. 'If my father's got one, it can't be *his* knife that was sticking out of rotten old Emden's back.'

'How do you deduce that the knife was sticking out of Mr Emden's back? You mentioned it once before, I noticed.'

'Well, wasn't it? "Stabbed in the back." It's almost a proverb or something. I mean, you'd have a job to stab a man in the chest if he saw you coming. If anybody came at me, to stab me in the chest, I should pick up a chair. He'd look pretty silly stabbing the seat of a chair!'

'Clement,' said Dame Beatrice with unwonted severity in her tone, 'kindly seat yourself beside me on this bench. We must have no secrets from one another. That is to say, you must have no secrets from me. Answer my questions truthfully.'

'I'm not going to sit on any benches,' said Clement. 'And I'm not a liar.'

'Oh, yes, you are – both the one and the other.' Before he realized what was happening, she had taken his wrist in fingers which seemed to the boy to be made of steel, and had jerked him to his feet. He gave a yell of anger, but the next moment he was seated beside her and was rubbing his wrist. 'Now', she went on, 'for the questions, and don't imagine that I shall let you go until you have answered them to my satisfaction.'

'Suppose I can't?' He spoke sullenly, and without looking at her.

'You will be able to. First, since you get no pocket-money, why were you able to hire mules for yourself and Chiquito to make the journey to the cave of the dead kings? Quickly, now.'

'I – I had some money then.'

'Stolen?'

'I – you can't steal off your parents! Anyway, they shouldn't keep me so short.'

'The money came from Mr Emden.'

'It didn't! I took it off my father's dressing-table.

There's always loose change he takes out of his trousers' pockets at night. I sneaked in, first thing in the morning. He was asleep, so I helped myself. Why shouldn't I?'

'Your morals are no business of mine. I shall get your father to confirm your story, of course.'

'All right, then! The money did come from Emden. It was hush-money.'

'What were you to keep secret?'

'Shan't tell you. It's no business of yours!'

'You knew your father possessed an island knife, didn't you?'

'I suppose so.'

'When did you – shall we say – borrow it?'

'It wasn't me who killed the old swine!'

'That, at least, is the truth. No boy of your age would have had the strength to drive a knife in as far as that was driven in.'

'Oh, wouldn't he!' said Clement, annoyed. 'Just you feel that!' He flexed his biceps.

'*Buen Dios!*' said Dame Beatrice, prodding the slight bulge on his upper arm. 'And now tell me whether you had not *examined* the bodies in the cave when you told us that they totalled twenty-four.'

'Oh, you win!' said Clement disgustedly. 'That was when I spotted that one of them had a knife in his back.'

'We make progress. Look here, Clement: do you realize that until you tell everything you know you may be in very great danger? While you keep back information you are, perhaps, the only menace to the killer. Once all is known, you will be of no more interest to him than anyone else. Use your intelligence, child.'

'I'll – I'll think about it,' said Clement. 'May I go now?'

'Of course.' She watched him walk towards the terrace, kicking a stone before him, his hands in his pockets and his lips pursed (she guessed) in a whistle of indecision. She remained where she was. Clement reached the terrace, gave the stone a particularly vicious kick, and turned back

'It's only this,' he said. 'That knife in Mr Emden's back belongs to Mr Peterhouse.'

'How do you know?'

'I was with him when he bought it. It had a nick in the handle that you couldn't mistake. Did you notice it when you saw the body?'

'Yes, I did. What did it remind you of? – the shape of this nick, I mean.'

'It's like a crescent moon.'

'Yes, I noticed it particularly.'

'Does Mr Peterhouse know you noticed it?'

'No, but he is going to be told. Anything more?'

'No.'

He began to turn away, and then swung round again. You understand why I told you I didn't know whether you could buy an island knife, don't you?' This time he walked, whistling cheerfully, to the terrace and leapt up the steps.

'Our young friend', said Mr Peterhouse, appearing from behind a bush, 'seems to have removed a weight from his conscience, doesn't he?'

'This time, the weight was on his mind. He has transferred the burden to me. I, on my part, propose to pass it on to you. When did you lose your island knife?'

'What do you mean? I hope you're not telling me that my knife was found in Emden's back!'

'That *is* what I am telling you.'

'But it's impossible!'

'Why?' But she felt she knew the answer.

'Why? Because, dear lady, my island knife is still in my possession. I can show it you if you wish.'

'I should very much like to see it.'

'I'll get it at once.'

When he brought it, Dame Beatrice saw what she had expected to see. On the black hilt of the knife was a whitish nick the shape of a crescent moon.

'You have been framed,' she said, giving him a frightful leer. 'Or, rather, there was an attempt to create an illusion that you are a murderer. And, of course,' she added thoughtfully, 'it could be so.'

'What could be so? You don't really think ...?'

'What don't I really think?'

'That I would do such a dastardly thing as to kill Emden and then fake a new knife to look like the old one.'

'And why don't you think I might think that?'

'For one thing, you would not be safe if I really were the murderer. There are no witnesses to this conversation.'

'That's where you are quite wrong,' said Clun, stepping from behind the bush which previously had sheltered Peterhouse himself. 'I've heard every word. And I'm inclined to think, you know, my dear sir, that Dame Beatrice has got something there. It must have been the easiest thing in the world to nick that second knife and pass it off as the original one.'

'I have more brains than that, you young ass. And don't call me your dear sir, you wretched little gaol-bird!'

'Here, steady on! Don't kick a man when he's down.'

'But that is by far the most sensible time to kick him,' said Dame Beatrice. 'Ask Mrs Lockerby's brother. He will tell you.'

She walked away, leaving the two men scowling at one another. Clun capitulated.

'Sorry,' he said. 'I didn't mean to rile you. What's your theory about the murder? The D.B.E. has got it into her head that it's one of us, you know, but personally I plump for one of the dagoes. Seems far more likely to me, especially as I hear, on reliable authority – i.e. the chambermaid on my corridor – that Emden was inclined to spree about with the local ladies. No Spaniard, however mixed his blood, is going to stand for that.'

'I am inclined to agree with you, Clun. I accept your apology, although I don't think your joke was in the best of taste. I don't see why you and I (who must, I imagine, be suspected, as Dame Beatrice has this bee in her bonnet about the English tourists) should not exercise our wits to find the killer. What do you say?'

'Nerts!' said Clun forcibly. 'Don't be a silly old josser. I'm not sticking *my* neck out. I don't want an island knife, chipped hilt or not, in *my* back, I can assure you, and that's what's likely to happen if inexperienced amateur sleuths, among whom I count myself, begin trying to identify murderers.'

'I am *not* an old josser,' protested Mr Peterhouse. 'All the same, I see your point of view.'

'Quite, quite. After all, what's one D.B.E., more or less, compared with our valuable selves? Let Dame Beatrice do the detecting.'

Dame Beatrice had guessed the turn the conversation would take when she left the two men. She went into the lounge and saw Mrs Angel seated at one of the small writing tables. She took the nearest armchair and fixed her sharp black eyes on the back of the scribe's neck.

Mrs Angel, flicked over the pages she had written, read them through, folded them, and placed them in an envelope which was already addressed. Dame Beatrice noticed that she had not used the hotel note-paper but some thin airmail sheets which she tore from a large-sized writing-pad. Having stamped her correspondence, she put it into her handbag.

'A very interesting continent, South America,' said Dame Beatrice, as Mrs Angel stood up.

'South America?' Mrs Angel blinked at her. 'I've been writing letters without using my spectacles. I shan't be able to see a thing for the next twenty minutes. Yes, I suppose it is. They have some most wonderful birds which I should very much like to see in their wild state.'

'The giant condor of the Andes?'

'Well, yes. I was thinking more of the brilliant-plumaged birds of the tropical forests. The condors – well, one might not be in the best position to appreciate how interesting they are.'

'That is very true. It must be a grisly experience to realize that rapacious birds are waiting for one to die.'

Mrs Angel gave her a very direct glance.

'Are you going to sit here for a bit?' she inquired.

'I had thought of doing so.'

'Good. One or two things we'd better straighten out. I take it you don't make much progress in your search for Emden's murderer.'

'It depends upon what you mean by progress.'

'I see. Close as an oyster, eh? Are you *really* any nearer a solution?'

'People *will* pop up from behind bushes when I am in the garden, you know. It makes an investigation of murder very difficult. It is so confusing to discover that the Owl has overheard one's conversation with the Pussycat, and the Fly one's remarks to the Spider, not to speak of the Owl's having taken in what one said to the Fly.'

'I don't know what you're talking about.' Mrs Angel looked as puzzled as she sounded. 'I know you're a very clever woman, and if what you say is overheard, then I take it that you mean it to be so. What are you after? To get some of these people mad at one another in the hope that one of them will shout out something indiscreet and provide the clue you're looking for?'

'That could happen, of course, but, if it did, it would be a by-product, so to speak, of my intentions. No; I am working on a question of motive.'

'But there are enough motives among our little colony to crowd a raft,' said the fresh, young voice of the American girl. 'I could give you most of them myself.'

'*You* eat fried chicken,' said Mrs Angel. She got up and walked out, throwing 'Disgusting!' over her shoulder.

'Well!' said the girl. 'What eats *her*? It's all my fault, I guess. If Pop has said once I shouldn't horn in on matters that are none of my business, he's said it two million times. If I had a dollar for every time I've had my ears slapped down for just that one little thing, I would be the proud possessor of two Grand right now. I'm terribly, terribly sorry, truly, if I crossed your line.'

'It appeared to me that Mrs Angel welcomed an excuse

to leave me. What are these motives for murder of which you speak with such confidence?'

'I guess you will have chiselled them out of folks by now, but here goes: Pop Peterhouse and his precious orchids ...'

'One moment!' Dame Beatrice fished out a small note-book. 'Mr Peterhouse and his orchids. This may or may not be new to me, but as I desire no Beatrice (except myself) who, like a lapwing, runs close to the ground to hear our conference, I propose that we adjourn to some secluded spot. I perceive that you are carrying a towel. That, surely, indicates a desire to bathe. Are you a swimmer? Could you bathe from a boat on the bay?'

'Surely. That's a swell idea.'

'I doubt it. The tides are slight. We will go to Villa Tendresa by car, and hire the boat there. Is there anyone you would care to have go with us?'

'No, no. Give me five little minutes, and I'll be right back.'

'Meet me in the Plaza de Toreadores, then. It is the easiest place from which to hire a car. One has a choice there, and can attempt to avoid those vehicles whose coachwork is held together by string.'

It was a delightful day. The sunshine, even in the Plaza de Toreadores, which was at sea-level, was tempered by a breeze. Dame Beatrice chose her vehicle and astonished the driver by preferring to stand in the sun while she waited, instead of sitting in the car or remaining in the shade of one of the dusty trees which cloistered all four sides of the Plaza. Bits of paper blew about and a lounging group of youths made remarks in the island Spanish. There was not a girl to be seen at that time of day until the young American turned up to be greeted by Latin wolf-whistles and scandalous invitations.

The car tore across the Plaza and on to the coast road. This ran along past the landward end of the Mole, climbed through cultivated land, mostly sugar-cane, and descended to Villa Tendresa in the arm of a beautiful bay.

'Talk first, swim last,' said Miranda, whose name, in spite of Shakespeare, Dame Beatrice associated immediately with Sunnybrook Farm. 'The boatman looks dangerous. Do you think you should tell him that the money you pay for the boat-hire is all the money we have?'

'He will not remain with us. He has a little skiff with an outboard engine and will tow our boat out into the bay, anchor us, and abandon us until we wave to him to come out and bring us in.'

When they were anchored out in the bay, Miranda said: 'Those orchids.'

'I had heard from Mr Peterhouse himself that he collected them, but I should hardly have supposed that an island in this latitude could provide the rare specimens he postulated.'

'It does not. His orchids are sheer boloney, and Emden found it out.'

'How do you know?'

'Emden made a pass at me. He does it to every girl, I guess. I saw it coming and played him for a sucker, but Poppa smacked him down. I guess mine is an old-fashioned Poppa, at that, because he has no idea a girl can take care of herself when it comes to wolves. Anyway, near the beginning, Emden told me about how he had always wondered whether Peterhouse really collected orchids, because to say you collected orchids might mean anything, so one day he followed him into the mountains and where does he go, do you suppose?'

'Well, he did admit that twice he had been taken prisoner by bandits.'

'Taken prisoner my foot! He had a rendezvous with them. So Emden said, and I don't see why it wouldn't be true. The bandits here are sheer Oklahoma. They couldn't kidnap a tortoise. No, I figure Emden was right, and Pop Peterhouse had a date with them.'

'And the reason?'

'Ah, there you have me all mixed up. I just sheerly

don't know. And I wasn't letting on to Emden I was curious. I just said, "Oh, yeah? So what?" Then I slid off the raft – we were sunbathing on the raft way out by Santa Catalina, but I saw to it there were folks all about and around – and swam ashore. I was just crazy to know the answer, of course, but I was not going to let Emden rib me, so I kept quiet, figuring that he sure would spill in the end. He did not.'

'But you believe he was telling the truth?'

'Well, he's been bumped off.'

'That does not necessarily mean that Mr Peterhouse bumped him off, you know.'

'That is so. Well, I guess that's all I can tell you. You'll be kind of disappointed, no doubt, I haven't got more of the dope. Dope? Say! What do you know! It could be just that little old thing!'

'Not packed in boxes filled with damp moss, or however Mr Peterhouse is supposed to pack his orchids. I am most grateful for your information, however. It remains, I fancy, to find out what Mr Peterhouse *does* send to Kew Gardens, if he doesn't send orchids.'

'You think it's some other kind of plant? Gee, that's too bad! It ought to be something exciting!'

'It may be. And, don't you see, *if* Mr Peterhouse has a partner at Kew – well, the Gardens are so utterly respectable that nobody would think of their being connected in any possible way with illegal and mercenary exploits.'

'What about your British Customs and Excise? Not much that's illegal gets past *them*, if some of my friends' experiences are anything to go by.'

'I know. That's the point. Mr Peterhouse's parcels – if he *is* doing something wrong – must *appear* to be innocuous enough. Have your swim, dear child, while, to use your own idiom, I figure it all out. Incidentally, if I may say so, your Americanisms remind me of a Mayfair girl trying to speak Cockney.'

Miranda went in like a seal and swam like a mermaid. Dame Beatrice watched her, but only the surface of her mind was on the graceful, golden body and the rainbow drops cascading from the dipping and flashing arms. Her thoughts were concerned with the murder by a gang of thugs of an unloved husband in England; the hysteria of a young widow on the first expedition to the cave of the dead men; the unwanted attentions of a man who finished by getting an island knife in his back and who had been raised to regal status after his death; the pimps, trulls, and trollops organized – or not – by a watcher of'birds; a metamorphosis of orchids; a coward who ran away and left his companion to die; a Spanish hotel-keeper who had a jealously guarded daughter and a South American son; the brigands who might be more bloodthirsty than they seemed; last – and it was very much inclined to be least – she thought of a man who had been in prison for manslaughter (probably with extenuating circumstances). For all his brash manners and reckless face, Dame Beatrice liked Clun.

CHAPTER 9

The Lotus Eater of Puerto del Sol

By the time that Miranda had climbed back into the boat, Dame Beatrice had done with speculation and had made up her mind. Without more evidence there was nothing else to be done on Hombres Muertos. She therefore sat still and let time pass until the arrival of a liner returning to England put an end to the period of inaction.

'You're not leaving us!' exclaimed Peterhouse, when the hotel porter put her luggage in the entrance hall. 'And with the problem still unsolved!'

'I sail today.'

'But how did you get a stateroom at such short notice?'

'I cabled.'

'But when, dear lady?'

'A fortnight ago.'

'Dear, dear! You had tired of us all as soon as that?'

'Oh, no. But there are matters at home that need attention.'

'Ah, private affairs! I see. Forgive me. I did not intend to appear to be prying.'

He insisted upon going down to the Mole to see her off, and arrived with his arms full of flowers. Dame Beatrice deduced, without much difficulty, that he was greatly relieved to be able to assure himself that she really did intend to leave the island.

'Good-bye, Mr Peterhouse,' she said. 'It is charming of you to bring me bouquets and escort me to the ship. Perhaps we shall meet again one day. The island is quite, quite charming and your society has been most delightful.'

She was about to board the liner when a taxi skidded to a halt on the cobbled surface of the Mole, and Caroline's brother Telham came rushing to the end of the gangway.

'Stop! Stop!' he cried, waving vigorously. Judging, correctly, that the command was directed at her, she turned inquiringly.

'Dear me, Mr Telham,' she said mildly. 'Ought you to excite yourself like this on such a very warm afternoon?'

'Just thought you'd like to know', said Telham, 'that the murderer Clun is making his getaway. Only waited until your back was turned to take himself off to Puerto del Sol.'

'Not *another* of our number attempting to become a troglodyte, surely?'

'Our number! Good heavens! Don't you class me with that swine! He's booked in at the Hotel Flores. Well, there you are. It's up to you now.' He signalled a taxi and took himself off.

'I can't make that young man out,' said Peterhouse, who was still standing at the end of the gangway. 'Have you ever wondered ...?'

'Whether he killed Emden? Yes, of course, I have. On the other hand, if he did, there seems to be no motive. Well, good-bye, again, Mr Peterhouse. Remember me to the orchids.'

With this Parthian shot, she walked up the gangway and went immediately to her stateroom where she found a stewardess and gave her Peterhouse's bouquet to put in water. The ship called at three more small ports on the island, and travelled leisurely, remaining several hours at each port so that passengers could go ashore. The first of these ports was not more than a seaside resort and was known as Puerto del Sol. In view of the tidings she had received from Caroline's brother that Clun had journeyed there, Dame Beatrice did not go ashore, but spent the hours that the ship remained in port in annotating her case-book. It made interesting reading. She considered each case on what appeared to be its merits, occasionally reserving judgement.

First she thought over the activities attributed to Mrs Angel. They were not incompatible with one another.

She made a note, against Mrs Angel's *dossier*, of the fact that Señor Ruiz had a son in South America who made what might seem to be a surprising number of visits to his home. This fact might lend colour to Pilar's dark disclosures of Mrs Angel's profession; it might also have coloured Pilar's prurient imagination. In other words, it remained extremely doubtful whether the chambermaid was a reliable witness.

The case of the attentive and gallant Peterhouse had points of similarity with that of Mrs Angel. Both, having appeared innocent, if not particularly lovable, beings, were accused of what might loosely be defined as subversive activities. But with Peterhouse, as with the reputed procuress, the imagination of the islanders might well have provided him with a nefarious source of income which, in actuality, he did not possess.

Then there was Clun. She knew, from a vast and lengthy experience, that nothing was more likely than that a killer would be prepared to kill again, and one of her reasons for returning to England was to find out the details of the manslaughter charge which Clun had had to face. On the other hand, between manslaughter and murder there was an unbridgeable gap. She could not see Clun as a murderer.

The islanders, including Ruiz, she had already dismissed from her mind. Her eyes travelled over the pages of notes she had made respecting Ruiz, his son, and Pepe Casita. Suddenly she made a rapid hieroglyphic which, if anyone else could have deciphered it, would have read: 'Luisa Ruiz herself?' She shook her head. She did not believe it. Luisa could take care of herself where men were concerned, and without the help of a knife.

'But we must leave no stone unturned,' she said to the steward who brought her some coffee. The boy smiled as he set down the tray.

'Certainly not, madam,' he said soothingly. 'Will you be going ashore?'

'Not today. Are you on shore leave?'

'Yes, madam. It's my turn for a make-and-mend. Anything I can do for you?'

'There is. I have a young acquaintance staying at the Hotel Flores. I wonder whether you would call there and leave a message?'

'Certainly, madam. Glad of something to do. It's quite pretty round and about here, but there's not much fun. We're hardly ashore long enough to pick up a girl and, anyway, I'm not much of a one for these island types.'

Dame Beatrice wrote decipherably on a page of her notebook and tore it out.

'The name is Clun,' she said. 'It doesn't matter whether you see him personally or not. There's no answer.'

She had written, 'Keep an eye on Peterhouse if you can.'

The voyage home was soon over. The ship docked at Southampton where Dame Beatrice's chauffeur, the sober and respectable George, awaited her with the car, her secretary, and her secretary's baby son.

'Fancy cutting short your holiday like this!' said Laura reproachfully, when her employer was settled in beside her. 'I thought, and hoped, that you were going to have a good three months' rest. Didn't you like the hotel?'

Dame Beatrice, who had given no hint of the happenings on Hombres Muertos, said:

'Let the story of my experiences keep until after dinner. Then I will tell a tale to curdle the blood.'

'*Not* another murder?' exclaimed Laura. 'Oh, dear! And I've been out of it all because of *This*!' She indicated her son, asleep in his travelling cot. 'I can't wait to hear all about it. But if there's been a murder I don't see why you've come home. Have you made the island too hot to hold you?'

'I hardly think so. I have come to England in search of evidence. I have a very strong feeling that the story began over here. If it didn't, I shall be none the worse off except for the price of my fare.'

The story was a good one, and Laura thoroughly enjoyed it. If it lost nothing in the telling, neither did it

gain anything, for Dame Beatrice was scrupulously accu-
rate. She concluded by saying:

'So you see why I felt I had to come over here. If my
ideas are wrong, at least I shall have cleared away some of
the undergrowth and can see the problem afresh.'

'It will be a frightful fag devilling through oceans of
newsprint to find out about deaths when you don't even
know when they occurred, though, won't it?' asked
Laura.

'So much so that I propose to get the devilling done
for me.'

'Right. I'll go up to Town first thing tomorrow. I can
stay in Kensington, I suppose? I'll have to take Junior
with me because of feeding him, but I can leave him,
between feeds, for four hours at a time. Kitty will come
and look after him. She does nothing nowadays but rake
in the cash from those beauty parlours of hers.'

'You are not going to take him or yourself to Kensington. Why have I a grand-nephew in Fleet Street? Bonamy
Lestrange will love to look up the details and will find
them twice as easily as either you or I. Tomorrow we will
telephone him and set him to work. And now for another
matter. How would you like to take the baby for a short
holiday to Hombres Muertos? I feel that an eye should be
kept on the guests at the Hotel Sombrero and, as you
would be there *incognito,* so to speak – that is to say, having
no obvious connexion with *me* – you would be a very
valuable source of information. What do you say? The
ship I came back in takes a couple of days only to turn
round, so you must make up your mind at once. I have
booked a stateroom, so there wouldn't be any trouble
about that. Ring up Robert and see what he thinks. The
climate would suit the baby, I am sure.'

So, three days later, Laura and her infant son found
themselves off the Scilly Isles, heading south and west for
the Island of Dead Men, and, long before she was tired of
the voyage, Laura was ashore at Reales and *en route* for
the Hotel Sombrero, where a room had been booked by

cable. At parting, Dame Beatrice's final instructions had been:

'You have *carte blanche* to follow your nose. I cannot tell you what to expect, but I think you may need to put in one or two days at Puerto del Sol to see what Mr Clun is doing with himself. Do not rush into any difficult or dangerous situations. If you are undecided at any point, think of your husband and son and *do nothing at all.*'

Laura, as Dame Beatrice was aware, was temperamentally incapable of carrying out this particular instruction. For Laura to do nothing was a mental and physical impossibility.

'Jolly nice for you,' said her husband, when he was apprised of the plan for her to take a holiday on the island of Hombres Muertos. 'Be good, and please be careful. It's rather interesting that the bloke Clun should be there. He did in a chap – manslaughter, of course – just over three years ago, and I believe a fellow called Emden and another called Telham came into the case. Witnesses for the prosecution, if I remember. Keep an eye skinned for Telham. He had the name of being a dark horse, I think, but, of course, it wasn't my case, so I may not be abreast of the facts.'

'I expect you are,' said Laura. 'Can you come to see me off?'

'I don't see why not.'

He did, in due course, see her off, and she and the baby arrived at the Mole of Reales less than a fortnight after Dame Beatrice had left it. Laura regretted that the voyage had to end, for she loved the sea and would never travel by air if she could help it, but she was keenly anxious to meet the guests at the hotel and to see how far her estimate of them coincided with that of her employer. Allowing for the considerable difference in their ages, Laura and Dame Beatrice thought alike about people, and Laura already had the feeling that she knew Mrs Angel, Peterhouse, Caroline, Telham, and Clun, and of the Drashleighs and their adopted son she had received such a vivid impression of a cranky couple with the power to experiment on a defenceless child that she looked forward eagerly to entering the lists against them and giving battle. Laura was, theoretically, at least, on the side of little boys and against their adult persecutors.

'And now,' she confided to her own small son as the taxi took them to the Hotel Sombrero de Miguel Cervantes, 'we have to keep an eye on things for a bit, so do your stuff.'

The baby chumbled his fist and smiled at her.

It proved easy enough to keep an eye on Dame Beatrice's fellow-guests at the Hotel Sombrero. The sociable Mr Peterhouse and the (possibly) anti-social Mrs Angel appeared to regard the baby as an introduction to Laura. She welcomed their interest as soon as she knew who they were, and, Luisa Ruiz proving to have a way with, as well as a devotion to, Gavin junior, he was often given into her charge. Laura, thus freed, was soon acquainted with Caroline and Telham also, for she went swimming with them and astonished both by her remarkable speed and efficiency in the water.

She had been wondering how to introduce the subject of Emden's death without betraying the fact that she knew Dame Beatrice, and had still found no safe way of doing this when Telham set the ball rolling by mentioning the matter himself. He, his sister and Laura one day were lounging on the raft which was anchored out in the bay. He suddenly said:

'You haven't been to the cave of dead men yet, have you?'

'No. I've heard about it, of course. I'm curious about it, naturally. Is it horrid?'

'Caroline and I think it is, but it's definitely one of the sights and you ought not to miss it. I wonder old Peterhouse hasn't made up a party to include you. He regards the cave as his own property, I believe. He certainly shows it off as though it is. Still, even with him you need a native guide.'

'Why? Doesn't he know the way to it?'

'Oh, yes, but there are the bandits, you know.'

'Bandits? How jolly that sounds! What sort of bandits?'

'I don't really know. If you feel charitable you'd better ask Peterhouse. The old bore claims to have been captured by them twice. He'll like to tell you all about it. He swears the cave's haunted now.'

'I should think it most likely, with all those dead men in it!'

'Oh, it's not those. It's a chap who used to live here. Somebody did for him and put his body in the cave with the others, and fixed him up in the robes and death-mask of one of the kings, but nobody knows who did it. We had Dame Beatrice Lestrange Bradley staying here at the time, and she began looking into the thing, but it seems she got discouraged. The fellow must be pretty brilliant to have got the better of *her*. I understand she's acquired a reputation as a sleuth. However, she left at the end of a month, so, apparently, she realized the job was hopeless.'

'Why was the murder done? Does anybody know?'

'Only the killer, I imagine. My personal opinion is that it was a revenge job, and, with those sort of deeds, unless you've got a low-down on the dead man's past, you're stymied.'

'Let's swim back to the beach,' said his sister. 'I'm starving.'

'The man I've got *my* eye on,' continued Telham, sitting up, 'is a certain Clun. A nasty bit of work, if ever there was one. Besides, he's slung his hook, always a pointer to guilt.'

'Has he gone far?' Laura asked this disingenuous question in what she hoped was a manner unlikely to arouse suspicion.

'He's at Puerto del Sol, a little place further round the coast. Of course, if you're going in for killing, this island is the ideal place. The police here don't seem to trouble themselves about anything except agitating for more pay.

Clun's done time already for killing somebody in England, so I suppose he dared not tackle his man there.'

'Wasn't it rather short-sighted of the victim to come to live in a place where he could so easily be murdered?'

'Oh, do come along,' pleaded Caroline, before her brother could answer. She balanced herself on the edge of the raft, waited for a wave to lift it the way she desired, and dived in. The other two followed, and the three swam ashore.

That evening, before dinner, which, as was the island custom, did not appear until between nine and ten at night, Laura broached the subject of the cave to Peterhouse, and was greatly intrigued by his flat refusal to go anywhere near it.

'I used to enjoy making up parties and taking them along,' he said, 'but, since poor Emden's body was found there, I seem to have lost interest.'

'I've heard something of the murder – I suppose there's no doubt it *was* murder? – from Mr Telham. What a dreadful thing to happen on a lovely island like this!'

'Indeed it was. Emden, of course, was a mystery man. Dressed like the peasants and annoyed the local girls, to put the thing in a nutshell, so some disgruntled islander bumped him off.'

'So you think the murderer was a native of Hombres Muertos?'

'Between you and me, I wouldn't put it past the landlord here, old Ruiz. He's a full-blooded Spaniard and as proud as the devil. If Emden had molested Luisa, the fat would have been in the fire. A Spaniard doesn't stop to think, you know.'

'I heard that the corpse had a knife in its back. That doesn't sound like the work of a proud Spaniard, does it?'

'He may not have done the job himself. He probably hired Tio Caballo, or one of his gang.'

'His gang? Not the bandits?'

'Who else? When I inform you that they have captured

me twice, you will understand what manner of persons
they are.'

'Very daring,' said Laura, tongue in cheek but not
betraying the fact.

'Oh, I wouldn't say *that*! Safety in numbers, you know.
But if you wish to visit the cave, dear lady, it is a simple
matter to arrange a party and a guide. I'm sure Ruiz will
be only too pleased to accommodate you, and there are
several new people in the hotel who would join in. I will
ask Ruiz myself, if you like.'

'Thank you. I should certainly like to go, but I can't
leave my child all day with Luisa, so I think, after all, I
had better postpone my visit. Isn't there anything else of
interest? – a steamer trip, perhaps? I love being on the
sea.'

'You could go to Puerto del Sol. It's a beautiful little
place, and you don't need to wait for a liner. You can go
by coast road, and, of course, the local steamers call there.'

'Are they clean and well-run? I don't want my child to
pick up germs or fleas!'

'The steamers are run by a Dutch company and are
spotless. You would enjoy the trip, I feel sure. And when
you get to Puerto del Sol you may run into a man named
Clun. He stayed in this hotel until Dame Beatrice Bradley
went back to England.'

'Oh, the psychiatrist! I've heard of her, of course. Do
you mean there was a connexion between her leaving the
island and this Mr Clun going to Puerto del Sol?'

'I don't know what the connexion was, but I rather
think there was one. Still, it may have been coincidence.
The only thing is that they certainly seemed very thick
while she was here. I heard Clun had been in prison in
England for manslaughter, but I don't know that that
had any bearing on the matter.'

'Surely he didn't tell you so himself?'

'No. I had it from somebody or other – I can't remember who told me. Do you think it a very long step
from manslaughter to murder? Dame Beatrice, I gather,

interests herself in questions of sudden death, and, after all, manslaughter and murder are allied under that heading, are they not?'

'I've never thought about it. It would depend upon what kind of manslaughter, wouldn't it? I mean, if you killed somebody by driving your car carelessly, or under the influence, or something of that sort, it wouldn't be the same thing, in my opinion, as hitting somebody in a fit of temper and killing him.'

'But it seems that's what Clun did. He told Dame Beatrice – I overheard it at the lunch-table, I remember – that he hit a bit too hard.'

'And you think that a man who did that once by accident – well, anyhow, unintentionally – might do it again, meaning to kill? I don't know what I think about that. Well, how do I recognize this dangerous gentleman?'

'He's a dark-haired, saturnine fellow, quite young – thirty, perhaps – with a devil-may-care look on his face. If you stay a day or two at the Hotel Flores you'll be sure to spot him.'

'That is as far as it will get, I expect. I don't see myself tapping strangers on the shoulder and asking them whether they're Mr Clun.'

She arranged a passage for herself and the baby without difficulty, and the local steamer was all that Peterhouse had claimed for it. The trip round the coast took four hours and landed the passengers at Puerto del Sol at two in the afternoon, so that they were in time for the three o'clock lunch at the Hotel Flores.

The hotel was small compared with the Sombrero and looked like a typical Spanish house. Its windows were shuttered in green and it had the traditional balcony over-looking the street. In charge of the hotel was a relative of Ruiz, a certain Señora Galjos, moustached, magisterial, and kindly, who impounded Gavin junior at sight, sighed and crooned over him, told Laura the story of her own confinements and, in effect, took charge of mother and child in a manner which brooked of no argument.

There were so few guests at the Flores that Laura had no difficulty in recognizing Clun from the descriptions she had been given by Dame Beatrice and by Peterhouse.

'One person I can knock off the list of suspects, I hope,' she thought. 'Not that Dame B. suspects him, if I'm any judge of her reactions.'

The bathing facilities at Puerto del Sol were even better than those at Reales, and Laura was almost an amphibian. Her swimming excited interest and admiration, and at the end of the second day she found herself Clun's guest at the hotel cocktail bar.

'I suppose you know, queen of naiads,' he said, at the third drink, 'that you're consorting with an ex-gaolbird?'

'Really?' Laura squinted into her glass. 'That's interesting. I've met a few in my time and heard about a great many more. My husband's in the C.I.D., you know.'

'Is he? Pity he wasn't here a month ago. At least, not so much here as in Reales.'

'Reales? Oh, you mean the murder.'

'You've heard about it?'

'I came here from the Hotel Sombrero. Mr Peterhouse was eloquent upon the subject.'

'Old Peterhouse? Oh, yes, he would be. Did he advance any theories?'

'Two; one definite, one under correction. That is to say, he committed himself to saying, that he would not put murder past the landlord, Ruiz.'

'It is also to say that he told you a little about my own past history and permitted himself to wonder whether breaking a man's neck by accident might not lead to sticking a knife in a man's back by design. That's about the size of it, isn't it?'

'Yes,' said Laura, who saw no reason for disagreeing. 'That was about the size of it.'

'It wasn't Ruiz,' stated Clun, swigging the liquid in his glass round and round and watching it. 'My bet, for what it's worth, is that it was our very dark and nervous horse Telham. Did you meet him?'

'And his sister. I swam with them, in fact.'

'As you have with me. Are you, in other words, a copper's nark, handsome Mrs Gavin?'

'No, I'm not, but I *am* holding a watching brief. You're not unintelligent, Mr Clun. Can it be that prison has sharpened your wits, or have I given my game away?'

'So Dame Beatrice has *not* left the field of battle! I had a feeling she wasn't the type to desert a good cause. Tell me more. Have another drink if it will help.'

'No more, thanks. You have one on me. As you've almost penetrated my *incognito*, I'd better help you to the rest.'

'Wait a minute,' said Clun. 'Don't say anything you're likely to regret. You're like me, Mrs Gavin. Say or do first, and think afterwards. Steady, now.'

'It's all right,' said Laura. 'Nice of you, but I've got to trust somebody, and, as I don't know whom Dame Beatrice really suspects, I might as well trust you as anybody else. I'm Dame Beatrice's secretary and general dogsbody, and I'm here to hold the fort while she looks for some evidence in England. There you are. Now you know all about it, and I shall be grateful for any constructive suggestions. Oh, and, if you don't mind, please don't tell anybody else who I am.'

'Have you been to the cave of dead men?'

'No. I can't take my son there. I don't know why. It's just one of those things.'

'I understand that. But couldn't you go there now? Señora Galjos seems to have adopted your kid.'

'Can one go there from here? – easily, I mean? I've got to keep young Gavin fed, you see.'

'You can go to Polje by car in a quarter of an hour. From there you'll have to hire a mule, but, even then, half an hour's climb will do it. Allow a quarter of an hour to inspect the cave, and there you are!'

'Oh, well, that seems all right. How do I collect the mule? The car is easy enough.'

'There are always mules at Polje. Fix up with La Galjos to look after the infant and let's go.'

With the mental reservation that she would keep an open mind upon the subject of Clun's *bona fides* and an open eye upon his antics, Laura agreed, and the excursion was fixed for the following morning. They set out with three other visitors and a guide at half past six in order to avoid the hottest part of the day, and the time for the journey was much as Clun had indicated. They got to the cave before half past seven and Laura had her first sight of the dead men.

'There are twenty-three,' she said. 'I should have thought it would be twenty-two now. Wasn't one thrown down the mountain-side or something?'

'Good Lord! The bandits must have resurrected him. Well, what do you think of the set-up?'

'Impressive, very. There's one thing I want to know.'

'How long the late Emden could have remained disguised as the twenty-third man if that little mosquito of a boy hadn't seen twenty-four bodies before the killer had had a chance to get rid of one of them? And that's interesting, too, you know, because, surely, there was one without the trappings?'

'I don't know. It hadn't even occurred to me, I'm ashamed to say. Well, there's nothing more to be done here. I ought to talk to that boy. So far he hasn't crossed my path.'

'When he does, you'd be well advised to boot him out of it. The kid's poison. Mind you, it isn't his fault. Well, there's no more to see, I'm afraid. Shall we be getting back to breakfast?'

'I hoped to see the bandits,' said Laura. 'I thought this was one of their haunts.'

'Only when one comes without a guide. Union rules, you know.'

There seemed nothing useful for her to do in Puerto del Sol and she did not feel justified in remaining there merely to enjoy all the sun and the sea, so she returned to the Hotel Sombrero and soon found an opportunity of asking Clement about the twenty-fourth body in the cave,

for Laura was not a believer in mincing matters where
the young were concerned.

'What was he like to look at?' she asked bluntly, having
introduced the subject with equal brusqueness.

'Oh, him!' said Clement. 'He was just a sort of
mummy. That means that Mr Emden was already there,
togged up and with a mask on his face. He wasn't nifty,
though. The air was perfectly fresh. How soon do bodies
go bad?'

'It depends on all sorts of things, I believe. Look here,
people seem to have the impression that all twenty-four
were robed and masked. You don't appear to have told
anybody about the mummified type you saw.'

'No, I didn't, actually. After all, it would be a matter
of common sense. Besides, as soon as I saw it – it was
rather like a monkey, you know – I sort of guessed what
had happened.'

'How do you mean?'

'Well, Emden was pretty well disliked, and what I
think is that somebody came here to do him. Definitely, I
mean. With murder in mind, somebody followed him
here.'

'Followed him to the island? What made you think
that?'

'Well, you know my friend Chiquito?'

'No.'

'He's a semi-Spaniard, like most of the people here, and
there aren't many things he doesn't get to know. Their
lives are a bit dull, I imagine, so they gossip a lot and
have a grape-vine and a bush-telegraph and all that.
Well, Chiquito told me that Pepe Casita told him that
his girl, the maid Pilar on the first corridor, said that
Emden was in the most fearful funk as soon as Dame
Beatrice and the rest of that mob landed and came to stay
at the hotel. He – Emden, you know – hopped it at the
first possible minute, and you can't help putting two and
two together, when you realize that, once he left the Sombrero, he was never seen alive again.'

'That isn't certain, is it?'

'Well, the murderer saw him, of course. And do you know who *I* think did it? I think it was Mr Telham. He's got a hang-dog look. You watch him and see.'

CHAPTER 10

Botanical Information

LAURA was determined to earn her unexpected holiday. She felt she had gained very little by her first attempts, for her duty, as she saw it, was to obtain a first-hand impression of the guests and staff at the Hotel Sombrero and (although she had kept any hint of this from Dame Beatrice) to give the bandits and the troglodytes the benefit of her scrutiny.

'I'll knock off the troglodytes first,' she confided to the baby, as she gave him his morning six o'clock feed. 'So do yourself proud, cully, while you're at it, as I may be late for the next one.'

She breakfasted off rolls and coffee at seven, went into the Plaza and woke a taxi-driver.

'*Cavernas,*' she said.

'*A solas?*' The driver looked astounded.

'*Sí, sí!*'

'*Madre de Dios!*' It was clear that for a young woman to venture alone to the country of the cave-dwellers was unprecedented.

'*Con presteza!*' urged Laura, unconcerned with questions of precedent but merely with the necessity for haste. '*Como el viento!*'

The driver contrived to emulate the speed of the wind so successfully that Laura began to wonder whether her command had been strictly necessary. They bounced, swerved, climbed, and ricocheted up the mountain-side at a reckless speed which brought them to the caves in what she felt must be record time.

The troglodyte girls were already at work on the banana plantations or in the cigarette factories, or (thought Laura, with visions of the bird-loving Mrs Angel) getting themselves shipped off to South America, so the only

people at home were the old women and one or two
unkempt, unshaven men. At the end of a baffling and
fruitless hour she returned to the taxi-driver, whom she
had told to wait, and bade him take her back to the hotel.
It was some time before she realized that he was doing
nothing of the kind, but just as it dawned upon her that
they were on a very different route from the one by which
they had come, the taxi drew up, the driver got down,
and two tall, thin men appeared in front of a bit of scrub
behind which they had been hiding.

'Hold-up,' thought Laura. 'Oh, well, I wanted to see
the bandits, so this is it.'

The driver opened the door of the cab and bowed as
she got out. The two thin scarecrows bowed. Laura
inclined her head and graciously extended her hand. In
turn, the bandits kissed it.

There followed a staccato conversation in the island
patois. Even if they had spoken Spanish, it was so fast that
Laura could not have followed what was said. At last one
of the bandits turned to her and told her, in fair Spanish,
to pay the taxi. Laura shook her head. She needed the
taxi to take her home, she explained. The three men
smiled. Laura, on an inspiration, declared that she had
to feed her baby at ten o'clock and that it was already
half past nine.

'A baby?'

'Yes.'

'A boy?'

'Yes.'

'How old? – Ah, a *small* baby.' They looked at one
another, shrugged, spread out thin hands, and jerked their
heads at the taxi-driver. 'Take her.'

'And those men are followers of José the Wolf?' asked
Laura, when she had reached the Plaza again, and was
out of the car.

'Of Old Fool Uncle Horse,' the driver said, raising his
eyes heavenwards. Laura added a considerable tip to the
fare, since she deduced that the taxi-driver had missed a

fat rake-off from the bandits if they had decided to hold
her to ransom, and walked into the hotel.

The leisurely breakfast, served until eleven at the Hotel
Sombrero, satisfied Laura that she could manage to exist
until lunch-time. She dawdled over her last cup of coffee,
and then went on to the terrace. She had not been there
long before Luisa Ruiz came out. Pretending to rearrange
the cushions on the empty chair next to Laura's, she said
in a low tone:

'My brother is here.'

'Your brother? From Spain?'

'From Spanish America.'

'That's nice for you. How long will he stay?'

'Until his business is done, I think.'

'Oh, I see. Shipping cargo, or something, I take it.
Must be a jolly country, South America. I've never been
further than the West Indies.'

'That is the best thing. Nobody was clever enough,
intelligent enough, good enough, to leave it at that.
Always they wish to go west, further west, and more west
still. What is this madness, Señora, that makes for the
west, for the sunset, for disillusion – for death?'

She flicked a speck off the last cushion, gave Laura a
slight smile, and disappeared inside the doorway. Laura
decided to keep an eye open for the South American
brother. She had heard of him from Dame Beatrice, but
there had been no reason to think that he would be home
so soon. She wondered whether it was his usual time of
year for a visit, but decided that this could not be so. If
it were, surely some hint of it would have been dropped
to Dame Beatrice, if not by Luisa herself or by Señor
Ruiz, then certainly by the garrulous and artless (although
possibly prevaricating) Pilar, the beloved of Pepe.

However, Laura was greatly intrigued, when she went
down to the beach to sun-bathe, to see Mrs Angel with a
swarthy, broad-shouldered young man whom she took to
be the son of the house of Ruiz. All the ugly gossip about
Mrs Angel's profession came crowding into Laura's

ever-open mind. It looked like the gathering of the
vultures, she decided. She wished she could get near
enough to overhear their conversation, and was trying to
work out some way by which she could carry out this
wish, without appearing to eavesdrop, when the young
man, who had been facing her, got up, bowed, and Mrs
Angel, turning, beckoned Laura to join them.

'Our dear Señor Ruiz's son, Don Ricardo, Mrs Gavin.
Quite a famous man,' she said, effecting the introductions.
'Ricky dear, this is Mrs Gavin, from England.'

'Not famous. Or, if so, only because of my cherished
Mrs Angel, an angel, no?' said Don Ricardo, speaking in
English. 'Please to join us, Mrs Gavin. I am about to
order a bottle of wine. It is never too hot to drink wine.'

Laura joined them, but the conversation sustained itself
on a general note and her curiosity remained unsatisfied.
Unless there was something to be made of the fact that
Don Ricardo and Mrs Angel had a good deal to say to one
another and appeared to be on very good terms, the
answer (said Laura to the baby a little later) was a lemon.
She kept her eyes open during the next few days, however,
and it was most noticeable that Don Ricardo spent a great
deal of his time in Mrs Angel's company. For a young
man who thought enough of his home and family to pay
them an expensive visit every year without fail, this was a
curious circumstance, Laura thought, and one well worth
reporting to Dame Beatrice.

Her next encounter was with Peterhouse – her next
significant encounter, that is. He joined her on the following morning when she was in the garden.

'You are particularly interested in flowers?' he asked,
in a strangely gentle tone.

'Indeed I am; and, on the present occasion, they
delightfully occupy my thoughts,' said Laura, in unconscious imitation of Dame Beatrice's mode of speech.
She waved a hand to indicate the glowing, sub-tropical
garden.

'You are a *connaisseuse*?'

'Not of flowers – unless, perhaps, orchids.' She introduced the gambit unblushingly.

'Ah, yes. Most interesting. But there are no orchids worth talking about on Hombres Muertos, Mrs Gavin. Personally, I much prefer to experiment in growing Alpine plants.'

'Not orchids? I thought one of the other guests told me ...'

'Oh, no. There are no orchids which would justify the attention I lavish upon *Helliborus niger*, for instance. You know the plant, of course?'

'Sorry to say I've never heard of it. At least, not under that name.'

'I apologize. I refer to the Christmas Rose, known in Switzerland as *Schneerose*. I may tell you that I have reproduced it here in a very different type of soil from the humus chalk and dolomite soils which are its natural habitat. Moreover, I have caused it to flower (I have sent specimens to Kew to prove this) in what appears to be its close season, August. Not only have I succeeded with that. I think of *Pulsatilla montana*, the mountain anemone. It is really a southern Alpine valley plant, although it can be found up to an altitude of seven thousand feet. However, I can grow it at twelve thousand feet here, and *not* in a chalky soil. Then take *Pulsatilla vernalis*, the spring anemone! A lovely plant, and one that requires the sunlight. I am not altogether surprised that I get it to flower in October, considering the difference in climate, but still I account it one of my successes. So I do *Pulsatilla baldensis*, a typical Tyrolean mountain plant. Well, if not altogether typical, it certainly belongs to the Dolomites.'

'The Dolomites! Ah, yes!' said Laura, attempting to stem the flow. It was impossible.

'Then take *Tiroler Windröschen*, and what *do* you say to *Pulsatilla alpina sulphurea*?' asked the merciless botanist.

'The yellow anemone?' said Laura, guessing boldly. 'Well, it is a more important-looking plant than either

Vernalis or *Baldensis*, in my opinion, but that is purely a matter of choice.'

'Knowledgeable, knowledgeable,' said Peterhouse, collaring the batting once more. 'I like the way *Sulphurea* has that delicate suggestion of blue on the underside of the petals. The very sturdy bracts, too, and the tinge of red where these meet the main-stem of the plant are most attractive. In any case, I'm very fond of yellow.'

'There is plenty of sulphur, in every sense of the word, on Hombres Muertos, I suppose,' said Laura, faint but pursuing. Peterhouse shook her off again.

'I must show you specimens of *Rhododendron terrugineum*, the rusty-leaved Alpine rose, a tremendous plant,' he said. 'It grows to a height of more than three feet in the Swiss Alps, but here I have obtained a height of between five and six feet, and *my* flowers are larger than anything you'll ever see in Europe. Then take *Rhododendron hirsutum.*'

'The hairy rose. And that reminds me,' said Laura, desperately casting about for means of escape, 'I *must* go and see after my infant.'

'Mind you,' said Peterhouse, taking no notice of this plea, 'I am interested only in *poisonous* plants.'

'That sounds rather sinister. Do you mean that *everything* you've mentioned is poisonous?'

'Indeed it is. I might attempt to grow the Alpine campions, the soldenella, the lilies; the Alpine crowsfoot, the lady's-slipper orchis – a beauty, that! – the gentian; I could experiment with the erica, which – I don't know whether you've seen it? – is not unlike the heather; with the Noble Liverwort, that strange flower of three different colours. The cyclamen might attract me; the charming yellow violet, the graceful columbine, the saxifrage, (most famous of Alpine plants, and greatly loved), the auricula, the aromatic wormwood. ...'

'But none of these is poisonous?'

'Exactly, madam. None is poisonous.'

'You have interested me very much,' said Laura,

truthfully; for here, she felt, was a mind not altogether sane. 'Thank you. And now I must fly.'

She acted upon the word and literally fled.

'Atalanta! Atalanta!' called Peterhouse after her. She took no notice, but continued with loping strides towards the veranda. She leapt up the steps and bounded into the nearest public room, where she sank into a chair and metaphorically mopped her brow.

'That man Peterhouse', said Mrs Angel, materializing in uncanny fashion at her elbow, 'is a menace and a pest. In my opinion, he is quite insane.'

'He certainly does pin one down,' said Laura. 'He's been talking to me about Alpine plants.'

'Alpine plants? That's a change, then. I was told that he specialized in orchids.'

'So was ...' Laura was about to add Dame Beatrice's name, but recollected herself in time. 'So was I. At least, *he* didn't tell me, but I know I got it from somewhere.'

'He is a rogue, a charlatan, and a blackmailer. He blackmails poor old Ruiz, you know. That's why he's able to live here free of charge.'

'Good heavens! Is he really living free of charge?'

'Of course.'

'But what hold has he got over Ruiz?'

Mrs Angel wagged her head.

'Ask *young* Ruiz,' she said.

'Yes,' said Laura, determined to take this particular bull by the horns, 'why does young Ruiz come home so often? It must be awfully expensive to make that long voyage every year.'

'You've been listening to Pilar's tales. You really shouldn't take any notice of her. She is utterly lazy and utterly unreliable. I heard she even puts it about that I have the most undesirable commercial interests in South America.'

'You soon put that right, I suppose?' Laura was anxious to hear all about the undesirable element in Mrs Angel's commercial interests. Mrs Angel looked past her and fidgeted with the fringed edge of the arm of her chair.

'To speak sooth, no, I did not. It is better, I find, to take no notice of calumny. Evil rumours die all the quicker for not being contested.' She seemed about to say more, but changed her mind. 'I always thought that another guest along your corridor used to talk far too much to Pilar. Did you ever meet Dame Beatrice Lestrange Bradley? She is, I believe, quite famous in her own line.'

'She's a psychiatrist, a doctor of medicine, and is connected in some way with the Home Office,' said Laura, watching to see what effect the last bit of information would have. She was disappointed. Mrs Angel's face betrayed nothing except polite interest.

'Of course, living in England, you would be more in touch with such things than I am, making my life here as I do,' she said.

'Aren't you ever going back to England?'

'No, no. There is nothing for me to do in England. All my interests are here and in South America. Occasionally I go over there; not often; I cannot afford it. Young Ruiz has offered to pay my fare if I would like to go more often, but I do not care about life in a big city and my interests can be looked after just as well here.'

'And, of course, cattle and *guano* are more to do with men than with women, I suppose,' said Laura, probing wildly. Mrs Angel smiled.

'I am not primarily concerned with cattle *or* with *guano*,' she said. 'I do wish you would let me see your baby asleep. I always think a sleeping child is one of the most beautiful and satisfying sights on earth.'

'Of course you can see him asleep. He's probably asleep now, if you'd care to come up.' She had seen, through the open doorway, the stealthy approach of Mr Peterhouse, and she dreaded, above all things at that moment, a continuation of her conversation with him, or rather, a resumption of his botanical monologue. She got up and stretched her vital, magnificent body. 'Come on, Mrs Angel. Let's go.'

Even Mrs Angel's ecstatic and sincere admiration of the baby did not recommend her any more kindly to Laura. Her mysterious references to her South American concerns, however, and the suggestion that Peterhouse was blackmailing old Ruiz and that young Ruiz was willing to pay Mrs Angel's fare to the South American continent if and when she desired to visit it, had aroused detection fever in Laura. She must unburden herself to Dame Beatrice at once, she decided, and ask her to reinforce the garrison in person.

She got rid of Mrs Angel, fed the baby, went to the post office in the Plaza, and sent off a cable. She was both laconic and cautious, but she tried to indicate that she had found out some things which called for investigation. Whether the discoveries would prove to be mares' nests was anybody's guess, but this she did not indicate in the cable.

CHAPTER II

Down to Earth

DAME BEATRICE'S young relative did not take long to produce the information she wanted. She had been in London less than a week when documentary evidence arrived in the shape of a great bundle of typescript.

Dame Beatrice ordered a pot of coffee and set to work. Young Lestrange had done a successful bit of research, and she was able to follow the complete and enthralling stories of the death of Ian Lockerby and the trial of Clun. One thing was immediately clear. There was a connexion between the two men. Lockerby had been an acquaintance of Clun and had given evidence at his trial.

She studied the reports about Clun. The evidence was clear. He had been accused of the manslaughter of a man named Empson after both had been drinking. Clun's own story to Dame Beatrice, that he had hit too hard, was borne out by facts. Unfortunately for him, it seemed clear that he had instigated the quarrel. He had not been able to plead self-defence, and, to do him justice, had not, in the end, attempted to do so.

The other story, that of the death of Ian Lockerby, was more involved and far more interesting. Dame Beatrice made a summary of the evidence and added her own footnotes. Ian Lockerby, it appeared, had been a man of thirty two and was known to have had a violent temper and a nasty tongue. He was said to have had a liking for practical jokes of a cruel nature and to have taken pleasure in humiliating people, even when they were supposed to be his friends. He seemed a man born to be murdered.

The story of his fight with a gang of street louts had been told in court by Telham. The two men had been on a pub-crawl and Lockerby, at the time when the fight began, was considerably the worse for drink. According to Telham's evidence, one of the louts had been pushed by another, deliberately, so that he fell against Lockerby.

'It was enough to start Ian off,' the report ran. 'He began to set about the gang. I did my best to help, but it was two against eight or nine of them, so I shouted to Lockerby to scram, and began to run. I'd been knocked nearly silly by that time, and I'd seen the glint of a knife.'

Later, he had felt ashamed and had gone back. The gang had disappeared and Lockerby was dead. Telham had rung the police and had remained beside the body until they arrived.

It was the story that Dame Beatrice already had heard from Caroline. It certainly shed no light on the death of Emden. She made a note of the name and address of the public house beside which Lockerby had been killed, and then returned to the typescript and re-read the medical evidence.

A knife in the back ... signs that the body had been severely kicked after death had occurred. ... It was a nasty enough little business. It had happened before, and in the jungle of gangstership it was likely to happen again. People were more and more inclined to avoid going to the rescue of the victim in such circumstances. That Telham had been the only witness willing to come forward was understandable, too, although his descriptions of the young thugs were so vague as to be of little use to the police. Dame Beatrice shook a determined head and gathered the typescript together. She put it into a drawer and went off to look at the public house outside which the fight was said to have taken place.

It was a dingy little house in a side-street, and was unimpressive both within and without. In the saloon bar a rheumy-eyed man in his shirt-sleeves and a red knitted waistcoat was gloomily polishing glasses.

'Sherry?' he said, when she had given her order. He appeared to ruminate. 'Dark or light?'

'An unusual question,' said the elderly lady. The man looked surprised.

'I don't get much call for sherry,' he explained. 'More beer and stout, if you get me. Shorts – whisky and gin. Sherry – no. Port, now, port's a different matter.'

'What did the murdered man drink?'

'Ah, if I could get a few more of *his* sort, trade would look up, trade would. Ah, look up it would, good and proper. Once the murder got put in the papers I made six months' turnover in a matter of weeks. Not as he drunk anything here. Past closing time, I reckon. No, he never come in.'

'But, I gather, once the murder was out, others did come in. People have morbid fancies, have they not? I confess to a similar taste for the macabre.'

'Sherry, you said?'

'Dry, if you please.'

'Don't please me. Don't *not* please me. It's your gullet it's going down. Half a dollar. Ta, ma. Ah, morbid. That's the word. Mind you, there was a lot about that business as was very, very peculiar. One thing as puzzled me was how they never got a single one of the gang as did it. The police, they come here time and again to know what I could tell 'em, but, in the finish, I couldn't tell 'em nothing. "No sound of it come in here," I says. "Never knew as there was anything going on. Singing and 'ollering? Not on your life! Not in *my* 'ouse," I says. "Always quiet and friendly in 'ere. *Should* 'ave heard something of a dirty scrap like that," I says, "but, oath or not on oath, I never." But I don't understand *why* I didn't, if you take me. Not as I said that to *them*!'

'I should think the explanation is that he was set upon and killed elsewhere,' said Dame Beatrice, starting, she hoped, a hare. She was disappointed.

'If *so*,' said the barman, 'what about the evidence given in court by his pal?'

'Indeed, yes. What about it? Were you present at the inquest?'

'What about my opening times? You can't run a job in a pub *and* gallivant about amusing of yourself. I see his

picture in the local paper, though, and I wouldn't put it
past him to have done the job hisself. One pair of boots is
as 'andy as another when it comes to kicking a feller's
teeth in, that's as clear as the daylight, that is.'

There seemed nothing more to be gained. Dame
Beatrice drank a second dry sherry for the good of the
house and went home. After lunch she re-read the typescripts. She was not particularly impressed by the fact
that, if there had been a fight outside the public house,
the barman had heard nothing of it. There was no
window giving on to the street, and the doors, like those
of most public houses, were sturdy and fitted well. In any
case, as the man had said, it had happened, most probably
after closing time.

The typescripts, in themselves, were of no further help,
but they did give the name of the doctor who had first
examined the body. As she was a fellow-professional, she
thought that there would be no difficulty in obtaining an
interview with him. Neither was there. Doctor Brownlow
knew of her reputation and replied, over the telephone,
that he would be delighted to accept her invitation to
lunch with her at her club and that his morning surgery
finished, with luck, at noon at that time of year, when his
patients were mostly on holiday.

He presented himself at half past one, refused sherry or
a cocktail and drank tomato juice. He was a lean, grey-
haired man of fifty who acted as police doctor for his
district and was honorary surgeon to the local football club.

'I'm a physician by training,' he said, shaking pepper
over his soup, 'but I know enough about bones and
muscles to deal with footballers' injuries. Now, what do
you want to know about this young fellow found scuppered
outside the Old Bull and Bush?'

'Everything you can tell me. I've read the newspaper
reports, but there are usually one or two details which
don't get into the Press.'

'I can't think of any in this particular connexion,
though.'

'The weapon?'

'A thing like the knives they sell to Boy Scouts.'

'Had only one blow been struck?'

'No. But I formed the impression, when I performed the post-mortem, that the first blow had caused death and that the others had been inflicted after death had taken place. The blow which was the fatal one was in the centre back just below the shoulder-blades, and it had penetrated the heart. Copy-book stuff, in short.'

'But there were other wounds?'

'Yes. Several. You'd expect that, if he was attacked by a gang.'

'Are not razor-blades more common than knives in these cases?'

'Well, I expect it depends on the gang leader. If he decides that the trade-mark is a knife-wound. ....'

'Yes, I see. What about signs of a struggle?'

'None. It would have been a quick job.'

'But I understand there was a fight, and that the murdered man's friend – his brother-in-law, incidentally – ran out of it.'

'Oh, the chap who telephoned! Well, I dare say there was a scuffle, and then the first knife-thrust did the trick.'

'What was the weather like?'

'A fine night, but very dark.'

'Were the public houses still open?'

'It was after midnight when I was called.'

'That is very interesting, but, of course, it is clear enough what must have happened. The man who ran away must have taken a long time to make certain that the gang had gone before he decided to go back. It would be quite in keeping with his character, as far as I have been able to judge it. Was the body, so to speak, hidden away?'

'Well, I gather you've seen the public house. The body had been dragged some distance from where it had fallen. The clothes had that appearance. When I saw it first it was in that passage-way beside the men's convenience, well out of the way of passers-by.'

'It seems strange that Mr Telham found it. I suppose he had a torch and made a thorough search. I wonder how far from home the murdered man was? I don't remember reading his address in the reports.'

A further examination of the typescripts that afternoon did not produce the address, so she rang up her grand-nephew.

'Same address as Telham,' he replied. 'That's in the typescript, surely?'

'Yes, thank you, it is. I didn't realize that it was the same house. Then they *were* a long way from home.'

'Well, you don't usually pub-crawl in your own locality – not if you're having a real night out, you know. What surprises me is that there were only the two of them. You usually go in a body, so to speak, and stand the rounds in turn. I once had to drink fourteen pints on a pub-crawl. Tell you the whole sordid story at some time.'

Dame Beatrice replaced the receiver. She felt she had food for thought. The picture, as she had first conceived it, had changed. The fight had not been heard from inside the public house – that she could allow to pass as a strong probability – but that there might have been a roistering party engaged in getting drunk with Telham and the murdered Ian Lockerby she had *not* allowed for, any more than she had given consideration to the fact that the Lockerbys might have had Telham – who, after all, was unmarried and was devoted to his sister – as a member of their household. She wondered what had happened to the house, and whether the people in it, if it was still occupied, could give her any further information.

She summarized her knowledge again, adopting a different view-point. First, there was nothing in the medical evidence to suggest that the murder necessarily had taken place after the public houses closed. Secondly, the body had been dragged from the place where the fatal injury had been inflicted into a passage-way where it might have remained unnoticed until the morning. A man lying apparently dead-drunk near the entrance to a public house privy was not likely to have been the recipient of help or the object of concern. Even a possible Good Samaritan would have done no more than give the prone figure a shake and advise it to get up and go home.

So far, so good, thought Dame Beatrice; but other thoughts obtruded themselves. Telham, already connected, in a sense, with the death of Lockerby (which he might or might not have been able to prevent), had arrived at the Hotel Sombrero in a state of nervous tension. His behaviour with regard to Clun showed the state of his mind. Right, thought Dame Beatrice, and natural enough, if he blamed his own cowardice for Ian Lockerby's death. There followed the so-far-unexplained and sudden exit from the hotel of the philandering but otherwise seemingly harmless Emden. There was no obvious connexion between the arrival of the ship's party and the flight of Lothario, but it remained a curious and interesting feature, the more so as Emden himself, soon after his disappearance, had been murdered. There was also the coincidence that the murdered Lockerby and the manslaughtering Clun had been acquainted with one another before Clun's conviction.

Then, Telham was not the only person to exhibit nervous strain. Still unexplained were Caroline's outbursts on the occasion of her first visit to the Cave of Dead Men. She might have had guilty knowledge of the death of Emden; she might have had a recurrence of the feeling of horror her husband's murder had engendered; she might even be *clairvoyante*. Dame Beatrice shrugged her aside, but only temporarily. Caroline's reactions would bear further examination.

She considered afresh her grandnephew's theory that Lockerby and Telham had been not a *duo* but a frothblowers' chorus. She shook her head. It was an untenable theory. Interested, like other psychiatrists, in the phenomenon of the post-war street gangs, she realized that the gangs only went into battle where they were certain of success. The nearest analogies, she thought, were the

Mohawk or Mohock gangs of unruly, cruel, and cowardly
youths (of good family, too!) who were the terror of the
old and the unarmed in eighteenth-century London. No.
Whatever else was uncertain, it did not seem possible that
Lockerby and Telham had been members of a party large
enough to engage the street youths on anything like equal
terms.

There remained the interesting but possibly unrelated
facts that the deaths of Lockerby and Emden had both
been obtained by knife-thrusts, and that, in both cases,
the knife had been left in the wound. Exhaustive inquiries
by the police had failed to produce evidence against the
hand which had struck down Lockerby, and the Yard's
fingerprint experts had found no traces on the hilt of the
knife. That produced another interesting speculation.
Did knife and razor gangs habitually go about gloved?
Dame Beatrice went to the telephone and rang up Detective Chief-Inspector Robert Gavin. He was not, he
announced, an expert on gang-warfare, but he thought
that, in summer, the gangs were unlikely to wear gloves.
In any case, he added, the majority of the gangsters were
'unknown' to the police.

'Curiouser and curiouser,' said Dame Beatrice. 'And
I am not referring to the gangs and their glovelessness.
How is Laura?'

'Into mischief, I strongly suspect, in spite of the
restraining influence of my son and heir. Come and have
dinner with me somewhere. I'm pining away. You've
robbed me of the wife of my bosom and sent her gallivanting to Hombres Muertos, so the least you can do is to help
relieve my lonely estate of grass widower.'

'No. You come and have dinner here with me, and I'll
despatch George to Hampshire forthwith to bring back
Henri to cook our meal. Left to his own devices and without the incubus of a back-seat driver, he can be there and
back in under four hours. You had better have a good
substantial tea and we'll dine at nine.'

During Laura's holiday, Gavin was sharing a bachelor

flat with a friend, but the friend, another policeman, had been called to a case which was proving too hard a nut for the county police to crack unaided, so Gavin was glad enough of a change from a lonely dinner. He turned up in Kensington at eight and announced that he had come early to gossip, in case he was called away.

'Not that I expect to be,' he added, tucking Dame Beatrice's arm in his and leading her to the settee. 'Now, then, you put your feet up. You've been gadding and are tired. I can always tell.'

Dame Beatrice, who was never in the least tired, gave an amiable cackle and let him fuss. He had long since been treated like a favourite son and relished this position in the household.

'Now,' she said, when he had settled her with cushions and a foot-wrap, 'sit where I can see you. Listen carefully. I want you to pick all the holes you can in my argument.'

'Police holes?'

'And defending counsel holes. And any other holes you can think of. I don't want to be right, so I shall be most grateful for any proof that I'm wrong.'

'You're never wrong, Dame B. But fire away, and I'll whack in the dynamite and blow you sky-high. It's the island business, I suppose? Made up your mind who did it?'

'Not entirely. But I don't like what I know.'

'Something fishy you've discovered?'

'Plural. Some things, and odd rather than fishy, if I interpret that word aright.'

Gavin grunted in Gaelic.

'We – I say we, meaning the police – questioned that chap Telham pretty closely, you know,' he said. 'There was a theory, at one point in the inquiry, that he'd done the job himself and that his story of being attacked by a Teddy gang was just so much boloney.'

'Really? But that is just what I myself have been wondering. Theoretically it would fit rather well. What made the police suspect Telham?'

'They thought his story was pretty thin. It was obvious that his sister's marriage wasn't altogether a happy one, and it was known that Telham was very fond of Caroline. Tell you what. If you like to come along to the Yard at some time I'll manage for you to have a look at the police records of the case. You can't take them off the building, of course, but you can sit in my office and study them to your heart's content. They'll tell you a lot that never got into the newspapers. How about it?'

'I should be most grateful. And now you would like something to drink.'

'Lots and lots of beer, please. Shall I ring the bell? What are you having? Sherry?'

'No. You shall mix me a White Lady and we will drink Laura's health.'

'If I know Laura, she's as brown as an Indian by now, with the sea and the sun. I suppose Hombres Muertos is a bit of the Garden of Eden, isn't it?'

'Complete with more than one serpent.' She regaled him, as he drank his beer, with the rich and vivid histories of the people she had met in the Hotel Sombrero de Miguel Cervantes, rounding off the tale with Pilar's account of the illegal and horrid enterprises of the bird-loving Mrs Angel. It was doubtless regrettable of him, but Gavin choked with laughter.

'I'd like to meet the old girl,' he said. 'By heck, though, you know, Dame B., what with her cynical activities and old Peterhouse's sinister orchids and the Ruiz boy in South America, Hombres Muertos sounds like one of civilization's hot spots, doesn't it? And that chap Clun – you say you've found a slight connexion between his case and the one you're on? Well to me, he sounds just the lad.'

'No, he doesn't. He wouldn't put a knife in a man's back. That's one of the things I don't much like about these murders. They're rather nasty ones.'

'Dirty, yes, that's true. Still, the fifteenth-century Italians had a word for it, and who are we to criticize the fellow-countrymen of Andrea del Sarto and Fra Lippo Lippi?'

'It is all too obvious, I suppose,' said Dame Beatrice, following her own line of thought. 'It all ties up far too neatly. The jealous brother, the stabbing, the stupid story about the street gang, not one member of which has ever been found, the flight from England, the unbalanced outbreaks of anger, the second stabbing, the otherwise inexplicable behaviour of Caroline in the cave of the dead men ...'

'Ah, yes, but what would be the motive for the second stabbing?'

'That's just the point. There doesn't seem to be one unless Lockerby's murderer suddenly realized that, in coming to Hombres Muertos, he had come to the place where lived the one man who was in a position to give the game away – in other words, the one and only witness of his crime.'

'But why should the murderer have gone to Hombres Muertos? Never mind. You come along tomorrow for the dossier, and see what you think when you have read it.'

CHAPTER 12

The Case Against a Brother-in-Law

DAME BEATRICE spent an interesting and instructive day in Gavin's office. Supplied with police notes and the signed statements of everybody who could possibly have been in a position to give any evidence whatever concerning the cause of Lockerby's death, she read and scribbled, read and scribbled all day except for a short break for lunch in a restaurant where they knew her and would serve her quickly.

The police certainly had pushed Telham as hard as the law allowed. Time and again he had been interrogated. His signed statement, however, bore out the verbal answer he had given at the very first interview, when he had telephoned the police and they had come to inspect the body. It was obvious that, if Telham *had* committed the murder, he not only had planned it exceptionally carefully but had had the intelligence to anticipate the line the police would take with him and had prepared answers to their questions. Moreover, his statement had the merit of simplicity. He had attempted no embroidery and had dug no pit for his own feet.

In addition to the statement, written in the formal if stilted language of the police, there was also that other, far more illuminating statement given in Telham's own words and taken down in shorthand. Dame Beatrice studied the two side by side, but the signed statement was a fair enough précis of the other. She put it aside, and concentrated on the shorthand version.

'We had been out for the evening and both had too much to drink. Lockerby had taken much more than I had, and I was worried about getting him home. We had started out by visiting big, respectable pubs, but at the fourth one they would not serve us and advised us to get out. I wanted to call it a day, but Lockerby got mad at being refused a drink. He blasted the place to hell and said he knew somewhere where they *would* serve us. I suggested we went home. I was thinking of my sister and how she would blame me if I took him back completely plastered. He said that I could do what I liked, but that he was not going home until he had had another drink.

'I did not like to leave him, seeing the state he was in. I thought he would get himself in trouble. He was fighting drunk, but not helpless. I mean, he could walk all right and his speech was all right – a bit thick, but not really slurred – in other words, he had reached the dangerous stage. He was always a quick-tempered chap and I felt he might go too far if I was not there to look after things.

'We tried a little pub in a back street and there was a barmaid. She served us all right. I do not know whether she spotted that Lockerby was canned. I do not know the name of the pub. It is the one in Kidling Street. Lockerby had a double whisky and asked for another. He was served. He drank up and banged his glass down on the counter for another. The chap who was with the girl behind the bar told him they had run out of whisky. Lockerby swore at him but I managed to haul him out before anything happened.

'On the way to the bus stop we came to another small pub and Lockerby said he was going in to have a last drink, but the pub was shut. It was then we ran into the Teddies. There were a dozen or more. They were a bit noisy but I did not believe they meant any mischief at first. As we passed, one of them charged against another and sent him sprawling into Lockerby, who was taken off balance and fell into the gutter. The Teddies laughed, and one of them pushed him in the side with his shoe. I do not call it a kick. It was more a bit of cheek, I should say.

'Lockerby got up and charged at them like a mad bull. He was a tough, heavy chap and I think his punches and open-handed slaps across their faces really hurt. Some of them attended to me, and some to him. I could hear him grunting and they were cursing. I soon had enough of it. I shouted to him to run, and made a dash for it, believing he would follow. I thought they would not chase us into the main road, and none of them did, but Lockerby did not come. I looked out for a policeman, but there was not one about. I made for the bus stop, but then I thought I probably looked a bit of a mess.

'I decided to try for a taxi, but there was no taxi-rank along there and I did not see a roving cab. Then I thought I had been a heel to leave Lockerby scrapping with the bunch of Teddies, and I ought to go back. I went back and the street was quite deserted and the pub was shut, as I said. There was no sign of Lockerby and I felt he was bound to have got the worst of it, one against a mob. I thought he might have concussion and be wandering about, not knowing what he was doing, or he might have been kicked unconscious.

'The lights in the little pub were still burning, so I could see he was not in the gutter or on the pavement. Then I thought of the passage, and there he was. I did not know straight away that he was dead, but he was so cold I thought he must be. I did not spot the knife in his back. The rest you know.'

Dame Beatrice screwed the top on her fountain-pen. Gavin looked up from his work.

'Any luck?'

'No luck. One question and one cynical remark.'

'Shoot.'

'What caused Telham to "think of the passage", do you suppose?'

'He may have required to use the convenience, you know. Or he may have thought that Lockerby, feeling bad, had staggered into it after the gang had finished with him. It wouldn't be at all an unlikely thing.'

'Quite. It was very convenient for Telham that he "did not spot the knife", I thought. It saved him from fingering it and leaving prints which would have to be explained.'

'I say! You *have* got it all worked out, haven't you? But, even if you're right, we shall never get him now. There simply isn't any more evidence anywhere. Of course, the case isn't closed. You can take it that we've still got an ear to the ground. I can tell you more. The police are still rounding up Teddies and making searching inquiries into alibis. They'll leave no stone unturned, as the saying is. But what makes you so certain it was Telham?'

'Oh, but I am not certain. I am not certain at all. The only thing is that it would have been so easy for him to have done it. And, you know, just as, in John Gay's time, all evil deeds were laid upon the gin, so, nowadays, it seems to me, the same is true about the street gangs.'

'What do you propose to do now? Is there any other way in which I can help you?'

'Not unless there is a guilty connexion among Lockerby, Telham, and Emden.'

'You think Telham killed Emden, too?'

'Only if he or Emden killed Lockerby.'

'Aha! You have an alternative theory!'

'A remarkably sketchy one, I fear, but, all the same, I should like to test it. You see, the medical evidence is surprising if Lockerby really was killed by a gang. Almost all the bruises appear to have been inflicted after death. Now, in my experience, the average Teddy boy makes himself very scarce indeed when there has been real trouble. The gang would know at once that Lockerby had been stabbed. The killer would say so, and they would all be off in no time. They would not remain and kick the body.'

'Oh, I don't know. They're abysmal young brutes, some of them.'

'Yes, when it is safe to be brutal. It was not a street gangster who killed Lockerby, Robert. The body had been dragged, too, remember. I have a very strong feeling that a gang would have left it lying where it dropped.'

'Oh, I don't know. There's the human instinct to hide the traces of wrong-doing, isn't there? It's inborn. All children have it.'

'Quite. But it's not a herd instinct, it's a personal one.'

'You are building up the case in the same way as the police built it up, but, as Telham couldn't be shaken – What did his sister have to say?'

Dame Beatrice selected another document.

'My husband and my brother often went out together to get a drink. They were very good friends. When they did not get back I was anxious, but there was nothing I could do, as they had not said where they were going. I went to bed at just after midnight. When I next saw my brother it was in company with a police officer who broke the news to me of my husband's death and told me there would be an inquest.'

'I quite understand why she had to make a statement to the police,' said Gavin. 'They were firmly convinced that Telham was guilty. Her talk about the two men being good friends, and so forth, was just a bit of whitewash, most likely. All the same, I don't see what else she could have said. Besides, not many women would be parties to the bumping off of their husbands by their brothers.'

'It may have been an extremely unhappy marriage. From my knowledge of her, Caroline is both sensitive and neurotic.'

'Yes. The police wondered whether, in fact, she was an accessory, you know. I should think there has hardly been a case of murder with so little evidence available. Our chaps could get nothing out of the people at the pub and they couldn't even trace the origin of the knife. The makers turn out hundreds every year, and send them all over the place. Inquiries were of the usual exhaustive pattern, but all the evidence was negative or abortive.'

'Including Telham's refusal to attempt a description of any of the gang who were supposed to have attacked the two of them. How much was he himself knocked about, I wonder?'

'It isn't difficult to inflict a few bruises on yourself and even a tentative razor slash or so. You know, you're an insinuating monster. You've almost convinced me that Telham did do it. And I know Anson, who was in charge of the case, thought he had. Why don't you have a word with Anson? I'll find out what he's doing and send him round when he's got a spot of time. I'll call you up and warn you when he's coming.'

Detective-Inspector Anson was an expert on Boxer dogs. He brought one with him and in a quarter of an hour had convinced Dame Beatrice that if Boxers instead of humans had inherited the earth, heaven would be present laughter and hell a complete misconception.

'As to Telham,' he said suddenly, flattening out and restoring the creases in his dog's face, 'he's guilty all right, but we'll never prove it. Did you ever read the ballad called *The Cruel Brother*?'

'Indeed, yes,' Dame Beatrice admitted. 'But *he* killed his sister, not her husband.'

'A distinction, not a difference. Telham can't do without his sister, you see.'

'What makes you think that Telham killed Ian Locker-by?'

'Common sense. It was done in the pub convenience, of course. Plenty of water available to wash away blood-stains. Everything. Oh, he did it all right. I only wish I could pin it on him.'

'You know,' said Dame Beatrice suddenly, 'I don't believe a word of it. And I've thought as you have – until now. But now I know it is wrong. We have to look else-where for our murderer.'

'I wish you could convince me, ma'am. If we had another line to go on, we might be able to do something. It gets under my skin to have a case rest like this. One thing I'm certain about. This was no street-gang murder. Much too tidy.'

'I agree completely. This murder was very carefully planned; so carefully, in fact, that there must be some indication, somewhere, of the identity of the planner. Meanwhile, my place seems to be on Hombres Muertos, not here.'

'Oh, yes, your island, ma'am. Very beautiful, I understand.'

'Very beautiful and, strange to say, since beautiful islands have, on the whole, a sinister reputation, very innocent and pleasant.'

'The cave of dead kings, ma'am?'

'There's sun and moon, brother; there is also respect for dead kings, except that I do not think the murderer of Emden showed any respect for the dead kings, and it may well be that they will give some token of their resentment.'

'I say, is the old girl barmy?' asked Detective-Inspector Anson when next he encountered Gavin. Gavin grinned.

'What did she soak you with, dearie?'

'Dead kings.'

'How many of them?'

'I've no idea.'

'Twenty-four,' said Gavin, tapping him solemnly on the chest. 'Twenty-four, my good fellow. And there should have been only twenty-three. Remember?'

'I don't know what you're talking about. All I asked you was whether the old lady's screwy.'

'Don't you believe it, sonny. What else did she say?'

'Said that until my visit she'd been convinced Telham did it, but that now she doesn't think so, and that her place is on Hombres Muertos, a beautiful, innocent island. *Is* it beautiful and innocent?'

'According to her, apart from Emden's murder, it shelters a dope-runner and a white-slave trader, if that's anything to judge it by.'

Anson went away, solemnly shaking his head. Dame Beatrice went to the house where the Lockerbys and Telham had been living. A strictly unofficial visit to people she had never met needed a credible explanation, so she packed her black bag with the accessories carried by general practitioners, called up a private-hire car as

likely to be more reassuring to her pretended patient than
a taxi or her own car would have been, and, with her
usual brisk self-assurance, went to the address she had
found in the police files and rang the bell.

The house was an old one in the Maida Vale district
and had been converted into flats. There was no porter.
The front door, at the top of a flight of well-worn but
newly scrubbed steps, was opened by an equally well-
worn but slatternly daily help.

'Yes?'

'I am the doctor. May I come in?'

'Doctor?'

'Yes. Where is my patient?'

''Ow do *I* know? I only works for Mr Bellini, and 'e
ain't in, so it can't be 'im. There's old Mrs Barstow, on
the second floor, but she 'as Doctor Stopps.'

'Barstow is the name. Kindly show me the way.'

'You can't miss it. Up them stairs, second floor, door
marked with a four.'

Dame Beatrice ascended. An old lady and an invalid,
provided she possessed all her senses, was more than she
had dared hope for. She gained the landing and tapped
at the door marked with a figure four. It was opened a
crack, and a suspicious old face, much wrinkled and not
over-clean, appeared and studied her.

'Yes?' it said. Fortunately the note was merely inter-
rogative and not in the least belligerent or nervous. There
appeared to be a reason for this disarming attitude, for the
door opened wider to display a magnificent Boxer dog.
'Eat you as soon as look at you,' said its owner, with a
chuckle, 'so you may as well come in. The draughts on
this landing you'd never believe, unless you'd lived here
twenty years, as I have.'

'You stayed here during the war?' Dame Beatrice
clucked hopefully at the Boxer and entered a large, high-
ceilinged room which was furnished, in its various corners,
as a bedroom, a sitting-room, a kitchen, and a bathroom,
a screen round the latter proving not quite large enough

to hide a portable zinc tub and a clothes-horse holding a towel. A pile of newspapers and a horse-blanket near the foot of the bed indicated the sleeping-quarters of the dog.

'*Couchant*, Hector,' said Mrs Barstow, prodding the dog with a slippered foot. 'Yes, of course I stayed here during the war. Where else was there for me to go? And now, what's your business? I take it you're Doctor Stopps' locum. Where's *he* gone gallivanting off to? I suppose he thinks that because it isn't autumn yet, my rheumatism doesn't matter.'

'I'm afraid I know nothing either of Doctor Stopps or your rheumatism. I am interested in a patient named Lockerby.'

'Well, you needn't be. He got murdered months ago.'

'No, no. *Mrs* Lockerby. A nerve-subject. Depression. Sleeplessness. A tendency to hysteria.'

'You won't find her here. She's another gallivanting flibber-tee-gibbit. Really, you'd have thought even an unfaithful wife would have nicer feeling than to go running off to the Riviera with her husband's murderer. Oh, don't tell *me*! Brother, indeed! That Telham creature is no more her brother than I am! The dirty pair fixed it all up together, and *I've* never been certain which of them stuck the knife in his back, because *she* was out that night, too. Now, what's your business with her?'

'I am a mental specialist.'

'Oh, and I should think she needs one, too, the artful, scheming hussy! You're not a police doctor, are you? I thought they always had men.'

'Probably they do. Well, when is Mrs Lockerby expected back? It is most vexing not to find her here. I have received definite evidence of the state of her mind.'

'Downright wicked, that's the state of her mind, and I don't care who knows I've said it. She deliberately made that poor man drunk so that she and that Telham (as he called himself) could carry on together. It was absolutely shocking!'

'How did you know about all this?'

'Looking over banisters and listening at keyholes, of course. What else have I got to do with my time, except feed Hector and take him out? That's how I got to know Mr Lockerby. Many's the time, when the drink's been too much for him, I've told him to take Hector out for a run. They always brought each other back safely. No men ever go wrong when my dog has them on a lead. Once, when the poor man was feeling very low, he said to me, "Mrs Barstow, I'm going to drink all the money away. I'm not leaving anything to Caroline. She doesn't deserve it." And she certainly didn't, you know. But they murdered the poor man, between them, before it all went. I know their artfulness, and so I told the police.'

'The police came to see you?'

'Several times. They pretended to make notes, but I was never asked to sign anything. They didn't believe me, you see, *but I knew*!'

'It seems strange that they didn't believe you. Could you render chapter and verse?'

'Didn't see how to. I wasn't there when the deed was done, and they wouldn't believe that Telham wasn't her brother.'

'I expect they looked it all up, you know, and found that you were misinformed, and that Mr Telham *is* her brother. The police are very thorough.'

'Maybe they are, but I know what I know, all the same. Well, that rampole isn't here and nobody knows when she'll be back, so you've had your journey for nothing. And now, if you'll excuse me, I'm going to make Hector and myself a dish of cocoa.'

Dame Beatrice was not in the least surprised that the police had not been over-anxious to accept Mrs Barstow's disclosures at their face-value, but there were two points that she wanted to have cleared up.

'What about the relationship between Caroline Locker-by and Telham?' she inquired of Anson. '*Were* they brother and sister?'

'You've been talking to old Mrs Barstow, ma'am. I shouldn't place much reliance on *her,* you know.'

'She says she looks over banisters and listens at key-holes. Could she, by such means, be one jump ahead of the police?'

Gavin laughed when he heard of this encounter.

'The police can't hope to emulate, much less surpass, the activities of a lonely old lady with nothing much to do except to mind her neighbours' business. So, according to the old dear, there had been goings-on, had there?'

'She seemed to think so, but, of course, in these disastrous days, wishful thinking is on the increase.'

'I don't really think we can take much notice of her. How did she strike you? – as a reliable witness, I mean.'

'I would not call her reliable. Obviously she intends to believe what she wants to believe. All the same, I found her not uninteresting and far from unimportant.'

'Not unimportant?'

'Any stick does with which to beat a dog. Nothing is louder in any gate than a hog. All that glistens is not necessarily gold. Not to every policeman is unperishing truth told. Too many cooks can spoil the choicest broth. Not always with a wedding ring does a man plight his troth. If in the sunshine you choose to make your hay, there is not always much left to put by for a rainy day!'

'Chorus,' said Gavin, 'in which the cook and the baby joined – Yah! Boo! Sucks to you! The police will solve it before you do! Come out with me tonight and let me teach you how to rock and roll. Rock out of arms' reach and roll with the punch. Or don't you care about boxing?'

'Why does Mrs Barstow keep a Boxer?'

'Eh? Oh, you mean the dog? Yes, it doesn't seem a typical pet for an old lady, does it, now one comes to think? I remember Anson said his mind was on the seat of his trousers all the time he was talking to the old lady.'

'But a Boxer wouldn't hurt a fly!'

'If I were a fly, I wouldn't care to bet on that!'

'Do you think he means what he said?'

'About the seat of his trousers? Yes, I do, and I can't blame him, either.'

'But, my dear Robert, this may be of the first importance.'

'Don't try to pull my leg.'

'It is essential that we return to old Mrs Barstow and try to reconstruct the conversations she had with Detective Inspector Anson.'

'But Anson was playing the wag when he said he was scared of the dog. Why, he keeps a Boxer himself. He'd know that the dog was harmless.'

'That is just my point. He knew that the dog *wasn't* harmless. My dear Robert, bear with me for once. This may mark the turning-point of the case. To Mrs Barstow without delay. I hear the Gytrash panting at my heels.'

'The Gytrash?'

'Mentioned in *Jane Eyre*. An East Coast dog-ghost renowned from Essex to Yorkshire. Brought over here by the Danes, I rather fancy, and left as a legacy, particularly to the Fenlands, on which, as you probably know, it is as well to place no foot after dark. *Flat* land is as much more sinister than mountains as the ghostly midday is than the moonless night.'

Instead of going straight to Mrs Barstow, they sought out Anson. He admitted the soft impeachment.

'She'd set the dog at the alert,' he said. 'I don't really blame her, and I don't think it made any difference to the interrogation. One's prepared to be a martyr in a good-cause. Of course, I didn't take much stock in her evidence. She was convinced that Mrs Lockerby and Telham were not related, so I got Mrs Lockerby to produce the birth certificates. They were brother and sister all right, so the old lady's suspicions went for a Burton, and I regarded the rest of her tale as unreliable.'

Dame Beatrice went back next day to Mrs Barstow.

'I have been to the police about Mrs Lockerby,' she announced. 'Can you describe Mr Telham?'

'I see him in my dreams.' Mrs Barstow invited her

visitor to come in. 'I'm glad to hear the police are showing a bit of common sense at last,' she went on, when both were seated. She proceeded to give a recognizable – indeed, an unmistakable – description of Emden.

'And the unfortunate husband?'

'Medium height, heavy build and very dark – almost swarthy, in fact.'

'Ah, yes.' It was certainly not a description which, by any imagination, could fit Telham. 'Then there was a third man, or so I was told. Where did he fit in?'

'A third man? Oh, you mean Mr Karl Emden, I suppose.'

'Emden was the name, yes. The police are particularly interested in Mr Emden. You see, although I do not imagine the story' got into the English papers, the unfortunate Mr Karl Emden has been murdered.'

'What? Him, too? Good gracious me! Whatever next?'

'I have no idea.'

'But the poor, pale, soft young man! Whatever could *he* have been doing to get himself murdered? Why, he only came here visiting. Once a week he came, on Fridays, to make up a four at bridge. Whoever could have wanted to murder *him*?'

'That is what a good many people would like to know.'

'You said something about it not getting into the English papers. Was he murdered abroad, then? I always say you can't trust foreigners. That's the way *I* see it. Poor soul! Such a quiet young man, you couldn't think he could upset anybody, not even a heathen cannibal. Where did it happen?'

'On the island of Hombres Muertos.'

'Never heard of it.'

'None of the party ever mentioned it in your hearing?'

'Never, and it wasn't for want of me listening, I assure you.'

'What was the relationship between Mrs Lockerby and this Mr Karl Emden?'

'Cool and polite. Quite friendly, but nothing more. No,

no. It was what I have already told you. She was wrapped up in this fellow she called her brother.'

'How long had they been living in this house before the husband was murdered?'

'A matter of a year and a half.'

'Did you ever know Mrs Lockerby to be hysterical?'

'Only with her husband when there were quarrels. Of course, I will say he could be violent.'

'How violent?'

'Oh, not blows. I should have sent for the police if he had struck her. He used bad language and a lot of it. It was from him I found out that Mr Telham was not her brother.'

'Did he ever use Telham's name in the course of these quarrels?'

'Not that I remember. He called him a great number of things, but never Telham.'

'How did you know his name was Telham, then?'

'Letters.'

'Letters?'

'His letters came here and she used to pick them up where I'd left them lying on the mat. I always used to get to the front door first because, by the time the post came, the men had gone off to business and my lady was still in bed.'

Dame Beatrice confided the gist of this conversation to Gavin.

'It sounds a rum sort of set-up,' he said. 'The description of Telham fits Emden, you think, and Emden was clearly Telham. *Ménage à trois, et un mari complaisant, en effet, n'est-ce pas?* Well, it's all of a queer do, but the more I know of human relationships, the less I'm prepared to put anything past anybody. The puzzle, though, far from getting itself unravelled, seems in more of a mess than ever. I mean to say, if Lockerby didn't object to his wife's making a love-nest with Emden, why the need for either of them to bump him off? Do you think perhaps Caroline wanted a divorce and he refused to play ball?'

'Or did the chivalrous brother, the weekly visitor who made a fourth at bridge on Friday nights, remove the obstacle to a second and happier marriage for his sister?'

'Goodness knows! As I say, it appears to me we're as much in the dark as we were. Do you want me to tell Anson all this?'

'If you think it will help him. I cannot see that it will. However, it will very likely help *me* when I get back to Hombres Muertos. The trouble there, from the beginning, has been that we have not known how to ask questions or, rather, what questions to ask and of whom to ask them.'

'But now, you think, there are to be some interesting answers to be expected from Mrs Lockerby? What's she like?'

'Aged about twenty-nine and very charming. And very fond of her brother.'

'The real Telham?'

'The real Telham.'

'Is the fondness genuine?'

'Undoubtedly, I should say.'

'Well, you would certainly know. I can't say I envy you. You haven't freed one of your suspects by coming back here. You've only been offered a lot of irrelevant details and spent a great deal of valuable time.'

'I haven't freed any of my suspects, it is true; but there is no doubt that on one or two of them the searchlight of suspicion is differently focused. Before I leave London, I want to re-read my grandnephew's notes on the trial of Mr Clun for manslaughter. And now, is it fair to ask how much longer you can spare your Laura to the island of bandits and bananas?'

'Not very much longer,' said Gavin, 'sun-bathing and señores notwithstanding. In other words, keep her as long as you want her, of course. That, by this time, goes without saying.'

'And now to retrace our steps. What was all that about Mr Clun?' said Dame Beatrice. She looked up her notes.

CHAPTER 13

The Case Against a Killer

INTO the Crown Court of Assize came the judge's chaplain, the sheriff, then the judge, importantly dressed in red, followed by his marshal. The court stood. The judge bowed to counsel, who bowed in return, and to the jury.

Clun, immaculately dressed, stood in the dock and was flanked by two warders. The jury looked expectant, the witnesses stopped fidgeting, the Press poised their pencils. The judge's clerk, a thin man in spectacles, traditionally and unnecessarily called the court to attention, and the assize clerk read the indictment. The prisoner pleaded not guilty, but only as a matter of form. He knew he stood no chance of being acquitted, but his counsel had insisted on the plea.

He was given the opportunity to object to the jury or to any individual member of it. Then the jury, eight men and four women, were sworn, and the trial began.

'Members of the jury ...' the assize clerk opened the proceedings in a thin, clear voice – 'Clun stands before you, charged with the manslaughter of Ernest Everard in the foyer of the *Crown* Hotel, Pawsey, at 10.45 p.m. on the evening of 18 March. Upon this indictment he has been arraigned, and, upon this arraignment, he has pleaded Not Guilty. Your charge, therefore, is to say whether he be guilty or no, and to hear the evidence.'

At a signal from the warder nearest him, Clun seated himself, and counsel for the prosecution stood up to address the judge and then the jury. He put his case plainly and straightforwardly, in a dry and non-committal voice. Clun had been one of a party of men who had had dinner together at the hotel. It was a stag party, the tie between the diners being that of belonging to a local political club.

'It is not contested, members of the jury, that the parties had both been drinking heavily. It is not contested that the dead man had used insulting and intemperate language. You will hear from eye-witnesses that a scuffle took place, between him and the accused, at the top of a staircase leading from the dining-room to the foyer. You will hear that the accused acted under strong provocation; nevertheless, I submit that no provocation could be strong enough to justify the action of the accused in bringing about the death of Ernest Everard in the way you will hear described.'

Here counsel produced plans and diagrams for the inspection of judge and jury, and then called his first witness. This turned out to be Ian Lockerby.

'Your name is Ian Lockerby?'

'Yes.'

'You live in flat number fifteen, in Temple Mansions?'

'Yes.'

'You were the convener of this dinner-party?'

'Well, I'm the secretary, so, of course, I sent out the invitations.'

'So you sent an invitation to Clun and another to a Mr Ernest Everard?'

'No, I didn't. Clun was a member, but Everard came in place of one of the members who couldn't turn up.'

'Was that in order?'

'Well, no, not really, I suppose.'

'Will you clarify that answer, if you please.'

'What I mean is that we didn't usually admit non-members, but the member who couldn't turn up had paid for the dinner in advance and we couldn't refund him the money because the restaurant had it, and these chaps will never disgorge ...'

'Keep to the point, please.'

'I thought I was.' (Here Dame Beatrice's grand-nephew had noted in his report that it seemed, according to the newspapers, that Lockerby had flushed up and looked annoyed.) 'The point is that the fellow who should have come didn't want to have paid for nothing, so he'd arranged with Everard to settle for it. He thought we wouldn't mind, as we knew he was pretty hard up. He'd dropped a packet that week at ...'

'Please spare us these unnecessary details. What happened after dinner?'

'We were slung out.'

'That is not what I mean. When the dinner was over, and your party were about to descend to the foyer to go home, did you see Clun strike Everard?'

'Yes, I did.'

'Did you hear him say anything to him before, or as he struck him?'

'Yes, I did,' said the witness, with an apologetic glance at the prisoner, who gave an ironic smile. 'He said he would – am I to repeat his actual words, my lord?'

'Certainly,' replied the judge.

'Well, he said he would knock him cock-eyed and he hoped he'd break his bloody neck.'

'Fair enough,' muttered someone from the back of the court.

'What opinion did you form when you heard those words spoken?'

'I had no time to form an opinion. As he spoke, he up and did it.'

'Did what?'

'Punched Everard in the eye, so that he staggered towards the top of the stairs. Then Clun held on to the top banister post with his left hand and upper-cut Everard with his right so that the fellow simply went crashing down the stairs on to the stone floor of the foyer. Of course, nobody thought ...'

'In your opinion, then,' said counsel hastily, 'the accused fully intended to knock his victim downstairs and injure him seriously?'

'Well, I couldn't honestly swear to that. I shouldn't think he thought of actual injuries, don't you know, and, of course, he was devilish tight at the time.'

'He was ...?' inquired the judge.

'Too drunk to be responsible,' translated the witness.

'Yes, yes. Thank you, Mr Lockerby,' said counsel. 'His Lordship understands you, I am sure.'

Counsel for the defence rose.

'When you say that the accused was too drunk to be responsible, do you mean that he would not have acted in the same way if he had been sober?'

'I'm sure he wouldn't.'

'That is a matter of opinion, not of fact,' said the judge dryly. Counsel bowed.

'When you said that you were "slung out" – that is the expression I think you employed – you mean, I take it that the management requested your party to leave?'

'That's about the size of it. We were pretty well tanked up, most of us ...'

'Will the witness confine himself to the Queen's English?' suggested the judge mildly.

'Pardon, my lord,' said the witness sulkily. 'I should say that we had all had a fair amount to drink and were not altogether sober.'

'Your party was requested to leave,' pursued counsel. 'What effect did that have?'

'The blokes were a bit sore. That is to say' – the witness glanced towards the judge – 'some dissatisfaction was expressed. Then, when some of us were at the top of the stairs, after we'd got our things from the cloakroom, Clun hit Everard and Everard rolled down the stairs. He lay there, and when some of us went to help him and see what the damage was, we could see he'd busted his skull – er – he'd received a severe knock on the head which had broken the skin. We phoned the hospital but when the ambulance came it turned out that he was dead.'

The next witness was the doctor. He explained that the ambulance men had brought Everard to the casualty department of the local hospital, that he had been called at once to attend to him, but that he was dead.

'How long, would you say, Doctor?'

'A matter of half an hour, possibly less.'

'In other words, he was dead before he was removed from the hotel foyer to hospital?'

'Yes. I should say that something must have killed him immediately.'

'Was it the injury to his head that killed him?'

'No. That was severe, but the actual cause of death was, in common parlance, a broken neck.'

'A result of the fall?'

'It is not possible to say definitely.'

'Will you explain that, please?'

'From the nature of the injury, death *could* have been caused by a punch under the angle of the jaw, but I am not able to say that it *was* so caused.'

'Upon what do you base the supposition that such a punch might have broken the man's neck?'

'I saw the same thing happen at a boxing match once, and have heard of other instances.'

Counsel for the defence asked:

'Would it be a rare occurrence?'

'I have experience only of the one instance. I have heard of two others.'

'Were there not multiple contusions upon the body?'

'Yes, but they were superficial injuries. The serious injury, apart from the knock on the head, was a broken jaw.'

'Might not that also have been an effect of the fall?'

'Well, I deduced that it was the result of a heavy punch, but one cannot be sure.'

'Thank you, Doctor.' Counsel sat down.

'Call Charles Emden,' said the prosecuting counsel.

It was too beautiful, thought Dame Beatrice, re-reading her grandnephew's full and sufficient notes. That Clun, Emden, and Lockerby were all sewn up in the same parcel was matter more suitable to the dramas of Ancient Greece than to the world of the present century.

Karl Emden, it appeared, could not speak to the *fracas* at the top of the staircase, but he could, and did, provide contributory evidence in that he had been present at the beginning of the argument between Clun and Everard.

'You are Charles Emden?'

(Surprising what a difference an anglicized baptismal name could make, Dame Beatrice thought).

'Yes, I am Charles Emden.'

His home address followed and the witness acknowledged it.

'You were present at a dinner-party held at the *Crown* Hotel, Pawsey, on the evening of 18 March?'

'I was.'

'At the conclusion of the meeting you went to the cloakroom for your overcoat and hat.'

'And scarf and gloves.'

'Quite so. While you were in the cloakroom you overheard an exchange of remarks between the prisoner and the deceased?'

'Yes. They had a difference of opinion.'

'Can you tell us the subject of this disagreement?'

'Yes. Clun called Everard a dirty interloper and said he ought not to have gate-crashed the dinner, and Everard said that he'd paid as much as Clun had, and had a right to come. They argued like that for a bit, and then things got more personal, and they were shouting at one another, and then Clun hit Everard in the eye.'

'You are certain that Clun was the aggressor?'

'Well, I didn't blame him really. Everard had just called him a ...'

'Never mind that. Answer the question.'

'Yes, Clun hit him first.'

'Did you see what happened at the top of the staircase?'

'No.'

'How was that?'

'I couldn't find my cloakroom ticket, so I waited until everybody else had claimed his things and mine were left.'

'When did you next see Clun?'

'When I got to the foyer. He and some others were

standing beside Everard, who was stretched out on the floor at the bottom of the stairs – well, not so much stretched out, I suppose, as crumpled up. I said, "Has he conked out?"'

'What did you mean by that?'

'Well, we'd all had drinks.'

'Answer the question.'

'I meant he was drunk. I also thought he'd tumbled down the stairs because I saw there was blood on his head. Clun said, "Lord! I've been and gone and done it now! Get a doctor, quick!"'

Defending counsel rose.

'You are certain those were the words Clun used?'

'Quite certain.'

'What interpretation did you put on them?'

'Well, I knew he'd hit him in the cloakroom so I thought he was referring to that.'

'You did not think he meant he had killed him?'

'Oh, no. I thought he meant perhaps Everard had been partly stunned by the first punch and had stumbled downstairs.'

'Thank you.'

'Call Inspector Truebody.'

Inspector Truebody's evidence amounted to a disclosure of the accused's words when he was confronted by the doctor's verdict that Everard had been killed. These, it seemed, were:

'Well, I've bought it this time. I never meant it like this.'

Then the accused himself was called.

'Your name is Clun?'

'Yes.'

'You are twenty-six years of age and you live at number seventeen Murray Street?'

'Yes.'

'You attended a club dinner at the *Crown* Hotel on 18 March?'

'Yes.'

'At the dinner you learned that a non-member of the club was present?'

'Yes.'

'You took exception to this fact?'

'I don't like gate-crashers.'

'Answer the question.'

'I thought the dinner should be confined to members only. That was the rule.'

'Did you strike the deceased in the cloakroom of the hotel after dinner?'

'Well, he called me a ...'

'What he called you is immaterial at the moment.'

'But it isn't immaterial! It's the whole point! How would *you* like to be called a ...'

'The witness', said the judge weightily, 'is not called upon to ask questions, but to answer them.'

'Did you strike the deceased, as I said?'

'Yes.'

'And again, at the top of the stairs leading down to the foyer?'

'Yes, but ...'

'With the result that death ensued?'

'You can't prove that.'

'I put it to you that if he had not been struck he would not have died.'

'That's for the doctor to say.'

'According to the evidence, you said, when you knew Everard was dead, "Well, I've bought it this time. I never meant it like this." Do you agree that those were the words you used?'

'I suppose so. I don't remember.'

'Do you agree that, in the light of those words, you knew you had been responsible for his death?'

'How was I to know a fall would kill him?'

'I must remind the witness', said the judge, 'that he is here to *answer* questions.'

'All right, then,' said Clun violently, 'have it your own way. I did know I'd killed him. I slammed him hard enough, anyway. But, of course, I never meant it. I was drunk.'

'If you were in charge of a car and ran over somebody and killed him, do you think the confession that you were drunk at the time would exonerate you?'

'The two things are quite different. Anyway, I don't possess a car.'

'I put it to you that you cannot control your temper.'

'Yes, I can.'

'Well, if you can, shall we accept it that you did not?'

'Hang it all, I tell you I was drunk! I suppose I did overstep the mark. All right, then! I did it, but I certainly didn't mean to kill him. I didn't even *know* the chap very well. Do what you like! You can't feel more upset about it than I do.'

'Do I understand that the accused wishes to change his plea to one of Guilty?' asked the judge.

'Yes, my lord,' replied the prisoner before his counsel could answer. 'I plead guilty, and you can all go to hell!'

He himself went to prison for three years, and did not appeal against the sentence. He did not receive the good-conduct reduction of sentence. The report – Dame Beatrice's grandnephew had been thorough – showed that he had served the full time, a fact which Dame Beatrice had already deduced, since he had not lost the prison pallor until he had basked in the sunshine on Hombres Muertos.

Important points arose out of the account of his trial. Neither Lockerby nor Emden could be called a malicious witness. Both had been prepared to insist on the fact that Clun had been drunk at the time and, to that extent, not responsible for his actions. It seemed unlikely that Clun, from what Dame Beatrice knew of his character, would bear either of them malice on account of their evidence. They had been called as witnesses for the prosecution, but it was more than an even chance that they would have preferred to be called for the defence.

Another point of importance was that Lockerby must

have been killed while Clun was still behind bars. If Dame
Beatrice's theories were to remain tenable, and there was
indeed a connexion between the murder of Lockerby and
the later murder of Emden, then it hardly looked as
though Clun could be involved.

'No,' said Dame Beatrice to Gavin, as she parted from
him before returning to Hombres Muertos, 'I think we
can eliminate Mr Clun. It looks, on the strength of it,
that the murder of Karl Emden evolved from the strange
ménage à trois of which I heard from old Mrs Barstow,
unless – but, no, it must! I must be right about that!'

'You were thinking of Peterhouse, who, from all
accounts, may be a deep one, and the mistakenly-named
Mrs Angel, weren't you, just now?'

'Peterhouse might have thought of putting the body in
the cave. It would fit with what I know of his mentality.
And, if he did put it there, of course it would have been
the obvious thing for him to conduct us to the cave while
there were still only the rightful ·inhabitants there. He
would have wanted to be sure that none of us had any
reason to go and visit it when the twenty-fourth body had
been added.'

'What I *don't* understand', said Gavin, 'is why there
ever were twenty-four bodies in the cave at the same time.
A sensible chap wouldn't have taken the risk of leaving an
extra one about. He'd have got rid of it as soon as he'd
taken off its trappings to use them as a disguise for Emden's
body. That's the bit that doesn't make sense to me.'

'But I think he did get rid of it as soon as that,' said
Dame Beatrice.

'The kid was lying, you think, when he came back and
said he'd seen twenty-four bodies?'

'I think he was, but that, of course, would need to be
proved.'

'I should like to meet that youngster. The toe of a good
man's boot wouldn't do him any harm, I fancy.'

'He doesn't provoke that reaction as much as you
might expect,' said Dame Beatrice, 'but his story could

stand a more rigorous checking than any that I have so far given it.'

'We shan't be able to *do* anything, if you do pin the murderer down. There's no extradition from Hombres Muertos, you know. Of course, if the same chap turned out to be the murderer of Lockerby as well –'

'We must keep an open mind,' said Beatrice.

CHAPTER 14

Concerning an Uninhabited Island

HOMBRES MUERTOS presented much the same appearance as it had done on the morning when Dame Beatrice had joined Caroline Lockerby on the boat deck to admire the view. There were the same itinerant and noisy merchants, the same shrill and persuasive diving boys, the same prospect of jumbled town, cathedral tower, and serrated mountain ranges behind green hills.

She reached the hotel to find both Peterhouse and Laura on the veranda steps. She had cabled for a room and the delighted Ruiz had broadcast the news of her return. That accounted only partly for the presence of Peterhouse, for he had dogged Laura's footsteps unrelentingly ever since their botanic session in the hotel garden, and she had felt herself haunted and hunted. She greeted Dame Beatrice politely, as though they had no more than a passing acquaintance, since she did not know, until she had seen Dame Beatrice privately, whether their true relationship was to be made manifest to the other guests at the hotel, for Clun had been as good as his word and had kept the secret.

Peterhouse gambolled about the new arrival, escorted her to the reception desk, watched her being given her key, and was only shaken off at the exit from the lift. Laura awaited her opportunity, and, having seen him safely into the dining-room for a late but hearty breakfast, she went up to Dame Beatrice's room, the number of which she readily obtained from Luisa Ruiz, tapped, and was admitted.

'Well,' said Dame Beatrice, 'and what have *you* been up to, and how is my godson?'

'First things first: he's flourishing. Eats and sleeps. Good as gold. I can't believe he's *my* child.'

'He probably takes after his father who, by the way, sends love to you both and says that you are to stay as long as I want you.'

'Very nice of him. I suppose he's on a stag-party toot every free evening he has!'

'I have interested him in our island mystery. The consensus of opinion in London is that Telham knifed Lockerby; but who knifed Emden still seems a matter of detection.'

'On balance, it ought to be Telham, I suppose,' said Laura. 'But let me – unless you want breakfast –?'

'I breakfasted on board at eight.'

'Then let me tell you all my news and give you all my views.'

'By all means. The mattress on that bed perhaps will not need renewal or replacement so soon if you cease from bouncing up and down on it.'

'Oh, sorry. Yes, well, as I was saying, we come now to the mysteries of (a) Peterhouse, who, so far as I am concerned, has adopted the pernicious characteristic of an unwanted sticking-plaster, and (b) that very odd woman, Mrs Angel. Somehow, you know, I don't see her as a female Simon Legree.'

'You have picked the wrong man with whom to compare her, but I came to the same conclusion. Nevertheless, as the gentleman said in *St Joan*, there is *something* about her.'

'That's where my knowledge comes in,' said Laura. 'She's hand-in-glove, thick as thieves – any figure of speech you like – with Ruiz's son.'

'Possibly she is his mother.'

'His mother?'

'It would explain a good deal.'

'Good Lord! It would explain another bit of gossip I've picked up. She told me that Peterhouse the Barnacle blackmails Ruiz into keeping him here free of charge.'

'Indeed? No wonder he is hail-fellow-well-met with the other guests, if that is true.'

'He's a queer kettle of fish altogether, if you ask *me*. You know he's supposed to be an orchid-gatherer?'

'We exploded that myth. There are no orchids worth a collector's trouble to be found on Hombres Muertos.'

'No? Well, his speciality seems to be Alpine plants – the poisonous varieties. He was telling me all about them. I was bored to death, except that poison is always interesting.'

'No doubt, and I am obliged to you for the information. Is there anything more that you have learned?'

'I don't think so. Pilar seems a bit of a liar, but I expect you know all that.'

'Pilar's life lacks excitement, therefore she likes to live in her imagination. Nevertheless, you see, her tales, lurid and, I think, untrue (I doubt very much whether Mr Peterhouse is blackmailing Señor Ruiz, for example), have helped us, although not, of course, considerably. We must get Mr Peterhouse to show us his poisonous plants.'

'Do you really think he grows them?'

'I have every expectation of it, child. It may, or may not, throw some light on his mentality if he does. Time, as often, will show. What of friend Clun?'

'I don't know. He seems all right. I haven't seen much of the Drashleighs, but I rather like the kid Clement.'

'Yes. Clement is a host in himself. Did you visit the Cave of Dead Men?'

'I did. You know, our murderer is a moron. Who on earth would put a twenty-fourth dead man at a table where every visitor knew there ought to be twenty-three?'

'It was not quite like that, you know, Laura. The boy saw twenty-two orthodox dead men in their robes and masks, the murdered man disguised as the twenty-third of them. If he saw the real twenty-third king he saw him as a mummy, lying in a corner of the cave. As we know, this mummy was taken away and tossed down the mountain-side among the rocks where the brigands found him.'

'Oh, yes, the brigands! They're terribly funny! I just

mentioned I had to feed my baby and they almost burst into tears and begged me to go and look after him.'

'When was this?'

'When they stopped me, after I'd been to see the troglodytes.' She recounted the abortive adventure.

'Tomorrow', said Dame Beatrice, forbearing to comment on the sentimental conduct of the bandits, 'Mr Peterhouse shall take me to the Botanic Gardens.'

The botanic gardens were outside the city boundaries of Reales but less than half an hour's journey by car from the hotel. They were not particularly impressive, being small, by European standards. They exhibited a fair number of the indigenous plants of the island, but, otherwise, were uninteresting. Laura, acting on instructions, did not make one of the party. Peterhouse, enjoying his role, gave brief but adequate descriptive information as he and Dame Beatrice made the rounds, but he seemed uneasy with her, smiled often and nervously, rather in the style of Ben Gunn, and showed obvious relief when they were once more outside the gates.

'And now?' he asked, when they had gained the road which led in a northerly direction to the mountains but southwards back to Reales and the hotel.

'Much more anon,' said Dame Beatrice. 'What do you know about knives?'

'Knives?' He looked startled. 'Oh, you mean Emden. Of course, that's all over now. The island police have written it down to the bandits' account, which means that the incident's closed – or so says Pilar's Pepe. Personally, one can't help feeling rather glad it's all over. It made things very uncomfortable at the hotel. It was something outside the routine, and I love routine. I live by it. Besides, we're not used to the murder of English tourists on Hombres Muertos. It ruins the local colour.'

'The local colour', said Dame Beatrice, gazing up at the sky and out to the distant sea, 'appears to be mostly blue, and blue is the colour which is said to attract the most ghosts.'

'Ghosts?'

'Come, come, Mr Peterhouse! You are not going to tell me you do not believe in ghosts?'

'Haven't given them a thought since my boyhood.'

'You do not believe that the spirits of Karl Emden and of Ian Lockerby haunt this beautiful island?'

'Ian Lockerby? Mrs Lockerby's husband? Why, what happened to him?'

'He was knifed in the back, Mr Peterhouse.'

'Good heavens! Like Emden?'

'Exactly like Emden, except for the kind of knife. Yet, even at that, a sort of likeness arises.'

'Oh, really? How do you mean?'

'Ian Lockerby was killed with a knife whose owner cannot be identified.'

'Where was he killed? He was not killed here.'

'In a back street in London.'

'And you think whoever did it came here afterwards?'

'I do. And don't ask me what I have to go on, because I should find that far too fatiguing to explain.'

'And you're still determined to get Emden's murderer?'

'If, by that, you mean hand his murderer over to the law, the answer is that my chief consideration is one of identification.'

'And you think', said Peterhouse eagerly, 'that you're on the way to identifying him?'

'I have hopes. And now, I must thank you for your kindness in escorting me to the Botanical Gardens and in giving me the benefit of your vast knowledge of the plants indigenous to this island. Will you do me a further favour?'

'Surely, dear lady, if it lies within my power.'

'Will you take me to see the Rusty-leaved Alpine rose?'

Peterhouse, whose face had become solemn, brightened immediately.

'Certainly, certainly. Whenever you like. I shall be delighted to show you my whole collection. When would you care to come? It means a boat-trip, I'm afraid. My little collection takes root on the tiny island of Tiene.'

'Tiene? A curious name. I have never heard of it.'

'That is quite likely. The island is mine by purchase, and I named it myself. It is little more than a rock, but the soil is not volcanic, as it is here. I made my earliest experiments on Monte Voy, to the north-east of Reales, but met with so little success that I prospected, discovered Tiene, made an offer for it, purchased it, and – hey presto! Success!'

'Most commendable, I am sure. Could we go there this afternoon?'

'This afternoon? Admirable, if only the tide is right.'

'I have an idea that the tide *will* be right.'

Peterhouse gave her a very searching look.

'It is interesting that you should say that,' he remarked. 'I, too, have that very same feeling. The name of my island is Tiene. You won't forget, will you?'

'*Tiene.* He holds. Holds what, Mr Peterhouse? What dark and dangerous secret do you hide there?'

'Well, not bodies that have been knifed in the back,' replied Peterhouse. He spoke gaily. They got into the car which Dame Beatrice had hired, and beside which they had stood and talked after leaving the Gardens, and in a very short time were sharing a table for a rather late lunch at the Sombrero, where Señor Ruiz, as a signal honour, waited upon them himself.

They rested for half an hour after lunch, and met on the terrace at five. The boat, a small motor-launch hired from the harbour, took them round the south-east coast of the island and out to a speck on the horizon. This speck soon turned into a large rock with a tiny strip of greyish beach towards which the launch leapt like a beast that espies its prey. The boatman brought his little craft round with skill, and backed gently in. He and Peterhouse gallantly chaired Dame Beatrice ashore.

To the astonishment of the latter, a couple of donkeys, in charge of a small boy, were waiting at the top of the beach to convey them into the mountains.

'This', said Dame Beatrice, contemplating the animals

and their guardian, 'is luxury indeed. I fully expected that we should go mountaineering in the Swiss manner, roped together and carrying the alpenstocks which I felt certain you would have hidden in a cave among the rocks. But we are not, it seems, to bear a banner with a strange device, and I cannot say I am sorry.'

The sun streamed down on the little grey beach and the sand was hot beneath their feet. Above their heads towered a mighty cliff broken only by a defile up which, it appeared, the donkeys were prepared to climb. The travellers mounted their steeds, the boy clucked and walloped, the boatman returned to his launch, and the donkeys, after a preliminary pause for reflection, began to move onwards and upwards. Dame Beatrice turned her head.

'We are marooned,' she said. The launch was being shoved off-shore by the boy and the boatman, and soon they heard the chugging of the engine.

'Oh, they'll be back when we need them,' said Peterhouse easily. "The boy lives opposite. His brother brings him and the donkeys in an old fishing-boat. Then my boatman takes the child back in the launch, which then plies for hire until it returns for me here. It meant quite a bit of organization to begin with, but it works very nicely now.'

'I really must congratulate you. How high do we climb to see your plants?'

'We find several specimens at three thousand five hundred feet.'

'Really? That does not seem very high for Alpine flowers, but I should scarcely have thought this island rose to more than three thousand feet, in any case.'

'You can't tell from the beach. This mountain is very deceptive. There are peaks beyond peaks, you know. The path narrows here. I had better lead, I think.'

The defile had shrunk to a width of less than a couple of yards, and it wound and turned on itself and presented what seemed to be the blind end of a *cul-de-sac* time and again, only to writhe a way through. The donkeys plodded on as though they were accustomed to the route. The donkey-boy had provided the riders with sticks, but there seemed no need to use them.

As they made their way upward it became clear that the island was considerably larger than Peterhouse had indicated. The defile ended at last in an upland valley, heather-covered, not unlike a Scottish deer-forest. At the head of the valley were some scattered pines from which, disturbed by the travellers, flew several large blue chaffinches.

'I wonder whether Mrs Angel has seen and photographed such birds?' Dame Beatrice remarked. She had drawn level with Peterhouse, for they had left the defile and their donkeys were able to amble side by side.

'She got the Houbara bustard, really a North African native, and her black oyster-catcher,' Peterhouse observed. 'I have never invited her to Tiene, so she may or may not have seen the chaffinches. She wants the sand-grouse and the Canary chat, but she'll have to go to Fuenteventura to see them, or so she says. They don't breed here or on Hombres Muertos.'

'You seem to record her conversations with remarkable faithfulness. Are you, too, interested in birds?'

'Not particularly. You know, talking of Hombres Muertos, why not Mujeres Muertas? What is your opinion on that? If ever the sexes are to achieve completely equal treatment, I don't see why we men should die while the women live.'

'An interesting thought.'

The donkeys picked their way among the pines and came out on to an uneven, squarish plateau. Peterhouse growled at his donkey, in Spanish, to stop. He slid off, stiffly and awkwardly.

'We are here,' he said abruptly. 'Let me help you to dismount.'

Dame Beatrice did not wait for any help. Her donkey had stopped dead as soon as its companion had done so,

and she was standing beside him before Peterhouse had
finished speaking.

'I don't see your garden,' she remarked.

'I want you to see my cave first. I discovered it all by
myself. You will be the first of my friends to see it, but, I
hope, by no means the last.' He gave a sharp jerk to his
donkey's bridle and led the way across the plateau. Dame
Beatrice followed behind, her donkey delicately walking
in its companion's wake. Her left hand held the bridle.
Her right was in the pocket of her skirt.

At the edge of the plateau, which was at the end of a
fairly steep slope, Peterhouse stopped. With his free hand
he described a semi-circle in the air.

'What do you think of the view?' he asked. 'Come on
the other side of your donkey. You'll see much better if
you do.'

'I hardly think so,' Dame Beatrice replied. 'The view
from this angle is superb. I suppose that long smudge
over there is Hombres Muertos. How blue the sea is, and
how wide and remote the sky! But time marches on, Mr
Peterhouse. Where is your grotto?'

'My cave of Mujeres Muertas? Ah, yes, come along.
This way. This way.'

He jerked at his donkey's bridle and the patient animal
turned its back on the seascape and went with him back
across the plateau. They descended to the heather-
covered valley and then began to climb a slope away to
the left. Dame Beatrice took her hand from her pocket. A
small revolver nestled against her palm. It was pearl-
handled, toy-like, and deadly. Peterhouse did not turn his
head. The slope grew steeper. They passed among a few
more pine trees and there, at the right-hand side of the
way, was a mountain cave not unlike the one where the
twenty-three kings were entombed.

Dame Beatrice stood at the mouth of the cave. Peterhouse tiptoed past her, then turned, and beckoned her in.

'"Will you walk into my parlour?" said the spider to
the fly. Tell me more about your scheme to obtain the

dead women to people your cave,' Dame Beatrice suggested, holding up the revolver and gazing at it as though
she wondered how it came to be where it was. 'I can see
enough of the cave from here to realize that it is snug,
warm, dry, and nicely sanded. And how do you propose
to arrange your corpses? Are they to have a stone table
around which they will be seated to await the sound of the
Last Trump? Will they be embalmed? Mummified? Sun-
dried like the pirates at Execution Dock? Tell me your
plans. Do you need advice, help, or merely willing
victims?'

'Willing or unwilling, it matters nothing to me,' said
Peterhouse, swinging round to find an unwavering and
gleaming barrel pointed at his abdomen. 'You need not
think to frighten me with that thing.'

'Not even if it holds a silver bullet? Come, let us leave
the cave. I want to see your poison plants before we go.'

'Go? Go where?'

'Back to Hombres Muertos. Back to the hotel.'

'Do you think I'm mad?'

As Dame Beatrice had been attempting for some time
to assess him from this point of view, she did not reply.
She waved the revolver in an imperious but not an
impatient way, and intoned, in her beautiful voice, more
as an invocation than a command:

'On, Stanley, on!'

From the side of the cave appeared, as though by
pre-arrangement (which was the case), Laura Gavin and
the manslaughterer Clun. Peterhouse stepped back.

'Good heavens above!' he cried. 'How the devil did
you get here?'

'By boat, just like you,' Clun replied. 'You surely don't
imagine you're the only person who knows of this tight
little island, or the only one who knows you come to it?'

'Well, I don't call this nice!' said Peterhouse. He
turned to Dame Beatrice. 'You've double-crossed me!'

'There can be no double-cross, if I understand the
term, without a previous agreement,' said she. 'As we

made no agreement, and as I did not trust you merely to show me what you had agreed to show me ...'

'*Agreed* to show you?'

'Your poisonous Alpine plants. Now, Mr Peterhouse, justify my hopes, and then tell me why you choose to grow nothing but the poisonous varieties. What has South America to do with it? What the Hotel Sombrero de Miguel Cervantes? What my secretary, whom you took through the list of your favourites with such all-consuming zeal?'

'Nothing, nothing, nothing!' He uttered the words emphatically, as though he was answering each question separately. 'If you want to see the plants, come.'

'Just a minute,' said Laura. 'Let's have an answer. You'd better come clean, and then we shall know where we are.'

'Where *we* are, Mrs Gavin? I thought that you, at least, were my friend.'

'No, merely an interested acquaintance.'

'But what is it to do with you? Where's the connexion between you and Dame Beatrice? I perceive that there *is* a connexion, although, until you two met on the steps, I had not realized that it existed. Of course, I ought to have known that when you came and she went, just like that, there was something more than coincidence.'

'Categorically, then,' said Laura, waving a shapely palm, 'it concerns me because we are in joint session, Dame Beatrice and I, to expose impostors and to discover murderers. The actual connexion between us is that I am, and have been for many years – since I was twenty, to be exact – her secretary and amanuensis.'

'I see. So I am being vetted?'

'Exactly. So watch your step. I should be loth to see you overflown with a honey-bag, signior. Now, then, what about the potted plants? Fact, fiction, or camouflage?'

'Well, it's like this,' began Peterhouse. He was interrupted by being shouted at by Clun.

'Get on with your poisonous plants, you blinking, skullduggering hypocrite! *Allons!* – Or take the consequences!'

'Well, really,' said Peterhouse, mildly. 'All right, come this way.' He led them back along the route by which they had come, the donkeys following like dogs. When at last they gained the beach, he struck off towards the right. Dame Beatrice paused to stroke and pat the donkey which had borne her. Laura halted, too.

'What now?' she asked. Dame Beatrice cackled. Peterhouse looked back.

'Aren't you coming?' he called. There was a schoolboy shout.

'Wait for me! Oh, *please* wait for me! I'm coming, too!' Dame Beatrice turned to see Clement Drashleigh ploughing his way across the beach. Laura, at a nod from her employer, went to meet him.

'Hullo, Clement,' she said. 'What on earth are *you* doing here?'

'I don't know, really,' said the child, 'but I've come from Hombres Muertos because I got bored with the parents and made myself a nuisance. Pilar told me you'd all gone off with Mr Peterhouse. Well, I know this island. I've been over here before. It's very interesting. So I thought perhaps he'd brought Dame Beatrice here to show it to her, you know, so I thought I'd come.'

'But won't your father and mother wonder where you are?'

'I've no idea. I'm a lone wolf. But you ought to see the poisonous plants! They're just wonderful!'

'They do exist, then?' Laura looked doubtful. The boy laughed.

'I should say so. He's taking you to see them, isn't he? He took me once.'

'Did your people know?'

'Heavens, no! They don't care for Peterhouse at all.'

'Sensible blighters,' said Laura, under her breath. 'Well, here we go. Thank goodness Damè B. has brought a revolver.'

It proved a short way to go. A defile brought the party

on to a stretch of moorland. An ill-defined path led into a passage between rocks. At a thousand feet there was blooming the Christmas rose. Peterhouse led them onward and upward. The going was surprisingly easy.

'Well,' said Laura, when the exhaustive but not exhausting journey was over, 'I must congratulate you, Mr Peterhouse. Your experiments are an enormous success. What, exactly, is your object or plan?'

'Oh, I have none. A voice crying in the wilderness, dear Mrs Gavin. That is all your humble servant has ever aspired to be.'

Laura bent to inspect an attractive specimen of *Pulsatilla baldensis*.

'You must get a lot of fun, leading people up your garden,' she said. 'Is it really worth while, though?'

'Oh, I think so. I think so, you know.'

This elliptical conversation was interrupted.

'Mr Peterhouse saw the twenty-fourth body,' said Clement. 'I know he did.'

Peterhouse turned abruptly away from Laura.

'What was that?' he demanded.

'You heard,' said Clement rudely. 'What do you think I've been doing while I've stayed on Hombres Muertos? I followed everybody about. I heard all the conversations. I put a spoke in the murderer's wheel.'

Peterhouse was taken aback.

'You what?' he inquired feebly.

'You heard,' said Clement. 'And the murderer wasn't you, so you needn't get big-headed about it.'

'Do you know who the murderer was, then?' demanded Laura. Clement grinned.

'Maybe I do. Maybe I don't. Nobody does, I imagine. It was the perfect murder. I might have done it myself, for all you know.'

Peterhouse led the way down the mountain to the beach, but no launch was there to take the party back. They waited for half an hour, but there was no sign of any boat to take them back to Hombres Muertos.

Peterhouse began by showing resignation, then his mood changed, and he became very angry. He cursed, fumed, kicked the grey sand, and at last walked into the water and semaphored wildly with his arms. Dame Beatrice kept a covert eye on him. She was seated on the sand between Laura and Clun. Clement, a short distance away, was digging holes with the heels of his sandals, giving up this pastime occasionally to fondle the donkeys.

Peterhouse came out of the sea and addressed the adults.

'I can't understand it,' he said. 'I ordered the launch as usual. We haven't had tea, and, if this goes on, we shan't get a dinner either.'

'Oh, well,' said Laura cheerfully, 'we can always chew some of your alpine plants and get a good night's sleep.'

Peterhouse seated himself beside her, but soon got up to wander restlessly back and forth along the strip of beach.

'If it weren't for Clement, it would be an amusing situation,' said Dame Beatrice. 'His presence among us is something I did not foresee. I fear your fatal fascination has much to answer for.'

'I could always swim back,' said Laura. 'I wonder what the currents are like?'

'I have no control over your movements,' said Dame Beatrice, 'but I beg that you will not attempt such a feat.'

'There's my infant. By now he'll be raising hell for his dinner. Sorry, but I really must go.'

'Not on your Nelly,' murmured Clun. 'I'm going myself. You keep an eye on the kid and the old lady. Peterhouse equals Bughouse. He's a loony. So long.' He dropped his linen shorts to his ankles and pulled his shirt over his head. 'Bronze nude. Thank goodness I've managed to acquire a veneer of tan since I've been out of gaol. Excuse my back.'

Peterhouse was well up the beach and facing away from them as Clun waded into the water. By the time Peterhouse turned, he was striking out for the shadowy coastline ahead.

Dame Beatrice kept her eye on Peterhouse. As soon as he saw Clun in the water, he stood stock-still. Then he came galloping up to the women.

'What is he doing?' he cried.

'Swimming,' replied Laura, getting lazily on to her feet.

'But we must stop him! He is going out too far!'

'Oh, I expect he knows what he's up to. He swims quite well, I believe.'

'Shout to him, Mrs Gavin. A woman's voice will carry farther than mine. Shout to him to come back.'

'Not I. I don't believe in minding other people's business.'

'Dame Beatrice,' said Peterhouse, appealingly, 'can't I persuade *you* to stop him? So foolish to risk his life just to show off before ladies.'

'Alas!' said Dame Beatrice, shading her eyes with her hand and gazing seawards. 'I fear that my dulcet, ultra-feminine tones would scarcely carry so far. But do you shout, Mr Peterhouse. Imitate the unearthly cry of the foghorn, or the yodelling melodies of the Alps. You must surely have heard the latter many times in your search for the family of ranunculus.'

Peterhouse danced with impatience. Suddenly he rushed to the foot of the defile up which they had just climbed and came back with a collection of stones. He went to the water's edge and began to hurl the stones in the direction of Clun's bubbling head.

'Here!' he shouted, turning to Laura. 'Go and get a lot more!'

'No good,' said Laura, who was still on her feet. 'They're all falling woefully short. You won't attract his attention *that* way, you know. Much better leave him alone to judge for himself what to do.'

Peterhouse dropped on to the sand and dejectedly shook his head.

'Tell me,' he said, hitching himself backwards until he was seated at Laura's feet, 'has he gone to fetch help?'

Laura shrugged.

'The non-appearance of the launch was a put-up job, wasn't it?' she inquired. Peterhouse tittered.

'You answer my question, and I'll answer yours,' he said. Clement came strolling up to them.

'I want my tea,' he said.

'Well, you shouldn't have come here,' said Peterhouse. 'I didn't bargain for hungry children. Here!' He put his hand in his trousers' pocket and pulled out a piece of chocolate. What with the warmth of his body and the warmth of the day, it had become a revolting and fluid mess in a silver foil wrapping.

'I say! *Thanks!* Sure you don't want it?' said Clement, stretching out a grimy brown hand.

'Neither do you,' said Dame Beatrice. She twitched away the messy little packet.

'Give that back!' yelled Peterhouse. 'Oh, really, I beg your pardon! I suppose you know what's best.'

'In this case, yes,' Dame Beatrice calmly replied. 'I feel that I am *in loco parentis* to this child when his people are not present, and I am sure they would not care to have him eat chocolate in this condition. They are, as you are aware, somewhat particular, not to say faddy, where Clement is concerned.' She handed him back the chocolate.

'True, true,' Peterhouse agreed. He ran to the edge of the sand and hurled the packet of chocolate into the water.

'Oh, *slosh!*' said Clement, vexed. 'I *could* have done with that! I'm simply starving!'

'Poor child,' said Dame Beatrice kindly. 'I would not for the world deprive you of nourishment. Let us cast about. A little higher up I descried the prickly pear. Let us seek its habitat together.'

CHAPTER 15

Revelations of a Baby-Sitter

'I HAVE never', said Clement to Laura on the following day, as they sat drinking bottled lemonade, deliciously iced, under a striped umbrella on the beach at Reales, 'done any baby-sitting. It would be a new experience.'

'Well, you're jolly well not going to sit with mine. I wouldn't trust you an inch,' said Laura, gazing down at her shadowed son in his portable cradle.

'That's where you would be wrong, Mrs Gavin. Truly and honestly you would. I should be a model baby-sitter. I should be the prototype of baby-sitters. I should baby-sit *de luxe.*'

'Yes, you'd sit *on* the baby, not with it, I shouldn't wonder.'

Clement giggled. He had adopted Laura at sight, and as soon as he had discovered that she could sail a boat and was a far better swimmer than he was, his admiration for her had become almost sycophantic. Laura liked small boys and felt sorry for Clement. Besides, his faithful pursuit of her society had the supreme merit, in her eyes, of keeping Peterhouse at bay, for, since Clement's references to the murder, Peterhouse gave the impression of fleeing from the child's presence and of being terrified at the idea of being left alone with him.

'Well, can I baby-sit as long as you're there as well?' Clement demanded.

'Oh, all right. Go ahead. You can begin right now.'

'Do baby-sitters talk to their charges?'

'Not when they're asleep.'

At this moment Gavin junior opened his eyes, screwed up his nose, sneezed once for luck, and then brought up wind, making a slight grimace.

'He smiled at me! Did you see that?' cried Clement.

'He *likes* me to be his baby-sitter. Now he's awake, and I can talk to him. How do you begin speaking to a baby? And how do you know he's listening?'

'There's only one rule about *talking* to him,' said Laura, who held strong views on this matter. 'There's to be no baby-talk.'

'Oh, but I do so much agree, Mrs Gavin, I think baby-talk is absolutely stinking! I got it until I was nearly six! Imagine that!'

'I can't,' said Laura, shuddering. 'Well, that's all right, then. As to listening, well, your guess is as good as mine.'

'I know he'll listen. It'll be so interesting he's absolutely plumb *bound* to listen. Aren't you, baby? Do I call him by his proper name? What is it?'

'Hamish Alistair Gordon Grant Iain Sinclair. Add Gavin, for good measure, of course.'

'But his baptismal names make Haggis!' Clement was overcome by this discovery. Laura, who had invented all but two of her son's first names, grinned cheerfully. 'You're pulling my leg,' said Clement, still giggling joyously. 'All the same, I shall jolly well *call* him Haggis, and it's your fault if I do.'

'Granted.'

'And that's a pun!' yelled Clement, throwing himself about. 'See? Grant – granted! I suppose *you* can make jokes and puns all day!'

'More or less,' said Laura, squinting modestly down her nose. 'Anyway, haggis is a grand name for a grand food. Did you never try it?'

'No. I shouldn't think English people would like it. How is it made?'

Laura repeated the recipe for haggis as it was made in her own home. Clement produced his pocket-diary and took down the recipe from dictation. Replacing the book, he said:

'It sounds better than Mr Peterhouse's chocolate would have tasted. Still, it was decent of him to offer it to me. Laura – I *can* call you Laura, can't I? – you know,

Petrarch and all that – it's really quite respectful, if you
don't mind – what did you think about Mr Clun swimming out like that to get us rescued yesterday?'

'A jolly good effort.'

'He was lucky to spot that fishing boat and make the
men come and take us off. Golly, was I hungry by the
time we got to the hotel! I could have eaten a jelly-fish if
there'd been one on Tiene.'

'Yes, so could I. It's dreadful to miss your tea. I don't
know why I eat so much on Hombres Muertos.'

'Well, it's a boring sort of place, now the murder's all
washed up and finished.'

'What makes you think it is?'

'Well, isn't it? You see, until I turn squealer, nobody
can get any farther.'

'You underestimate our intelligence.'

'Quit kidding!'

'Oh, you've been talking to that girl from Boston, Mas-
sachusetts! Where she picked up that dreadful jargon of
hers I can't imagine.'

'From the films, I expect. I'd like to see a film again,
Laura. Do you think I'll ever be sent to school in England?'

'I'll do my best for you. You're not a bad kid in your
way.'

'Come off it! Do you really think Mr Peterhouse is
mad? You know that chocolate he offered me must have
been poisoned, don't you? Laura, is he mad?'

'A bit eccentric, perhaps. What is the object of your
researches into the life-history of the indigenous lizard of
this island, as Dame Beatrice would say?'

'Oh, Laura, don't change the subject! Do you know
what *I* think?'

'No, and I couldn't care less.'

'Oh, but you *must* listen to this! Do you know why Mr
Peterhouse wanted to keep us on Tiene?'

'I haven't a clue.'

'He'd been bribed to do it.'

'By whom?'

'I don't know, but I bet that's what it amounted to. Laura, will you get Dame Beatrice to tell them they *must* let me go to school in England?'

'Possibly. Tell me more about bribes.'

'Honestly, I don't know any more, but hasn't it struck you that Peterhouse knew Mrs Lockerby and Mr Telham? – before they came here, I mean?'

'How could it strike me? I wasn't here when they came.'

'Too right. You weren't.' He was silent after this. Laura brooded. The non-appearance of the launch which, according to Peterhouse, should have taken them off Tiene; the amount of time Peterhouse had wasted before he had taken Dame Beatrice to see his Alpine plants; his distress when Clun had swum out to sea; his fury (Laura remembered it with rueful amusement) when the fishing vessel – the triumphant Clun on board – had put in to Tiene to return the explorers to Reales; these were matters worthy of thought, and so was Dame Beatrice's action in causing Peterhouse to throw the chocolate into the sea.

'I shall tell the baby a story. He's not easily shocked, I hope?' said Clement, interrupting her thoughts.

'No, he's pretty broad-minded,' said Laura, bringing herself back to the present with an effort. 'I'm going to lie down on the sand. Do you want any more lemonade?'

Clement declined the offer of more lemonade, and squatted on his haunches beside the baby.

'There was once a very wicked man,' he began. The baby gurgled delightedly. 'You ought not to be pleased to hear it. You are even more broad-minded than I thought. This wicked man came to an island called Hombres Muertos and there he jolly well got himself bumped off. Yes, he got a knife in his back, and serve him jolly well right. What do *you* think, Haggis? Oh, yes, you're no end of a chap!

'You may not know it, Haggis, but only wicked men get themselves knifed in the back. It's done chiefly by girls. The men promise to marry the girls, and then they don't,

REVELATIONS OF A BABY-SITTER

and the girls get haughty about it, and it annoys them.'

'Too right,' agreed Laura. 'It annoys them to think that their charms, and their looks, and the scent they use, and the way they do their hair, and the things they talk about, don't appeal any more to the man, so then, if they're English, they bring a case against him and the man has to pay a lot of money.'

'Ah, yes,' said Clement, 'but if they're Spanish they knife him. Believe it or not, Haggis – and I wouldn't have believed it myself if Pilar hadn't shown me hers and told me she kept it very sharp for the first man who let her down – but they *do* knife him. And I dare say that English girls, if the man hasn't got any money, would either knife him or shoot him, and serve him jolly well right.'

'It could be, at that,' muttered Laura.

'All clear to you, so far? Right. Then let's get down to the details. I came to this island from the other, lousier one where my rather feeble people have a house, and I met this murdered man just before he went to live with the cave-dwellers. (By these cave-dwellers, I mean the living ones, Haggis. They live in terribly smelly houses made from the caves where there used to be a small fort. You ought to go up there sometime, when you can walk.)

'When I heard he had gone to the caves, I went there, too, but they didn't seem to know much about him – either that, or they were holding out on me. I told my Spanish friend – you must meet him, Haggis – and he said he didn't think this man – his name was Emden, if it interests you, Haggis – he didn't think this man had ever gone to the caves, not actually to live, I mean.'

'Dame B. didn't think so, either,' said Laura, under her breath. The story-teller was too much absorbed in his narrative to take any notice of this.

'Be that as it may,' he continued, watching the baby put its foot into its mouth, 'this man disappeared from mortal ken. What do you think of that, Haggis? Only, not *quite* from mortal ken, because I found out where he was. He was in the Cave of Dead Men. Well, he was a dead man, too, you see, so it was eminently suitable. What wasn't so eminently suitable was that one of the other dead men had had to make room for him, Haggis. Some-body had robbed the dead king of his robe and face-mask and put them on this new dead man. Whoever did it thought he was perfectly safe because the people from the hotel had already been to the cave and nobody was likely to go there again for at least another month. That's when the next ship comes in. I say, I shouldn't eat that foot if I were you, Haggis; you'll need it when you learn to walk, you know. I spoilt his little game. Only I think it was a *her*. Anybody can stick a knife in somebody else's back as long as they know where to stick it. Then the person dies; and that's what happened to Emden.'

'Her?' muttered Laura. 'The trouble is, *which* her? Don Juan gets his! Yes, but – Don Juan? That's the whole trouble. That's what makes the whole thing such a prob-lem. There simply isn't any evidence, because Don Juan *was* Don Juan. There are too many women mixed up in this sordid business.'

'No, there isn't any evidence,' said Clement, looking up at her. 'But I bet I've managed to put wind up whoever did it.'

'Have you? How?'

'Well', said the boy, in a virtuous tone, 'I don't think girls ought to stick knives in men just because the men manage to get out of marrying them and buying them a ring and taking them out, and so forth. I think it's a rotten thing to do. So I thought I'd let people know what this rotten person had done. That's why I went to the cave again and threw the poor old mummified king down the mountain. I knew someone at the bottom would find him, and that might make people wonder what had happened, and go up to the cave, and find there were still twenty-three men. I thought it might occur to the person – who-ever it might happen to be – that one of them didn't – ought not to be there. That being so, I thought that, sooner or later, they'd discover it was Emden, because he'd not been seen or heard of, you see, so that somebody would be for it.'

'Well, I'm dashed!' said Laura. 'I like the kind of bedtime story you tell my son, I must say!'

'He enjoys it! Look at him!' retorted Clement, waggling his finger at the baby. The baby crowed, gurgled, and kicked.

'Of course, it gets us no further,' said Laura, recounting the story, later in the day, to Dame Beatrice, 'but it's rather interesting that Clement should think a woman might have done it. Brings us back to Luisa and Pilar, I should rather think. I can't see Caroline Lockerby sticking knives in people. Can you?'

'I can imagine anything,' said Dame Beatrice, 'and it is more than time that we questioned Mrs Lockerby. We must take the bull by the horns, Time by the forelock and the tide which leads on to fortune, not to mention that the fault, dear Brutus, lies not in our stars, but in ourselves, that we are underlings.'

'Sang fairy-ang,' said Laura. 'No, but honestly, what do you make of Clement's disclosures?'

'I cannot tell until I have spoken to Señor Ruiz.'

Señor Ruiz was as helpful as his lack of knowledge allowed him to be.

''The little boy? Intelligent, yes. Mrs Lockerby? A very sad lady, one would say. I think she has had a difficult time with her brother. Of goings and comings from my hotel I cannot speak. The beach, the garden, the expeditions – who can say where any of my guests may be at a given time or even on a given day? This I say: you will know by now that neither I nor my Luisa had the urge to kill Mr Emden. That he was a louse is clear. That he dishonoured my Luisa is a misconception. Pilar may have killed him, but Pilar has not the mind which would have tried to disguise him as one of the dead kings. Pepe, too. He has no imagination, that lad. So we come back to where we begin. It is one of the English guests who has killed Mr Emden.'

'"I cheer a dead man's sweetheart – never ask me whose!"' said Laura, under her breath. Dame Beatrice patted her kindly on the shoulder.

'You have nicked the matter,' she said solemnly. 'But who was the sweetheart? That is the hub of the wheel.'

'The wheel must come full cycle,' said Laura idiotically. Her employer accepted this reading of the realities of the case.

'Exactly,' she said. 'So now we will talk again with Clement.'

Clement, summoned to a solemn conclave, was lyrical.

'I *said* there was dirty work afoot! I *said* it was too bad of my mother to go to see the dead kings without me! I *said* I'd have my revenge! I *said* ill deeds would follow the rising of the moon! I *said* I'd tell the world – and so I have.'

'Yes, but what?' asked Laura. 'Speak up, king-pin, and let us have all the dope – if there is any, of course.'

'"You wrong me every way; you wrong me, Brutus,"' declared Clement, to the astonishment of his hearers. 'I am *not* a king-pin, "but I am here to speak what I do know."'

'For heaven's sake, say on, abnormal child.' Laura stuck a sweet in his mouth to add weight to her words. Clement nodded his thanks and chewed dreamily for some moments. Then he said:

'I suppose I've listened to everything everybody's said in this hotel since I've been here, unless the people have been in bed. What do you want me to tell you?'

'Only that which is on your mind,' said Dame Beatrice. Clement chewed on, sucked, and nodded.

'Well,' he said, 'I suppose it all began the day you got here. Do you remember me pushing Mrs Lockerby into that pool?'

'Vividly.'

'I never realized a lady could be so tough.'

'Tough?' Laura pricked up her ears and raised her eyebrows.

'Tough is the only word,' Clement insisted. 'I had to hop it pretty-dam'-quick, I can tell you. "There was blood in the mate's eye."'

'Oh, tosh!' said Laura. 'You'd expect any normal person to be a bit annoyed if a wretched little half-bake like you pushed her into a pond.'

'Yes, I know,' agreed Clement, 'and I can see now that it was a fairly stinking thing to do, but, honestly, Laura, I thought she was going to brain me, and if she *had* brained me I think – well, never mind that.'

'You're not certain what your father's reactions would have been?'

Clement did not reply. He swallowed what remained of the sweet and then said: 'Come for a swim. I want you to look at my arms when I do my back-crawl.'

'They're not sufficiently relaxed after each pull,' said Laura. 'You look like a demented porpoise. Come on, then, but you'll have to go up to the hotel to get my things. I'm not going to sweat more than I have to in this heat. Pilar knows where everything is.'

When the instructional session was over, and coach and pupil were spread-eagled on the sand, Clement said:

'Laura?'

'Say on, boy-friend.'

'You know when I went to the cave of the dead kings?'

'First or second time?'

'First. I *didn't* see twenty-four of them, you know.'

'We had tended to suppose that, but don't let it deter you that we came to the conclusion you're a pestiferous, pernicious, and unskilful little liar.'

'Oh, well, that's a help. I just wanted to make old Peterhouse sit up.'

'Peterhouse?'

'Well, it must have been Peterhouse who hid Mr Emden, mustn't it? When nobody could get any news of him, you know.'

'Golly!' Laura sat up and stared down at the sprawling child. Clement closed his eyes. A smile of self-satisfaction wreathed his young, tender mouth. 'Take that smirk off your face, or I'll bounce my fist on your tum! Now tell me what you mean,' said Laura firmly.

'Well,' said Clement, 'I do a lot of thinking, and what I wondered was where on earth Emden was between the time he left the hotel and the time he was killed.'

'It wasn't a *long* time,' Laura pointed out.

'No, I know. But there must have been a day or two, Laura. Well, Dame Beatrice found out he'd never been to the troglodytes, didn't she?'

'How do you know that?'

'Pilar told me. Pilar knows everything.'

'And what she doesn't know she invents. Don't lose sight of that significant fact.'

'Did she invent what I said just now?'

'Partly. He *had* been to the troglodytes. He went to fix himself up as a lodger in one of the caves, but he never took up his option.'

'Well, but that's near enough, isn't it, Laura? I mean, he wasn't killed immediately, was he?'

'How do you make that out?' It was not that she disagreed; she was interested in his powers of inductive reasoning.

'Well, he wasn't dead when Peterhouse took that first party to the cave, otherwise he'd have *been* in the cave, wouldn't he?'

'Not necessarily. The body could have been hidden somewhere at hand.'

'Oh, no, Laura! The bandits would have known. We know they always keep a watch on the cave of dead men to kidnap anybody who goes without a proper guide. Look at what they did when *I* went!'

'And when *I* went, only I pleaded the blessed state of motherhood and got away with it! Yes, you've got something there. The bandits would have known. So what?' But she guessed what was coming.

'He was alive and hidden, Laura. And shall I tell you where?'

'If you like.'

'All right. *You* tell *me*, then, and we'll see whether great minds think alike.'

'Flattering both of us, aren't you? Here goes, then! He was hiding on Peterhouse's island of Tiene.'

'Got it in one! My cock-eyed parents wouldn't have worked that one out in a month of Sundays!'

'Fifth Commandment!' said Laura sternly.

'Yes, but they're not; they're foster-parents, and all they foster in me is a sort of dreary loathing. It's no joke being adopted by people you don't like or respect.'

'My heart bleeds for you. What's their opinion of *you*, Clement?'

'They think I'm a wart, I expect. Oh, well, never mind about them. Back to our dead sheep.'

'*Moutons* aren't dead, you half-baked oaf.'

'O.K. To recapitulate, (favourite word with my father when I don't understand what he's talking about), Emden wasn't dead; he was on Tiene. If you ask *me*, Laura, it was on Tiene he was killed.'

'*Eh?*' She was genuinely startled. 'Here, you come along at once and decant this theory in front of Dame B.'

'Oh, she's thought of it for herself, you bet,' said Clement. 'You don't really think she went with old Peterhouse just to see his crack-pot experiments with Alpine plants? Be your age, Laura!'

Dame Beatrice received the theory with an appreciative cackle and forbore to comment until she and Laura were alone. Then she said:

'We must talk to Mr Peterhouse.'

'Frighten him into a fit, you mean?'

'I think that is more easily said than done, but a word in season might bear fruit. Then, of course, there are the brother and sister. I have made up my mind to tax Telham with accomplishing the death of his brother- in-law.'

'I thought the police had already taken that line.'

'Not quite. They had no evidence on which to base a definite accusation. They went as far as they dared, but

Inspector Anson is both cautious and fair-minded. There is no reason why I should be either.'

'So you think you can bounce the truth out of him, do you? He's a dark horse and pretty deep, I fancy.'

'I don't expect to bounce the *truth* out of him, but there may be interesting repercussions. Then there is the question of Caroline. As far as I can see, she was the only person, except for Emden, (no longer an interested party), who profited in any way by her husband's death.'

'Money? I didn't know money had come into it.'

'It has not.'

'Oh, you mean the affair with Emden.'

'Exactly.'

'But Lockerby doesn't seem to have worried about that. At least, that's what I gathered from what you told me.'

'Caroline may have wanted to marry Emden. There was no thought of a divorce. I see Ian Lockerby as a coldly cruel man.'

'He seems to have had a pretty hot temper, doesn't he?'

'A hot temper when he was under the influence of alcohol, I fancy. Apart from that, I think he enjoyed the situation which obtained at that flat.'

'I can't see why Caroline didn't run away with Emden. She was living with him, it appears. Why didn't she push off and leave Lockerby on his own? It seems to me the obvious course to have taken.'

'I must ask her that. It is an interesting point which, incidentally, had not escaped me.'

'I bet it hadn't!' said Laura. 'I wish I could sit in when you tackle her. It should be an interesting interview.'

'I hope it will be a fruitful one.'

'By the way, why wasn't there any suggestion that Emden killed Lockerby? I should have thought he had as much interest in his death as Caroline. It looks to me as though he could have killed him and then come here, where there's no extradition.'

Dame Beatrice nodded benignly, then changed the subject and (as it seemed to Laura) with some abruptness.

'What did you make of our visit to the island of Tiene?' she inquired.

'Weird and wonderful. Did you think that Peterhouse would attack you?'

'The most striking and interesting thing about Peterhouse, so far as I am concerned, is the apparently serious deterioration in his mental condition since the death of Emden.'

'*Has* it deteriorated? Of course, I didn't know him quite as soon as you did.'

'I choose my words carefully, I trust.'

'Oh, I see. You don't think he's half as loony as he makes himself out to be.'

'Anxiety can produce strange results, of course.'

'Oh, I see. He's the type who might think that, because somebody has been murdered, he might be the next on the list.'

'If this were not Hombres Muertos, he might be quite right,' said Dame Beatrice.

'I decline to look puzzled and I refuse to plead for an elucidation of that enigmatic statement. Let's change the subject.'

'As you wish. Do not forget, however, that there are advantages, at times, in being regarded as irresponsible.'

'Don't I know it! I got out of various tiresome and time-wasting chores in my youth by affecting to be utterly unreliable. It's a jolly good defence mechanism. It nearly always works. "It's no good expecting Laura" – whatever it was I could have done. So you think Peterhouse's madness has method. But I still don't understand that crack about Hombres Muertos, so I *shall* change the subject. What do you think of that Bostonian who seems to have acted as my understudy when you were here before?'

'She found Mr Emden a nuisance.'

'I suppose *she* didn't do him in?'

'I did not ask her.'

'He does seem to have been a Lothario. No wonder he fled at Caroline's approach.'

'But, my dear Laura, we do not know that he fled at Caroline's approach. We have no evidence which bears upon the matter. You must not jump to conclusions.'

'Well', said Laura, 'I'm dashed if I can see why he should vamoose at anyone else's approach. It wasn't *you* he was scared about, was it?'

'I think he suspected collusion between me and Mr Clun. And that, if it is a fact, coupled with the very valuable suggestion which you offered a while ago, could lead to a solution of our problem.'

'As how?' asked Laura. But there was no reply.

CHAPTER 16

Permutations and Combinations

DAME BEATRICE chose her victims with care. After some
consideration she decided to begin with Caroline Lockerby, and, having invited her to sherry in the hotel garden
as a preliminary to lunch, stated her business unequivo-
cally.

'I may tell you', she said, when the waiter had withdrawn, 'that I have known for some time not only the
identity of the person who killed your husband, but that of
the man who killed Emden.'

'Yes?' Caroline looked at her, startled, her lovely
mouth slightly open. 'And have you any proof?'

'I will leave you to answer your own question when you
have heard what I have to say. Whether I can count on
your cooperation is, I am inclined to think, doubtful, but
we shall see. Let us begin with the extraordinary reaction
of Mr Telham to Mr Clun when arrived at the hotel. You
remember?'

'I – yes. You have to remember that Telham was on the
verge of a nervous breakdown.'

'From which verge he retreated rapidly. His behaviour,
on the day we visited the cave of dead men, was in marked
contrast to your own.'

'I was feeling the heat.'

'Quite, quite. May I put it to you that Mr Telham had
an acute attack of guilty conscience when he saw Mr
Clun's name on the ship's passenger list?'

'There was nothing for him to feel guilty about. He
could not help giving evidence at Clun's trial.'

'He could not help it, I agree. But Mr Telham is of a
chivalrous disposition and, I suggest, felt badly about
having helped to send Mr Clun to prison. I suggest that he
avoided him quite successfully on the ship but was horri-

fied to discover that they would be spending at least a month together at the same hotel.'

'Well, yes, the idea did upset Telham,' Caroline agreed. 'You see, we'd concluded that Clun would be emigrating, not coming to a holiday island like this.'

'Leaving his shady past behind him? I see. But perhaps Clun does not consider his past to be shady. He has plenty of self-confidence, you know, and is not sensitive. I should say that he regards the death he caused as a regrettable accident for which he has been over-severely punished.'

'He's a swaggering brute, and Telham did quite right to make it clear that we intended to have nothing more to do with him.'

'Exit Telham's guilty conscience, then,' said Dame Beatrice good-humouredly. 'Now what did you make of the flight of Mr Emden from the hotel?'

'I don't see it as flight. He had given a reason, it seems, for leaving. After all, he dressed in that eccentric way. It wasn't so extraordinary that he wanted to sample life as the troglodytes lived it.'

'You think not? But we found his dead body, not his living one, in a cave. What is more, I think you realized what had happened to him.'

'I? Good heavens, no!'

'You thought you saw one of the bodies move.'

'I was not feeling at all well that day. I was hysterical and silly, I know, but it didn't mean a thing.' Dame Beatrice let this pass, but Caroline suddenly added, 'It *was* the tall one which I fancied I saw move.'

'You were in an overwrought state, as you say. You must have had a bitter pill to swallow. You came here to join the man who had committed murder for your sake, only to find that, in two short months, he had gained for himself a most disreputable name among women and thought it best to leave the hotel.'

'How do you know that? How do you know I'd arranged to join that – that cock of the dunghill here? Nobody knew except Telham!'

'Nobody told me, of course. Perhaps you forgot that I left Hombres Muertos for a time, and went back to England. I discovered there a number of interesting facts and formed some theories based on them.'

'I don't care what you found out, or what theories you formed,' said Caroline. 'There's no extradition from here.'

'I realized that that particular fact went straight to the root of the matter. What I did not know, until I went back to England, was that there was a definite connexion between your husband and Emden, and that with Emden your brother could also claim old acquaintance.'

'There is no need to mention Telham again! I know I've been a fool and a madwoman. Everything that has happened has been the result of an infatuation for which I hate and loathe myself every time I remember it! I wish I'd never *heard* of Emden! Really, really I do.'

'Is it true that Emden lived in your flat, impersonating your brother?'

'Well...' Caroline looked across the semi-tropical luxuriance of the garden to a prospect of distant mountains... 'it wasn't impersonation in the way one thinks of that, but I *had* moved to another flat when – when I thought I couldn't live without Karl, and I'd persuaded Telham to let Karl call himself my brother and for Telham to stay in our old flat and come to us as a visitor in Karl's name.'

'To hoodwink the occupants of the other flats – old Mrs Barstow, for example?'

'So you talked to that old beast! I suppose she spied on us!'

'She was bored and lonely. You should have chosen a bigger block of flats!'

'What did she tell you?'

'Approximately the truth. Now, Mrs Lockerby, why did you let it be supposed that your brother killed your husband?'

'But I did nothing of the kind! I told you, as I've told everybody else, that Ian was set upon by a gang of roughs, and that poor old Telham took panic and ran off. I also told you that he went back and found Ian dead.'

'I am afraid that won't do any longer. And the police were not satisfied with that story, either.'

'No, they weren't. They talked about the bruises. There was a lot of fuss about those.'

'Quite so. The bruises had been inflicted after death, and it was not a gang who had inflicted them, but someone who hoped to make the death look like the work of a gang. Your brother must be very fond of you. How could you bear to expose him to so much danger?'

'I don't know what you mean!'

'In other words, then, I know – I am certain – it was not your brother who was with your husband that evening, but the murderer Emden. Emden it was who killed him.'

Caroline, who had been giving her answers without looking at her inquisitor, swung round. Her face was very pale and her eyes glittered.

'What on earth are you saying?' she cried. Then, suddenly, 'Oh, it's true! It's true! But Ian was a beast and a brute and as mean as sin! It was *my* money he was spending, and he terrified me into giving him all he wanted. He didn't care twopence about Karl! Karl could take me out, or live with me, or anything!'

'Oh, I see,' said the implacable little old woman whom she was facing. 'So now it is clear. Your husband had to be killed before he ran through all your money. But whose idea was it, I wonder, that he should die?'

Caroline turned away with a sob.

'What are you going to do about it?' she asked. 'So long as Emden is dead, there's nothing that anyone can do. And I knew nothing about it, I swear I didn't – nothing at all until he came back and told me. I was not an accessory, either before or after. Then Emden told me he already had a steamer ticket for Hombres Muertos and said I was to join him there as soon as the fuss was over. He swore it would look like the work of a gang, and I believed him. When he'd left, I told Telham. He is very fond of me, and said he'd see me through. The police questioning was terrible for him, though!'

'So I should imagine,' said Dame Beatrice. 'No wonder the young man was on the verge of a nervous breakdown when he left England. What does interest me is the rapid rate at which he recovered. Did he know, when we visited the cave with Mr Peterhouse, that Emden was dead? And, if so, did he know that the body had already been placed in the cave? – Not, as you say, that it matters.'

'It's getting too hot out here,' said Caroline, suddenly. 'Please let's take our wine to your room.'

They were sipping it, and Dame Beatrice was watching the colour coming back into Caroline's face, when there came a gentle tapping at the door. Then Pilar's voice, loud with expostulation, came through the match-wood panels.

'But, Señor, it is not for a *caballero* to enter the room of Dame Beatrice. Yes, your sister is with her. They drink wine together. Certainly their proceedings are amicable. What makes you to think that they are not? Wait, if you please, and I will find out what is the situation. When there is a bed in the room, gentlemen are not readily admitted unless one is ill or in love.'

She opened the door, entered the room, closed the door behind her, and stood with her plump back pressed determinedly against it.

'If that is the Señor Telham, I wish him to join us,' said Dame Beatrice. 'Kindly admit him, bring another wine-glass, then take your departure and please do not listen at the door.'

'I put it to you, Mrs Angel,' said Dame Beatrice, 'that you are the mother of Ricardo Ruiz.'

The bird-watcher stared at her.

'Yes. What of it?' she demanded. 'How do you know?'

'Your reaction when, in flippant vein at our first meeting, I mentioned that David watched Bathsheba – we were talking about bird-watching and binoculars at the time, if you remember...'

'Oh, that!' Again the bird-watcher gazed at the beak-lipped witch. 'I don't see why that gave the game away.'

'Oh, but it didn't. I merely filed it for reference. And the South American connexion also defeated me for a time.'

'That girl Pilar! I wish someone would put a muzzle on her, the lying little gossip!'

'Precisely. Therefore, as Pilar uses imagination rather than reality in her daily dealings with the guests here, I wondered what the truth was. When I saw you and Don Ricardo together, there was not much doubt.'

'My husband is alive. There were, and are, no grounds for a divorce. ...'

'Desertion?'

'Scarcely, since he lives in the same hotel.'

'Not ...?'

'The man who calls himself Peterhouse, of course. How else do you think he lives here free of charge? In any case, Ruiz is a Catholic and would not marry a divorced woman. We had our fling – then Ricardo. That is my story. I am a fairly wealthy woman. Ricardo had his education in Madrid, and I started him in a good business in Buenos Aires. He's repaid me. I have no regrets at all for what I did.'

'Why should you entertain regrets if you have done no harm?'

'I wouldn't say I'd done no harm, and, even if *I* thought that, Peterhouse wouldn't agree. He's been playing the martyred husband for more than twenty years!'

'It is curious and interesting that, in this case – I have to call it that, although the police are not involved – we have two wives with money and two condoning husbands.'

'Peterhouse doesn't condone what I did. He's never forgiven it. He never will. Not that he wanted me back, but he's made me – or, rather, poor Ruiz – pay for our midsummer madness.'

'Literally, or so it seems. A strange tangle of events. I wonder whether you will answer a question?'

'I can't tell until you ask it.'

'Have you ever been to the cave of the dead men?'

'Why, yes, of course. I went with Peterhouse when we first came here. We came for a holiday, you know! It seems something to laugh at now.'

'Do you remember what you saw?'

'Oh, that is not the only time I've been. Peterhouse sometimes accompanies the hotel guests and sometimes I do, and sometimes there is merely the guide.'

'When did you go there last?'

'About a fortnight before you came. This murdered man, Emden, went with me, and the American gentleman from Boston and his daughter. Emden tried to kiss the daughter or something. She complained to me about it, so I told Ruiz, and Ruiz told him he'd throw him out of the hotel if he had any more complaints.'

'Well, he did have more complaints. What about Luisa Ruiz?'

'She did not complain until after Emden had left the hotel – to go and live with the troglodytes, as we thought.'

'Oh, I see. And Pilar. Did *she* complain?'

'I doubt it. Not officially, I mean. I have not much doubt, though, that she told all the visitors on her corridor what sort of man this Emden was.'

'Would you be surprised to hear that one of the dead kings was a good deal taller than the rest?'

'Well, no, because *he* would be Emden.'

'There was no such discrepancy in their heights when you yourself visited the cave?'

'No, no. They all appeared to be more or less the same height. Besides, they may have shrunk, you know, whereas his corpse would have been comparatively fresh.'

'*Rigor mortis* would have passed off,' said Dame Beatrice thoughtfully.

'*Rigor mortis?* Oh, you mean the fact that the corpse had been made to sit down? Well, he had to, if the murderer wanted to make him look like one of the dead kings. It's all very puzzling, isn't it?'

'Not if one remembers that everything that has happened

is part of a logical sequence. There was only one flaw,
so far as I am aware, in the self-proposed murderer's pro-
gramme.'

'Oh? What was that?'

'He himself was murdered.'

'Emden? He intended to murder someone else?'

Dame Beatrice shrugged.

'It is a matter of opinion,' she said.

'What did you get out of Telham?' demanded. Laura,
when lunch was over.

'Nothing at all. He came to make certain that I was not
bullying his sister.'

'They're very thick, those two. What happened then?'

'He came, as you know; he listened, and he preserved
silence. Fortunately I had asked all the necessary questions before he arrived. There was nothing more that I
wanted from Mrs Lockerby. They are not fond of one
another; the fondness, I fancy, is entirely on Telham's
side. The young man appears to prize his sister's happiness
not only above rubies but above his own life and safety.'

'What did Mrs Angel have to say?'

'Those things which we knew already, but it was as well
to get her to confirm them. She seemed surprised when I
told her that I thought Emden was murdered before he had
an opportunity of murdering.'

'Murdering Telham and Caroline, who must know, I
suppose, that he murdered Lockerby? But surely neither
of them killed him? They're not at all the type. Caroline is
definitely squeamish and Telham is a born procrastinator,
wouldn't you say?'

'It may well be so. I shall know more, perhaps, when I
have spoken to Mr Peterhouse. And now there is something which you can do for me, if you will. You remember
that Clement claimed to have seen twenty-four bodies in
the cave?'

'Oh, but we know that was a lie! He took it back afterwards, you know.'

'I wonder who persuaded him to say it? You see, he went there the first time with a guide, was not molested by the bandits, and came back with this curious tale. The next time he went he was captured and, when rescued, said that the bodies were reduced to twenty-three.'

'Then you had your bit of fun with Jose el Lupe and his men, and disclosed the body of Emden with the knife in its back. I remember. Right. I'll bounce the truth out of that kid. There's one thing: it would hardly have been the murderer who persuaded him to tell a lie like that.'

'It depends upon which murderer you mean.'

Laura stared at her employer distrustfully.

'And I suppose you'll tell me next that there's nothing up your sleeve,' she said.

'I don't think there is, dear child. I have no intention of misleading you. One certainly needs to understand the psychology of the child Clement, but I think you understand him very well. I did tell you, did I not, that he went out of his way to inform me that, whoever had killed Emden, his father certainly had not?'

'Yes, you did. I thought it a normal reaction on the kid's part.'

'Did you? I did not.'

'Oh, really? You mean he loathes old Drashleigh enough to wish him hanged? Oh, no of course! It wouldn't come to that here, so there wouldn't be *that* motive. So you think this black-hearted lad had method in this madness of defending his father? No, I don't get it. Explain.'

'Oh, nonsense!' said Dame Beatrice. 'Don't you remember the reason he gave for rallying to his father's defence?'

'Yes, I do. He told you that Emden had punched him, and that his father did not know. But what was the object of telling you all that?'

'Although he is basically intelligent, he is, of course, still very young and, for that reason, still simple-minded. His intention was to mislead me into believing that Emden was his enemy. The opposite, I fancy, was the case.

Emden was using and bribing the boy, but with what evil purpose it is not possible to say until you persuade Clement to talk. There is nothing for him to fear, and he is greatly attached to you, so you stand some chance, I feel, of obtaining the truth.'

'I'll do my best.'

Dame Beatrice, sleuthing diligently some time later, found Peterhouse pottering round the grotto of the hotel. The grotto was of natural origin and had been added to with more imagination than good taste. It consisted of a series of uneven caverns which had been deepened from the natural fissures to form cool, dim summer-houses in which were wooden benches of so-called rustic type, possibly picturesque but very uncomfortable as seats. These natural-cum-artificial arbours formed three sides of a square and in the middle of the square there was a pool (the one, incidentally, into which Clement had untimely thrust Caroline at an early stage in their acquaintanceship) and in the middle of the pool a fountain. Peterhouse was attracting the fish in the pool by scattering crumbs of cake for them. It was mid afternoon and the grotto was the coolest outdoor part of the hotel.

'"The Compleat Angler,"' remarked Dame Beatrice, stopping to watch. 'Have you ever tickled trout, Mr Peterhouse?'

'Not I,' replied the horticulturalist, straightening up. 'Why, dear lady, do you ask?'

'A pleasantry,' replied Dame Beatrice, waving her hand. 'A preliminary skirmish before I ask you some very personal questions.'

'I saw you in conversation with Mrs Angel. I suppose she told you we are man and wife. Don't believe a word of it. The woman is mentally deranged.'

'Why did you throw your packet of chocolate into the sea the other day?'

'What packet of chocolate?'

'The one which you offered to Clement and which I would not permit him to accept.'

'I don't remember the incident. It didn't take place at this hotel.'

'No, no. It took place on your island of Tiene.'

'Really? I have a very poor memory, I fear.'

'So you have forgotten that you married the woman who is known as Mrs Angel? You must keep a diary, you know. Bigamy is a serious offence.'

'Nothing is a serious offence on Hombres Muertos, dear lady. We are all dead men here, and among the dead there is the harmony of disinterested mercy.'

'That remains to be proved. But I spoke in jest. I dislike to think that you would commit a serious crime.'

Peterhouse shook his head.

'You underestimate me,' he said. 'The chocolate, of course, was poisoned, as you guessed. I had never tried the effect of my distillations on any human being, and I thought the boy, unwanted and, you must admit, extremely tiresome at times, would be a suitable subject for experiment.'

'Quite, quite. Which particular aconite did you use for your purpose, I wonder?'

'Wouldn't you like to know!' He squatted on his heels beside the pond, scattered a few more crumbs, then slid his hand into the water, scooped out a fish, and flung it at her. Dame Beatrice picked up the streak of silver as it writhed in the dust and gently replaced it in the pond.

'And now,' she said, seating herself on the stone surround, 'sit beside me and sing me songs of Araby, or, if you prefer it, tell me tales of fair Kashmir.'

Laura, prowling restlessly, found them, half an hour later, deep in a learned discussion of the best ways to cook and use English edible fungi. Dame Beatrice gave her an almost imperceptible signal to stay. Laura sat down on the coping and dabbled her fingers in the water while she listened to the gastronomes conversing.

'Well,' she said, as she and Dame Beatrice strolled towards the cliff path which led to the beach, 'he didn't *sound* particularly insane.'

'He is perfectly sane on the subject of edible fungi.'

'Yes. I suppose you mean there's the converse.'

'I beg your pardon?'

'I mean, the opposite of edible, which, in the case of fungi, is apt to be poisonous, isn't it? And that's him riding his hobby horse again!'

Dame Beatrice looked at her admiringly.

'Do you really think so?' she asked.

'I think it was because he knew you'd rumbled that the chocolate he offered Clement was poisoned with his awful ranunculus plants that he threw it into the sea so that you couldn't send it anywhere to be analysed. That's what *I* think.'

'I don't think the chocolate was poisoned, but I wanted Peterhouse to think I thought it was.'

'Why should you? I don't see the point.'

'Do you not? Does it not strike you that Peterhouse is our *deus ex machina?*'

'Well, yes, but we can't possibly prove it, can we?'

'I think we can. Señor Ruiz is chief witness for the prosecution.'

'Poor old Ruiz! How can he be?'

'You have realized that there is no extradition from Hombres Muertos?'

'Yes, of course. That's why crimes can be committed with impunity, as they say.'

'But there is such a thing as deportation, you know.'

'Deportation?'

'Certainly. Señor Ruiz is an important man in Reales. He would not stoop to murder, but I think he has it in his power to get rid of a nuisance.'

'That lends a different complexion.'

'So do cosmetics, dear child, but the facts remain the same.'

'Meaning that you can't alter the construction of bones? I couldn't do less than agree. But where does this lead us?'

'It leads us to the anatomy of the twenty-third or – if you prefer it – the twenty-fourth man.'

'You mean because he was taller than the others?'

'I do. The interesting feature is that the one man who ought to have noticed the difference forbore to comment upon it.'

'Peterhouse?'

'Exactly. He, of all people, accustomed as he was to leading parties to the cave, should have realized at once that one of the dead kings was noticeably taller than the rest. In other words, he *must* have noticed it.'

'But forbore to comment? I say, that opens up a field of thought.'

'No, no. It leads to one conclusion.'

'Oh, dear! He's a nuisance, but I don't dislike Peterhouse. Can't you get him out of it? It would be nice if you could. Anyway, why should he do it? There were people with far better motives. What about Telham, for example?'

'Motive is almost always the weakest link in a chain of evidence. Means and opportunity – those are usually considered more important.'

'Means? Well, the proved possession of the knife should settle that. But, then, dozens of people on the island possessed a similar type of knife, and – oh, of course, Peterhouse must have had two.'

'Opportunity?'

'You mean the island of Tiene. He could easily have killed him there. But why should Emden have gone to Tiene with Peterhouse? That's what I still don't understand.'

'There was no doubt that Emden had to leave the hotel.'

'No, that seems clear enough. I think I see what you mean. Peterhouse offered him shelter?'

'It seems that he did. I can get no further until I have talked with Peterhouse again.'

'You be careful, then. If Peterhouse did kill Emden he's a dangerous man.'

'So was the late Dan McGrew, of doubtful fame.'

CHAPTER 17

Brother Cain

'I wish', said Dame Beatrice, 'that you would tell me the whole story. I know you may have killed Emden. I can guess the reason. There appears to be no judicial penalty here for what you did, therefore I see no reason why you should refrain from telling me all.'

'I remember nothing of it,' said Peterhouse. They were sitting in deck-chairs on the beach. Peterhouse had an umbrella of extraordinary size and hue stuck in the sand to protect him from the sun. He was wearing sun-glasses and shorts and his bulging, pink torso reminded Dame Beatrice vaguely and not unpleasantly of her nephew's Large White pigs. She herself was full in the sun, a smiling, saurian old woman, ageless, implacable, kindhearted.

'Very possibly not,' she said. 'Freud, despite those who would discredit him, was sound on the subject. He averred, if you recollect his writings, that we forgot what we choose to forget. Memory, in fact, is selective.'

'Really? Well, dear lady, since you insist, I will endeavour to prove him wrong. I will delve into my memory, poor though it be, for the details you require. I don't know how far you look upon human life as sacred?'

'I don't know, either. I suspect that we all imagine our own lives to be sacred, but I feel that most of us are not nearly as certain when it comes to the lives of other people. Colour of skin, too, makes a difference; so does ideology. Let us by-pass the matter for the moment and argue it later.'

'Very well. I perceive that you think as I do. I killed Emden. That I do remember. What interests you is the reason. It is simple enough to state. If *I* had not killed *him*, *he* would have killed *me*. That was the situation in a nutshell. Are you satisfied?'

'Except in fairy stories, that which can be contained in a nutshell is of little importance. Tell me more.'

'Diamonds can be put in a nutshell.'

'I do not regard diamonds as important.'

'Lives have been hazarded and lost because of them.'

'We are asking ourselves why Emden's life was lost.'

'Ah, yes. It was not long before he ferreted out the truth about me.'

'That you have been living on blackmail?'

'Really, dear lady, you use harsh terms! Put yourself in my position. My wife had a child by Ruiz. Was I not entitled to compensation?'

'I have no idea. I presume that you must have been an inadequate husband, but in what particular way I do not inquire. Marital infidelities have various roots. So Emden discovered your secret – by talking to your wife, I presume?'

'He was an insinuating kind of man. I have never met a cleverer fellow where women were concerned.'

'Still, I hardly see what use he could make of his knowledge – in the way of gain, I mean.'

'He intended to marry Luisa Ruiz. She has no idea that Ricardo is anything but her full brother, and Emden thought he could force Ruiz to give consent by threatening to enlighten Luisa. Ruiz is very fond of his daughter and would hate her to know the truth.'

'But I think Luisa *does* know the truth. She must have noted the affection Ricardo had – forgive me, but I do not think of her by your name – for Mrs Angel. I myself hold the opinion that Emden tried to compromise Luisa, thinking that, by so doing, he could force her father into consenting to their marriage, but it seems that he reckoned without Luisa's strength of character. She appears to have been annoyed, not carried away, by his blandishments.'

'He was accustomed to the conquest of women. I do not imagine – supposing you to be right – that it would occur to him that Luisa could resist him. She must have told her father of the matter, I suppose.'

'Yes, she did, and Señor Ruiz was extremely angry about it. He was determined to get rid of Emden out of the hotel, and even threatened to have him deported. I am of the opinion that this was a particularly powerful threat in this particular case. You may or may not be aware that, once back in England, Emden would have placed himself in jeopardy of being tried for murder.'

'I did not realize that, but, now I come to think of it, he did say to me once – it was when you arrived at the hotel in company with Clun – he saw (to use his own expression) the writing on the wall.'

'How very much mistaken he was! I knew nothing of his connexion with the murder of Ian Lockerby until very much later.'

'Ian Lockerby? Mrs Lockerby's brother-in-law?'

'No, her husband.'

'I see. He killed her husband with the intention of marrying the lady! No wonder he made a connexion between your appearance and his probable fate! You may have me to thank for that! I take all the English papers and as soon as I saw your signature in the hotel register I remarked upon your august connexions. He saw the Home Office tracking him down, I suppose.'

'Interesting. So then he persuaded you to hide him on your island of Tiene, and there you murdered him.'

'But you must not think of it like that. It was not murder; it was self-defence, dear lady.'

'Ah, but you poisoned his wine!'

'But I did *not* poison the child's chocolate! It was cruel to have made such a suggestion! Why would you not let him eat it?'

'I wanted to warn you that I knew all. I will tell you the rest of the story, if you like. Emden, who, I agree, was a thorough-paced villain, bribed you to hide him on Tiene. You may live at the Hotel Sombrero without payment, but, if I may put it bluntly, you are woefully short of money to spend.'

'Well, that is perfectly true. My wife holds the purse-strings. Always has. A mean-spirited person is the self-styled Mrs Angel! Angel, indeed!'

'Emden then suggested that Ricardo Ruiz – or do you prefer to call him Ricardo Angel or Ricardo Peterhouse? – should be decoyed, on his next visit, which was about due, to Tiene, there to be murdered, and his South American papers confiscated. These papers were to become the property of Emden, who hoped, with their help, to enter South America, from which, again, there is no extradition. In other words he hoped to achieve his personal safety by going to live in a place to which the English law could not follow him.'

'That is correct. But I did not see myself tackling Ricardo with such an object in view. Ricardo dislikes me, you know, although I doubt whether he is aware of the fact that his mother is my wife. I did not think he would come to Tiene at my invitation. Emden threatened me when I told him this. He frightened me very much. I am not a bold man, Dame Beatrice, and I'm no longer young.'

'I sympathize greatly with people who are not very brave, but the thought that you murdered Emden is abhorrent to me. Did you fear him as much as all that?'

'I did indeed. I was afraid, I tell you, that if I did not kill him he would kill me. I really had no choice. He was a mad dog. You would agree that it is not wrong to kill a mad dog?'

'The analogy is not sufficiently close. Emden was not mad, and I see only one reason why he should have killed you.'

'But that is just it! He was afraid I would sell you the information that he was in hiding on Tiene. He told me so. He told me he had me at his mercy, and would have no more compunction in killing me than in killing a snake. Yes, he actually called me a poisonous old reptile! It was that which gave me the idea.'

'Of doping his wine from a distillation of your Alpine plants, I presume?'

'Well, yes. But it was his own fault, really. I should

never have thought of it but for his calling me names.'
Peterhouse suddenly chuckled. '"Very well" I thought.
"You little suspect, my good young man, that I have it in
my power to be exactly that!" You don't blame me for
having such a thought, Dame Beatrice, do you? Yes, I
doped his wine and, while he slept, I stabbed him. And
you yourself have proved to me that I was fully justified in
what I did. He had killed in England a man who was in
his way, so, you see, there is no doubt that he would have
killed *me*, and stolen my island of Tiene.'

'I fail to see how that would have helped him to get to
South America. However, where was the killing done?'

'In the cave of dead women that I showed you. I took a
little sand from the seashore and the small amount of
blood from the wound was soon covered up. And nobody
suspected, nobody at all, until *you* came along. What really made you suspect me, I wonder?'

'How did you get the corpse to the cave of dead men, to
disguise it as one of the kings?' Dame Beatrice demanded.

'Ah, that,' said Peterhouse, shaking his head, 'that I
cannot remember.'

'How long were you with him on the island of Tiene?'

'An hour or two each time. I was not missed. We are
here, there, everywhere, we of the Hotel Sombrero, are we
not? The beach, the town, the mountains, the bull-ring –
nobody attempts to account for where we shall be at any
particular time, and I went in the afternoons when many
take a siesta. In the very early morning I went to bring the
body from Tiene. Ah, I remember now! My friends the
bandits helped me. Tio Caballo and José el Lupe have
been my friends since I promised to pray for them.'

'And they helped you to dress the body in the robes of
one of the kings?'

'Exactly, exactly, dear lady. We bore him to the cave of
dead men and made him one of the kings. Believe me, I
have no compunction at all about what I did. I have rid
the world of a scoundrel. You are silent. Pray tell me your
thoughts.'

'I have been counting the waves,' said Dame Beatrice. 'The seventy and seventh is just about to come in.'

'Old Peterhouse?' exclaimed Laura. 'I can't believe it! What are you going to do now?'

'I am going to put it about that Peterhouse has told all. I shall give no details, but I want to make certain that the Drashleighs, Clun, Caroline Lockerby, Telham – oh, and Señor Ruiz – of course – all receive the same impression.'

'That Peterhouse has come clean?'

'Thank you. An old expression and not one that would figure in the vocabulary of a high court judge, but it expresses, no doubt, what I mean.'

'And what do you expect will happen then?'

'I expect violent repercussions.'

'Do I take it that one of the people you mentioned was actually engaged, with old Peterhouse, in a plot to murder Emden? But it happened so quickly after you got here! There wouldn't have been *time* to make such a plot with a perfect stranger and get it carried out and the body togged up like one of the dead kings, would there?'

'Yes, there would. Consider the time-sequence. Emden disappeared almost immediately we arrived. He was expecting Caroline and Telham, therefore it was not the sight of them which drove him from the hotel. As we said before, and as Peterhouse himself pointed out, it must have been the sight of Clun and myself in what, to Emden's guilty mind, was a partnership. Very well; Emden would have had previous knowledge of the little island of Tiene. A garrulous man such as Peterhouse would have told him about it long before we arrived.'

'Yes, I suppose he would. Anyhow, can we take it for granted that he did.'

'The next important move depended on Pilar. We may assume that Pilar gossiped as freely to Caroline Lockerby as she did to me. Pilar never wastes time.'

'That girl will trip over her own tongue one of these days!'

'We can take it that, as soon as the news of Emden's disappearance from the hotel was bruited, Pilar regaled Caroline with the stories, some true, some, no doubt, apochryphal, of his love affairs on this island.'

'Oh, I begin to see! Caroline didn't realize that Emden was scramming because of you and Clun and, as he thought, because of the shadow of deportation. She assumed, quite naturally, that he'd sent for her to come to Hombres Muertos just to humiliate her. She came to the conclusion that he didn't care twopence about her any more. She saw red, and told her devoted brother, I suppose.'

'That is how I see it. Telham did not know what course to take. He had seen his sister's unhappiness in her marriage and then he found her scorned and abandoned, as he thought, by a conscienceless libertine. He offered a reward, I imagine, for news of Emden. This was rather out of character, I feel, for he is as much of a procrastinator and often in as great a state of miserable indecision as his prototype Hamlet. This offer of a reward must have tempted Peterhouse into telling him where Emden was hiding. Then, I think, he bribed Peterhouse to murder Emden.'

'You mean that Peterhouse was so short of money that he could be used as an assassin? It doesn't seem credible!'

'Most murders are incredible to the people who do not commit them. You see, it would have taken at least two persons to get the body up to the cave of dead men and into the robes of the mummified king. I am inclined to think it took three.'

'Caroline Lockerby?'

'I think so. It would account for her curious outburst in the cave that day and for her brother's equally curious calm. *He* had released himself from the burden of indecision, and *she* began to realize the full horror of what had been done.'

'But what about Peterhouse's story that the bandits helped him?'

'I give it no credence. I fully believed Ruiz when he

told me that no islander would have dressed the body in
the robes and mask of one of the dead kings. Besides, had
you seen the timorous way in which the bandits ap-
proached the body when I was with them, you would
think, as I do, that they are entirely innocent of any com-
plicity whatever.'

'I see. What I really can't understand is that Peterhouse, knowing what he knew and what he'd done, took
that party of you to visit the cave after Emden's body was
there. You'd think that at all costs he'd want to keep
people away.'

'There are two possible explanations. He may have
weighed up the chances and decided that, as we new arrivals would be certain to want to visit the cave, it might
be as well to get our visit over before the corpse decompos-
ed and began to smell; or it may be that he had forgotten
the body was there. Some of his traumatic states are genuinely psychopathic.'

'But, apart from the money, which, no doubt, he
needed, how could he bring himself to do it?'

'There are no penalties here for murder, and Peterhouse has lived here a good many years. Most of his English inhibitions will have worked themselves out of his
system, so to speak, by this time.'

How Dame Beatrice did it, even Laura, who knew her
well, could not have said, but the news that all was known,
and that Peterhouse had confessed to having been bribed
to murder Emden, was allowed to seep into the conscious-
ness of those most nearly concerned. One morning neither
Caroline nor Telham appeared at breakfast. At lunch-
time they were still missing and Laura cocked a warily-
inquiring eye at Dame Beatrice. At four in the afternoon,
when lunch was over and the town was taking its siesta,
came José el Lupe sneaking up to the hotel. Dame Beatrice was in the garden, full in the sun, watching the
lizards disporting themselves on the warm stones of an
ornamental rockery.

The Wolf stopped short and bowed.

'You should, perhaps, pay another visit to the cave of dead men, Señora.'

'Very well, Señor. Thank you for your information. How is the backbone of our friend Caballo?'

'It has no ill-feeling now.'

Dame Beatrice strolled towards the house and met Clement.

'I don't want to live with Laura, after all,' he said. 'She is very inquisitive. She makes me tell her my secrets.'

'Very well, child. Of course, during the Middle Ages small boys acted as messengers of love. Where is she?'

'On the raft.'

'Go and find her. Tell her to bring Mr Clun.'

'What for?'

'Fun.'

'Can I join in?'

'No.'

'I had more fun running errands to Emden's women.'

Clement sauntered away and Dame Beatrice took her seat at the top of the cliff path. At the end of half an hour, Laura, Clun, and Clement appeared.

'Will you give me two shillings for a ride in a cart?' asked Clement. Dame Beatrice, espying the Drashleighs as their heads appeared above the top of the cliff at the last bend in the path, canvassed their opinion.

'It is very kind of you,' said Theodora Drashleigh.

'Yes, yes,' agreed Pentland. They sounded dejected. Dame Beatrice handed over the money and Clement strolled off towards the hotel gate. 'He says he wants to stay with us,' said Pentland Drashleigh. They continued on their way to the terrace. Laura gazed after them and smiled.

'Gavin would never have stood for Clement, anyway,' she said. 'My life-work has taken the only possible course and has included itself out.'

The cave presented the spectacle to which Dame Beatrice and Laura were accustomed, except that it contained two extra bodies.

'We did not know where to put them,' said Tio Caballo, materializing, a swarthy, unshaven, slightly Falstaffian ghost, from the back of the cave. Dame Beatrice had little need to examine the bodies. From the appearance of the injuries the brother and sister must have thrown themselves over the cliff.

'This presents a problem,' said Clun. 'It's either a double suicide or a murder and a suicide. It will complicate the funeral arrangements.'

'If those are the only things it will complicate, nobody will be unduly put out,' said Dame Beatrice. 'Personally, I see no reason why it should not be made to appear a mountaineering accident.'

'I wonder how much the bandits saw?' suggested Laura. She put the question to Tio Caballo. He shrugged and answered:

'I am a bandit, not a witness on oath. They died in any way you please, Señora. What was their sin, that they added a greater one to it?'

'They were accessories to the murder of the Señor Emden.'

'So?' He gazed fixedly at the broken bodies and crossed himself devoutly. '"Take what you will," says God, "and pay for it." They took what they would, Señora, and have paid.'